CHECKPOINT KALANDIA

CHECKPOINT KALANDIA

by

Dixiane Hallaj

 S & H Publishing
Falls Church, VA

S & H Publishing, Inc.
211 Park Avenue Falls Church, VA 22046
www.sandhpublishing.com

Publisher's Note: This is a work of fiction. Names, characters, places, and incidents are a product of the author's imagination.

Ordering Information:
Quantity sales. Special discounts are available on quantity purchases by corporations, associations, and others. For details, contact the "Special Sales Department" at the address above or email sales@sandhpublishing.com.

Checkpoint Kalandia/Dixiane Hallaj. ISBN 978-1-63320-018-0

OTHER WORKS BY DIXIANE HALLAJ

Born a Refugee
A Novel of One Palestinian Family

Caught by Culture and Conflict:
Illiteracy Among Palestinian Refugee Women

It's Just Lola
(a novel)

Aunt Nellie B
(a novel)

The 5th Wish
(a children's picture book)

http://www.dixianehallaj.com

Chapter I
❧KALANDIA UNDER CURFEW❧

The State of Palestine: Easier Said Than Done
Cox News Service; November 20, 2001

Angry Arafat cheered by UN audience: Palestinian leader blames Sharon for 13 months of violence
The Ottawa Citizen; November 12, 2001

Israeli restrictions placed on Palestine Relief and Works Agency criticized by speakers in Fourth Committee (Special Political and Decolonization)
Security checks and restrictions on the activities of the United Nations Relief and Works Agency for Palestine Refugees in the Near East (UNRWA), as well as its persistent serious financial situation, were highlighted this morning...the suffering of the refugees had been exacerbated by the measures imposed by Israel under the pretext of security.
M2 Newswire; November 2, 2001

Muhammad took a deep breath to ease the knots in his stomach. It didn't help his stomach, but by the time the soldier walking up the aisle of the bus checking identity cards reached his seat, Muhammad was able to extend his card with a steady hand. Luckily, the soldier heard neither the thudding of his heart, nor the voice screaming in his mind. The bus closed in around him. He struggled to breathe. Inhale slowly, count to five on the inhale. Exhale slowly, count to four on the exhale. Sweat trickled from his armpits. The soldier returned his card and Muhammad replaced it in his pocket.

He looked through the window at the cold gray sky and imagined he was outside with the sting of freezing November air in his lungs. Another soldier walked under the window, pacing the length of the bus. He never looked up, his eyes fixed on the long-handled mirror he carried. The soldier stepped back and nodded, indicating that he'd found nothing suspicious on the underside of the bus. Was he really looking for bombs, or was this just another empty delay? Why would anyone plant a bomb on a bus that carried laborers to their donkey jobs?

The bus moved forward with a jerk that shook Muhammad into another breath. He ignored the familiar shops and commercial buildings moving past the windows and focused on the ancient rounded hills behind them. His heart settled back into a quiet rhythm, and his sweat dried. The unheated bus turned from a coffin-like enclosure to a comforting womb carrying fellow workers, their warm breath mingling in the air. They would soon be comfortable enough in their winter clothes.

"You okay?" The stranger's question took him by surprise.

Muhammad nodded. "I'm fine now. Thanks for asking." He rode this bus every morning, and this was the first person that noticed his distress. "As long as the bus moves, I'm all right. I just get a little claustrophobic when it sits still." It wasn't the sitting still that did it. It was knowing he was trapped on the bus with the soldier and the gun.

He should follow this with something "normal" to let his seatmate know he really was all right. "Crummy day to have to work outside, isn't it?"

"I don't know about that. Any day I have work is a pretty good day to me."

Muhammad turned to the stranger next to him. It was like looking in a mirror, same dusky skin, dark eyes, dark curly hair in need of a barber, necks wrapped in black and white kafiya scarves tucked into puffy jackets. He'd be willing to bet the other man was wearing pajama pants under his ill-fitting trousers as well. The cold place inside him began to thaw. "I'm Muhammad." He held out his hand. The stranger grasped it with a laborer's calloused hand.

"Abdul Rahman, but everyone calls me Abed."

"Glad to know you, Abed." The ritual words were honest.

When they got off the bus at the terminal, Abed fell into step alongside Muhammad. "So, are you working on the new settlement, too?" Muhammad nodded. It bothered him to have to admit he worked on the settlements. He hated the settlements. Either Abed was a mind reader or his attitude showed on his face. "I resisted working there for a long time, too, but my kids have to eat."

"Yeah. Watch out for the foreman. He's a mean-spirited so-and-so. Always quick with the insults and taunts. One of these days he'll push someone too far."

The workday started like any other. Abed stayed close to Muhammad and kept his head down. Muhammad liked him even more when he saw how hard he worked at whatever he was asked to do. He didn't hang back when the truck of cement sacks had to be unloaded, and he kept up with Muhammad pounding nails into the scaffolding. The foreman strutted from place to place shouting unnecessary instructions and berating the men for not working harder. A couple of hours into the work, the rhythm of the hammers and saws faltered. Muhammad's own hammer moved slower as he glanced around to find

3

the cause of the disturbance. His ears located it before his eyes did.

"Your mother must have mated with a donkey to get someone as stupid as you," the foreman shouted at a man Muhammad soon recognized as his friend Shadi from Bethlehem. The sounds of construction quieted even more, and the foreman's voice rose in volume to fill the emptiness. "If you had any sense at all you'd know not to come back here like a whipped dog, crawling on your belly."

Muhammad felt the weight of the hammer in his hand. His arm trembled with the force of his grip. He barely heard the foreman's words over the voice in his head. *Throw the hammer. Make the words stop.* But the words didn't stop. They oozed out of the foreman's mouth like corrosive molasses, covering Shadi and spreading over the work site.

"What do you want from me? A welcome back party? You disappear for three days, come to work two hours late, and expect to have a job waiting for you?"

"But I was under curfew. Dheisheh Camp was closed. Today there were checkpoints. The bus waited for hours before it was our turn." Shadi's face twisted and for one awful moment, Muhammad thought he might cry.

The foreman looked as though he was enjoying himself. "That's not my problem. I've got my own deadlines."

Muhammad's vision narrowed. He watched the foreman's mouth move, spewing hateful words, but the rushing in his ears nearly drowned out the sound. He could stop the words. The arm with the hammer twitched and moved in an upward arc. A strong hand on his arm stopped the motion.

4

"You'd only be throwing your own job away, or worse. Think of your family. It won't help that guy, and you'll never get another job. It's not worth it." The words penetrated the thick fog of rage and echoed so deep within him that he wasn't sure if they were his own thoughts or the words of his coworker. He closed his eyes and inhaled deeply. No, it wasn't worth it. He had to think of Deena and the children. Shadi looked shrunken and withered as he walked away. Three days of curfew with no pay was bad, but loss of a job spelled disaster. As miserable as the job was, the money bought food.

Muhammad forced a smile and a nod. "Thanks."

Abed let go of his arm and they resumed their work. Muhammad took out his anger on the nails. He slammed the hammer down on ugly nail after ugly nail, pounding them into the even uglier wood. His soul cried at the ugliness of the reused wood he was making into concrete forms. His soul cried at the ugliness of the buildings slapped together to house more and more settlers. His soul cried at the injustice of life.

Why did he feel guilty about Shadi? The periodic curfews that closed the refugee camps weren't his fault. The jeeps, tanks, and troop carriers that patrolled the streets, forcing the inhabitants to stay inside their overcrowded homes until the curfew was lifted weren't under his control. Why did he feel guilty? He still had a job, and Shadi didn't. He'll go home with enough money to buy food for another day or maybe two, but Shadi will go home with empty pockets. Shadi might even walk the six or seven miles home to save the bus fare. Muhammad pounded another ugly nail and muttered to himself, punctuating each word with a blow of the hammer. "It ... could ... have ... been ... me."

The foreman called the lunch break. The hammers stopped and silence settled over the site. The men drifted into sheltered corners like autumn leaves, each with his brown bag. Today no easy give and take of small talk echoed through the unfinished construction, no laughter over jokes or stories of children's anecdotes. The sullen eyes of the laborers followed the foreman's progress across the lot and into the construction trailer.

Muhammad pulled out his sandwich. Before biting into it, he looked around at the other men. Satisfied that they were all eating, he sank his teeth into the pita bread and goat cheese sandwich. The first time Muhammad had noticed Shadi sitting without a lunch, he'd offered half of his own. Shadi had said something about the soldiers confiscating lunch bags at the Bethlehem checkpoint. Maybe that was true, or maybe the man went without lunch to leave what little food they could afford for his children. It happened. It didn't matter. Muhammad was thankful to have enough to share.

"If we'd all walked off when he fired Shadi ..." Muhammad left the sentence hanging. Abed, sitting next to him, shook his head and took another bite of his sandwich. He didn't have to say anything. They both knew that all the foreman had to do was snap his fingers and there'd be dozens of men scrambling for the chance to pound twice-used nails and mix cement and carry bricks up rickety ladders. Men like themselves, willing to submit to the long lines and humiliating searches at the checkpoints just to get work as a day laborer, subject to the whims of the foreman, the weather, or the guards at the checkpoints. It put food on the table.

Muhammad's anger cooled as exhaustion crept up during the long afternoon of back-breaking work. His feet felt like lead as he lifted them up the steps to the bus after work. He sank into a seat and stared vacantly out the window, grateful that Abed remained quiet. They breezed through the checkpoints on the way home. When he stepped off the bus at the Kalandia stop, he took a deep breath and gave his shoulders an almost imperceptible shake—his private ritual. He imagined himself shaking off the workday like a bird shaking water off its feathers.

He walked past the shops, staying on the main road through the camp as long as possible. He usually preferred a route that took the smaller side streets with their endless soccer games and running children, but in this weather, he stuck to the road with sidewalks. It was too muddy for the children to play anyway. Even the shops were uninteresting in the winter. With the awnings and outdoor racks of goods hidden away, the lifeless displays behind dirty windows held no appeal. He was tempted to buy a treat for the children, but that money would pay his bus fare tomorrow. He entered a side street, hoping no passing cars splashed mud on his clothes so he could wear them another day, and walked past tiny houses almost invisible behind high privacy walls of concrete block. Some had windows facing the street, but others, like his own, had sacrificed some of the precious ten meter by ten meter area for a tiny walled courtyard. The day seemed brighter as he turned into the narrow alley where he lived. By the time he opened the outer door, his smile was ready and his arms spread to receive the rambunctious twins that almost swept him off his feet with their greeting.

He snatched up Omar and Mustafa, one under each arm, and twirled around the tiny courtyard. Deena's musical laughter added to the giggles of the twins, and Muhammad set the boys down, keeping a hand on each one until they gained their footing after the dizzying ride. The boys ran into the house, and he gathered his wife in his arms, inhaling the clean fragrance of her hair. They shared a moment of quiet laughter as the burgeoning life within her womb protested their close embrace with a few strong kicks.

"Amal, how was school today?" His daughter was only eleven, but she took her responsibilities so seriously that he sometimes wanted to swing her around like her little brothers to make her giggle again. One look at her face told him that was the wrong question to ask. He gave her a quick hug on the way to the bathroom. Once he'd washed off the day's dust and grime, he'd be fully restored.

By the time he emerged from the bathroom, the stubby little table sat in the middle of the room with the sitting mats arranged around it. The boys, wonder of wonders, sat quietly in front of the television. He nearly collided with Amal as she brought the big plastic bag of bread to the table.

"I hate to disturb the peaceful moment."

Amal looked at the twins and gave a quiet laugh. "There's a new cartoon on today, and they've never seen it before." She leaned closer to her father and whispered, "Just don't tell them they might learn their letters if they pay attention."

Muhammad put a finger to his lips and winked. "It'll be our secret." He gave her a thumbs up signal and walked into the small kitchen. Deena was ladling steaming green bean stew into a large bowl. Her thick dark hair was drawn back and fastened with a rubber band, but small unruly curls escaped and lay on the nape of her neck, inviting his lips to push them aside and kiss the soft skin beneath. He resisted the temptation.

"Are you just going to stand there and stare?" Her voice softened the words.

"I'm not staring. I'm having my first course, feasting my eyes on the loveliest woman I ever saw."

"Flattery will get you everywhere, my love." She handed him the bowl and flashed him a smile. "Be careful, it's hot. Put this on the table, then see if you can corral those little scamps and get them washed up for supper."

Long before the ten o'clock news, Muhammad yawned and switched off the television. He opened the plywood door to the back room and tucked the quilt around the twins. Where did they get all that energy? They were never still, even in sleep.

Deena was in the bathroom when he came back to the main room. He moved the chairs from in front of the television and stacked them against the wall where the small table leaned with its stubby legs protruding like the arms and legs of some clumsy creature. Then he pulled the mattresses off the rack and set them side by side in the space in front of the wardrobe.

Deena emerged from the bathroom with her dark curls spread over the shoulders of her white flannel nightgown.

"You look good enough to eat," he said.

She smiled, and together they spread the sheets and quilt over the mattresses. He turned the lights out, relaxed in the nearness of her body, and told her about his new friend, Abed. He didn't tell her that Abed had probably saved his life. What purpose would be served by both of them worrying about the consequences of his temper?

Muhammad's eyes opened with the first notes of the dawn call to prayer. Reluctant to leave the warmth of the bed and the feel of his wife's body nestled against him, he listened as another mosque joined with its own call. Soon he heard a faint third echo from farther away. He allowed himself another two minutes before pulling back the thick cotton-stuffed quilt. At least his breath didn't make white clouds this morning. He lit the small kerosene heater. The chill would be gone by the time the children stirred. He heated some water to wash and shave and put the kettle back on for tea. By the time he'd left the bathroom, Deena was in the kitchen with a heavy sweater over her nightgown. He smiled at her back and proceeded to fold the bedding and place it on top of the spare mattress in the rack. Then he folded their two mattresses, lifted them atop the bedding and pulled the striped curtain across the rack for the day.

The sun was still a wan glow when he left for work, dressed in as many layers as he could wear and still move his arms. The bread and olives he'd had for breakfast turned to a lump in his stomach as soon as he walked out of the alley into the street. A troop carrier and two jeeps moved slowly past him. A cold wind that only he could feel chilled him to the bone, and he thrust his hands deep into his pockets and hunched his shoulders. He seldom

10

saw more than a foot patrol or two this early. Of course, foot patrols always had what he thought of as their sheepdog jeep somewhere in the area.

The closer he got to the terminal, the more the increased presence of soldiers oppressed him. He tried to focus on the street in front of him, but the uniforms and guns drew his eyes like a magnet. His footsteps slowed, and men, all headed for the buses, walked around him. Almost indistinguishable in the thick padding of clothing, they looked neither right nor left. He envied the others their ability to look straight ahead and ignore the soldiers. By chance, his eyes met those of a soldier leaning against a building smoking a cigarette. Their eyes locked, and Muhammad felt like an insect pinned to a corkboard, unable to move. Did his brother Selim see the eyes of the soldier who shot him? Sweat formed on his brow and his breath quickened. Something else caught the soldier's attention, and he looked away, freeing Muhammad to move on. Muhammad stumbled a few more steps toward the bus. He stopped for a deep breath and shook his head.

"Are you okay?" He looked up into a familiar face. His mind struggled for recognition as his body struggled for equilibrium.

"Abed." The name came back with the memory of yesterday's checkpoint crossing. "No, I feel a little dizzy. I'd better go home." He already felt hemmed in by so much military presence. He couldn't breathe. He remembered the weight of Selim lying on his chest, not moving. He'd never make it through the checkpoint today.

"See you tomorrow, then." Abed's words sounded cheerful, but his face showed his sympathy. No work meant no pay. Muhammad waved a hand in response. He shoved his hands in his pockets and turned back the way he had come. If he showed up bright and early tomorrow and did a little groveling, he'd probably be all right. As unpleasant as groveling to the foreman would be, it would be better than whatever might happen if he tried to get on the bus now.

Already feeling the humiliation of the apology, he walked with his head down and let his feet take the familiar path toward home. Hell, if they could breed a donkey with opposable thumbs, he could do the work— and that's what they think of their workers. Anger and frustration quickened his steps. More than soldiers and checkpoints trapped him. Even if the soldiers took the day off, he'd still be trapped in a job he hated, and terrified of losing it.

"Papa!"

"Uncle!" Muhammad looked up, almost surprised to find himself nearly home. Amal and Imahn stepped out of the stream of girls dressed in blue and white striped school uniforms and ran toward him. Only one year separated the two in age, but Amal barely topped her cousin's shoulder. The black pants they wore under their uniforms disguised the fact that Amal's uniform was too short, but nothing could disguise the too-short sleeves of her hand-me-down jacket. Why hadn't he noticed that earlier? Oh, because he left before her in the morning and came home so late they barely had time for supper and bedtime for the twins.

"Are you sick, Papa? Why aren't you at work?"

"I ... uh ..." Muhammad searched for a plausible answer. "Yes, I'm ... uh ..."

"Look, Uncle, there's Kareema."

"Kareema," both girls called in unison. The older girl's coat hung open and the green and white of her high school uniform stood out amongst all the elementary school blues. She waved, but didn't stop.

He raised his hand in greeting. Why was she in the Camp so late? She should already be in school, but it didn't matter. Whatever the reason, he was relieved not to have to explain his sudden sickness. When Kareema caught sight of him, she changed course and headed toward them. Muhammad realized that she would have passed the girls with only a wave, but to walk past her uncle would have been rude.

"Hello, Uncle Muhammad."

"Hello, Kareema. What's up?" Amal and Imahn talking about school drowned out his question. Muhammad watched Kareema shift nervously from foot to foot, and he put a hand on a shoulder of each of the younger girls. "Can't you see Kareema's in a hurry?" He couldn't mistake the gratitude in her smile as she dashed away.

"Papa—" Amal turned to him, but stopped in midsentence at the sound of her name. She waved at a passing girl, who hurried on when she saw Muhammad.

"If you hurry, you can catch up to your friend and have some time to talk before class." Muhammad gave them a grin. "Go on. You don't want to miss the latest gossip."

"Oh, Uncle, we don't gossip." Imahn laughed and her cheeks gained a touch of pink. She pulled Amal's hand and they jogged off before falling into step with their friend. He watched them until they disappeared into the stream of girls headed for school.

The faint but unmistakable sounds of machine gun fire came seconds after he turned into their alley. His shoulders sagged and the strength drained from his legs. Curfew—again. It might be his imagination, but it felt like the curfews were more frequent lately and they lasted longer. The sound truck announcing the curfew was still too far away to hear, but a jeep always drove in front of the truck and another behind it with mounted machine guns—guns that fired into the air with a sound that carried farther than the speakers. Maybe the girls were too busy chattering to hear it. Should he run back and get them? No, give them a few more minutes with their friends. They weren't far, and even a few minutes of freedom could be savored.

The bus that would have taken him to work had probably disgorged its passengers at the checkpoint already—passengers that would not be allowed to reenter the camp until the curfew was lifted. Thank God he wasn't on that bus. For once his "problem" was a blessing of sorts, but he still wanted to scream in frustration. If the curfew lasted longer than a day or two, he wouldn't even try to get his job back. He shook his head. He couldn't remember the last time they'd had a curfew that only lasted one day.

Deena's eyes opened wide when he came through the door. Her smile made his heart melt. "Do I hear machine guns?" He nodded. "Good. Then we have you all to ourselves today." Her arm went around him and she lifted her face for a kiss.

Inside, the twins were still having their breakfast. He left his shoes at the door and hung up his jacket, laughing at the twins' chatter. "If you stop talking and finish your breakfast, we can watch cartoons together." The chatter stopped as if by magic as the boys spooned their breakfast into their mouths. In the silence, he heard the distant sound trucks blaring out their unintelligible announcement. Did

14

anyone understand the words? Not that it mattered because everyone understood the sounds of the guns. They were getting closer. Was that a rifle shot?

"Papa, are you—"

"Be quiet, boys." The words came out harsher than he intended, and the twins instantly stopped talking.

"What is it?"

"Nothing, Deena. I'll be back in a few minutes." Another rifle shot punctuated the drone of loudspeakers.

"Be careful."

He paused long enough to slip his feet back into his shoes. The jacket would delay him. He crossed the courtyard with long strides and didn't even close the outer door behind him as he ran into the alley and sprinted to the street. Where were the girls? They should have been back by now. The machine guns announced curfew, but rifle shots shouted warnings, usually fired uncomfortably close to stragglers who didn't get off the streets fast enough, or next to windows if someone looked out and happened to catch the eye of a soldier. Muhammad had heard tales of soldiers having contests to see who could get the closest. No one ever won in that kind of contest, especially not the Palestinian. In a panic, Muhammad turned into the street and ran in the direction of the school.

Very soon he caught sight of the two girls walking toward him. They looked as though they didn't have a care in the world. His worry turned to relief and then to anger. How could they be so nonchalant? He waved his arm to indicate they should hurry and jogged toward them.

"You're not out for a walk in the park, you know," he said when he got close enough for them to hear. "Hurry up."

"Oh, Uncle, they're still on the next street over. We're fine." They were probably right, but he wasn't going to admit it to them. Soldiers were part of living under occupation; they were as much a part of the refugee camp as the trash in the streets.

He grabbed their hands and pulled them into a fast walk. "You girls don't seem to realize that a rifle bullet can travel a lot farther than from one side of the camp to the other." He let go of their hands and mimed shooting a rifle upward at a steep angle. "A shot meant to go over someone else's head has to come down somewhere, doesn't it?" His hand described a parabolic trajectory. "It could land here with enough force to do considerable damage. Getting inside when you hear gunfire anywhere in the camp is like looking both ways before you cross the street. It doesn't insure you against an accident, but it makes an accident less likely."

"Papa, you left the door open."

"Go in and get warm." He stood at their door and watched Imahn until she turned the corner at the end of the alley, a few feet from her door.

Amal was unusually cheerful when he got inside. "Today's wash day, so it's lucky the curfew came and I can keep the twins out of the wash water."

"I promised the boys we'd watch cartoons together after they finished breakfast. Come and sit with us."

"If you're going to sit with them, may I go in the back and try to get some math done?"

"Sure, I'll keep them quiet."

The kerosene burner heated water in the bathroom with a soft hiss. He pictured the large tub of water that Deena used to boil the sheets and white clothes. How *did*

16

she keep the twins safe when Amal was at school? He'd have to ask her later. The thought evaporated as the boys jostled each other for space on his lap.

Cartoons failed to hold his attention, and his thoughts slipped back to the increasing frequency of curfews. He tried to think back over recent curfews, but they all blended together in his mind. Maybe he should make tick marks on the wall like prisoners did, scratching on cell walls to record the passing of time. How different was his situation after all? They were all prisoners now, prisoners in their own homes.

"Mama, I'm going next door to get help with my math." Amal's voice, louder than usual so her mother could hear it over the sounds of washing, cut through his thoughts.

"What? Are you crazy?" He jumped up, tumbling boys to the sitting mat on either side of him. This was his calm responsible daughter? What was happening to her? "The answer is NO, and you should know better than to even ask. How can you forget there's a curfew?" He grabbed Amal's arm. She looked up at him with wide frightened eyes, her schoolbag slipping off her shoulder. She tried to pull her arm free and keep the bag from falling, but he tightened his grip.

"Muhammad." The sharp tone of Deena's voice made him look up. Once she had his attention, her lips drew up in a small smile and her voice softened. "Muhammad, no one is going to get shot. The girls have figured out a very clever way to see each other during the curfews. They figured it out during the last curfew." She dried her soapy hands, already wrinkled from wash water. "Come and watch." He released Amal's arm and followed the two out to the courtyard.

Amal shivered in the cold air, and Muhammad rubbed his hands together.

"Hurry up, Amal. I have to get back to the washing, and it's cold out here."

"I don't know what we're doing out here in our shirt sleeves, but I'm glad there's a ten-foot wall so no one can see us acting like idiots."

"Hush, Muhammad, that's not nice." Deena elbowed him in the ribs.

"Sorry, I was talking to myself." He put his arm around her to lend some warmth.

Amal took a small rubber ball out of her pocket and threw it over the wall separating their house from the neighbors. It hit the kitchen window with a soft thud and bounced off, landing somewhere on the other side of the wall. A hand appeared in the window and waved.

"What happens if no one hears it? Or it misses?"

"Then I have to wait until Imahn wants to visit me." Amal dragged an old chair into place near the center of the courtyard. Deena brought a board and propped one end on the wall and the other on the seat of the chair. Muhammad watched. Soon he heard Imahn and her mother talking to each other on the other side of the wall.

"Are you ready, Aunt Hanan? Imahn?

"We're ready. Come on over."

"I'm coming." Amal climbed on the chair and knelt on the board. She inched her way up the board to the top of the wall, waved at her parents, and disappeared on the other side.

"I don't know about that shaky-looking set up of boards." Muhammad shook his head. "I don't want to have to sell my mother's bracelets to pay a doctor to fix a broken leg if she falls." Muhammad laughed at his own joke.

"You know you're proud of her." Deena laughed and gave him a playful shove into the house.

"I suppose so. It's ingenious, but a little too rickety for my taste." He was still chuckling.

"What's so funny?" asked Mustafa.

"Papa said he wouldn't sell Grandmother's bracelets if Amal breaks her leg climbing the wall." Deena always answered their questions.

"That's silly," said Omar. "We ate Grandmother's bracelets."

"What you said is even sillier, Omar," said Mustafa with a smirk. "We can't eat gold."

Omar shrugged. "I know, but we must've because that's what Papa told me the last time I asked."

Deena tried to explain. "She sold the gold for food, and we ate the food. That's what makes it funny, because the bracelets are gone."

Mustafa's eyes widened in disbelief. "Is that true, Papa? Did Omar and I eat all the food from Grandmother's bracelets?"

"No, it's a joke about the bracelets. They were sold a long time before you were even born—even before *I* was born."

Mustafa looked at his brother. "It couldn't have been us, then."

Omar asked the inevitable. "Why?"

"Because when they came here, your grandfather couldn't sell his grapes and vegetables and they needed to have food."

"Why didn't he go to work like you do so he could buy food?"

"Because..." All the frustration and anger crashed in on him again. Because people can't always control their own lives. Because the world took away our land, and the people they gave it to took away our freedom. What would his boys say tomorrow when he didn't have money for food either? How could a four-year-old understand? He barely understood the concept of a downwardly spiraling economy himself. He had no answer for them. He looked at his hands—the hands that used to craft fine furniture commissioned by people all over the country. The hands that now pounded bent used nails into splintering reused wood to make scaffolding for more and more buildings to house strangers from America and Poland and Russia to take their land and their water. He may not understand the concept, but he lived the reality. His breath rushed in and out of his lungs like a bellows fanning the flames of anger. He needed to go outside; he needed to *do* something.

"Why don't you two get your jackets on and come out to the courtyard to help me?"

The twins scrambled for their jackets. "Help with what?"

"It's a secret."

Soon the sound of hammering echoed through the house and beyond. At least the hammering blocked the sounds of guns enforcing the curfew. Muhammad pounded his frustration into the nails, yet kept his voice low and even when he found small jobs for his boys.

It didn't take long for Deena to open the door to ask what all the commotion was, but the twins rushed to stop her from coming outside. "It's a secret, Mama."

Soon Hanan's voice floated over the wall, trying to insert a question between hammer blows. "It's a secret, Aunt Hanan." The twins' excited voices helped more in keeping their secret than their hands did in building the project. Halfway through his work, Muhammad brought the boys back inside to warm up. A glass of warm milk in front of the television soon distracted them.

Task completed, Muhammad stretched his back and cleaned up the scraps of wood. He came in and switched off the television the boys had abandoned. Moving toward the kitchen, he nearly tripped over the basket of wet clothes. "Deena? I'll take these out and hang them."

"No." The voice sounded tired. "Amal will do it when she gets back. I'm on the last of it now."

Wordlessly, he picked up the basket and, careful not to place anything in front of the new surprise, began to hang the wet clothes. He smiled at the thought that soon there would be diapers hanging in the courtyard again.

When Deena emerged from the bathroom with the last of the clean clothes, Muhammad intercepted her. "I'll hang them out. You'll catch a cold if you go out now after working with hot water all day."

"But it's women's work."

"If I can't do men's work, I might as well do women's work. You just sit and relax." Excited voices interrupted whatever Deena was going to say next. Amal burst through the door.

"Papa, you're so wonderful!" She gave him a tight hug.

The boys dropped their toys. "Did you see the surprise?"

"It's perfect!"

"What's perfect?" Deena was the only one in the dark.

21

"The ladder!" Amal grabbed her mother's hand and pulled her out into the courtyard. "Look what Papa made us. Now we can visit anytime we like. Isn't that great? And he made another one for the other side, too."

"Yes, Amal, it *is* wonderful." Deena turned to her husband. "Where did you get the wood?"

"I brought it from an old construction site a long time ago and stored it on the roof. I wanted to make a chicken coop or a rabbit hutch so we'd have meat during curfews." He couldn't meet her eyes. "I never got the rest of the wood." He would have had to buy the rest of the materials, and he never had enough money. He'd almost forgotten about the wood.

Deena's laughter surprised him. "That's all right. The ladder's much better than chickens. It's going to last a long time — and I don't have to feed it or clean up after it."

"Papa, it was so nice of you to make this just for me."

"Well, to be honest, I've been thinking about that wall since I saw you climb over this morning and thinking that your mother or I might want to climb over it."

"You and Mama?" Amal clapped her hand over her mouth to smother her giggles.

Her father laughed. "Even though you seem to think Imahn's the only person in that house, remember that her father *is* my big brother, and your aunt *is* your mother's big sister. We're all stuck at home during curfews, too. Maybe we'd like to visit Uncle Ali and Aunt Hanan to share a pot of tea. In fact, your mother's been working so hard all day, why don't we watch the boys and let her go right now?"

"No." Deena and Amal answered together. Amal grabbed her mother's hand and went inside. Deena spoke as she crossed the few steps to the door. "I still need to clean the lentils for supper."

Muhammad had no choice but to follow. He could understand Deena's objection, but Amal's reaction surprised him. "Can't Amal clean the lentils? You need a break." He overrode all Deena's objections with a promise of lighting the kerosene burner and getting the lentils started. He smiled and nodded as Deena gave him detailed instructions. "Just go and enjoy your visit."

Muhammad sat on a mat and put the tray of lentils on his lap. Amal sat next to him and the two bent over the pile, their heads almost touching. "Sometimes I think the farmers mix small stones in with the lentils on purpose to make them weigh more or maybe just to make more work for women," Amal said in a sullen voice. She looked through the lentils one by one and picked out all the little bits of stone and even the occasional twig. Her frown looked like more than just concentration.

"Is something bothering you, Amal?" Muhammad kept his voice low.

"No." A full minute passed before she changed her answer. "When I went next door, Imahn and Auntie were the only people home. Of course Uncle Ali's at work, and Jehad stays in town most of the time now so he can work whenever he's not studying, but Yusef still goes to school in the camp. He should've been home. I asked about him, and Aunt Hanan got teary and told me that he left early to go to a friend's house. They had something they wanted to do before school. He should've come home when they announced the curfew, but he didn't."

Muhammad remembered the rifle shots, and a small knot of fear formed in his stomach. He forced a smile. "I'm sure he'll be fine. He was probably talking with his friend and didn't pay attention. You know how Yusef gets carried away when he talks. When he realized there was a curfew, it was too late to be on the streets so he stayed with his friend." Muhammad hoped he was right.

Chapter II
❧ YUSEF'S MISADVENTURE ❧

The United Nations Must Impose A Peace Deal On The Middle East; 'It Is 10 Years Since The "Peace Process" Began. It Has Produced A Great Deal Of "Process" And No "Peace".
The Independent (London), December 6, 2001

Israeli troops enter West Bank villages after air raids; U.S. peace mission in jeopardy
Associated Press Worldstream, December 13, 2001

At least seven dead in Israeli attacks
United Press International, December 14, 2001

Israeli army arrests 17 Palestinians in West Bank
The arrests were made after about 100 soldiers entered the northern village late Tuesday, blocked all roads and imposed a curfew.
Agence France Presse; December 26, 2001

Hanan's eyes flew open and she gasped for breath. Her heart thumped so hard she thought the bed must be shaking. She reached for the light with quivering hands. It was only a dream. No, it wasn't "only" a dream. It was the worst nightmare she'd ever had. A small sob escaped her lips as she sat up and rocked back and forth. Yusef had been riding his bicycle to the store to buy enough bread to get them through the curfew. But it was only a dream. Yusef doesn't have a bicycle. She tried to shut out the rest of the dream. No, this is real life, and Yusef doesn't have a bicycle.

She swung her legs over the edge of the bed and slid her feet into her slippers. She couldn't sleep now. What if the dream came back? She shuddered and pulled on her bathrobe. A cup of tea should cure her wobblies. But in spite of her efforts, her mind went back to the dream. This time she said it out loud as she walked to the kitchen. "Yusef doesn't have a bicycle."

"Mama? What's wrong?"

"Nothing. I couldn't sleep so I'm making a cup of chamomile tea." Hanan put the kettle on and sank down on a chair to wait. The dream wouldn't go away. Yusef had been riding his bicycle, going for bread, and the soldiers stopped him. She closed her eyes and remembered. She didn't want to, but she couldn't stop. The soldier said the boy was breaking curfew, but the sound trucks had barely started blaring the announcement. He kicked the bicycle. The boy fell with it, and the dream soldier shouted in perfect Arabic. "I'm going to make sure at least one little Arab bastard never makes any more little Arab bastards."

The boy lay on the ground, helpless, his leg pinned under his bicycle. Tears ran down Hanan's face as she remembered. The soldier pulled back his steel-toed combat boot and aimed it at the boy's crotch.

"No. That wasn't Yusef." She covered her ears and shouted the words. She didn't want to hear the crunch of bone when the boot hit its target. Her body shuddered with sobs.

"Mama, what's wrong?" Imahn's arms wrapped around her, and she clutched her daughter to her. She drew comfort from the girl's embrace and struggled to stop the tears.

"I'm sorry I woke you, Imahn. It was silly of me to get so upset over a bad dream. That's all it was, just a bad dream. Yusef doesn't even have a bicycle." That was another boy in another curfew years ago, but the memory still haunted her. Reluctantly, she released her hold on

26

Imahn and walked to the bathroom to wash her face. When she emerged, Imahn had two small glasses of chamomile tea ready for them.

"Did you say you're going to get Yusef a bicycle?"

"Not after that dream."

"Do you want to tell me about it? When I was little, I used to tell Jehad about my bad dreams before I went back to sleep. It helps."

"Thank you, but not tonight. It's already fading." She picked up her tea to hide her false smile. That nightmare would never fade, but sharing it would only give Imahn nightmares.

Two more days passed without a break in the curfew. Hanan ignored the circles under her eyes the same way she ignored how jittery she felt. She made lists of things she needed to resupply the two houses. She tried playing cards with Imahn; she tried watching television, but she couldn't sit still. She'd scrubbed everything in sight to keep busy. She'd cooked a big meal in the morning, and she was going to send Imahn to tell Muhammad to bring the family over in the evening to share it, when a better idea occurred to her.

"Imahn, I'm going over the wall to clean Deena's house."

"Why don't you rest? You look tired." She *was* tired. She was so tired she could feel it in her bones, but sleep eluded her. Maybe cleaning another house from top to bottom would exhaust her into a dreamless sleep for the night.

"I'll send Uncle Muhammad over with the twins. You stay here and help with the boys."

Over Deena's objections, Hanan spent the afternoon scrubbing every inch of the small house. When she got to the kitchen, she kept Amal busy emptying cupboards so she could scrub the insides, and then had her reload the contents. She blinked back tears for a moment when she saw how close to bare the cupboards were. She had to invite them more often now that the ladders made it easier.

They had almost finished when Imahn came over the wall with a big grin on her face. "Did you hear the trucks? There'll be a two-hour break tomorrow morning. Yusef will be home."

"Yusef's not home?" Deena looked from one face to the other.

"He's at a friend's house. They're working on a school project, but we didn't expect such a long curfew." Hanan spoke with what she hoped was a matter of fact tone. She turned to Imahn. "Tell Uncle Muhammad we'll all be over in a few minutes. Put the kettle on because your Aunt Deena and I really could use a hot cup of tea."

Muhammad was withdrawn and silent at supper. Hanan knew he was unemployed once more. And Deena looked tired. Even though Hanan had tried to make her sit and enjoy the freedom of an afternoon off, she had insisted on working. Hanan found it hard to make conversation. Her thoughts kept returning to Yusef. Was he warm and fed in the safe cocoon of his friend's home, or in the clinic or hospital, or… ? She didn't let herself finish the thought.

"Who's your favorite teacher, Amal?" If she could get the girls chattering and giggling over school, she could stop trying to fill the silence.

The frenetic activity of the day had truly exhausted Hanan, and she didn't object when Deena and the girls said

28

they'd clean up. She gave the list she'd prepared earlier to Muhammad along with a handful of money. "If you get everything except the chicken and bread, you should be back within the two hours. I'll send Imahn for those because they're out of your way."

She could tell by his expression how much he hated holding his hand out for money. How could she soften that? She didn't want him to feel like a boy being sent on an errand. "Your ladders are a wonderful addition. Knowing I can always get to you makes me feel less isolated when Ali's in Ramallah working. It makes life easier." Her smile was genuine—the first one she'd had since this curfew started. "I don't know why you didn't think of it sooner."

Muhammad chuckled softly. "I guess I wasn't mad enough before." It was a cryptic sentence, but his chuckle warmed the cold fear within her.

That night Hanan took a couple of ibuprofen tablets before going to bed to ease the back pain that came from moving furniture and scrubbing floors. Pulling the covers up to her chin, she decided to concentrate on all the things she had to be thankful for. Maybe counting her blessings would ward off the nightmares.

Ali had what most men in Kalandia only dreamed of— a steady job with a decent salary. He was the head accountant at the electric company. Yes, she was sick of sleeping alone so often, but he had to stay in town when Kalandia was under curfew. Sometimes he misjudged and the curfew caught him inside.

He was lucky Layth always had room for him. Having an older brother with a house in town was another thing on the list of blessings. Ali had a lot of discretion about when he did his work, but it was his responsibility to meet all the deadlines. Even when the whole region was under curfew, the towns were often released before the camps, and he could accomplish an hour or more of work during a two-hour break like tomorrow's. If he was home, it could take the whole two hours to get to town, maybe longer if the checkpoints were crowded or the soldiers were being particular.

She reached over, grabbed his pillow, and buried her face in it. She imagined she could smell him. Ali was her rock. Just thinking of him gave her strength.

Hanan woke the next morning grateful for a dreamless night. She watched the clock tick its way toward ten o'clock in an endless series of endless minutes. Not trusting her own clock, she turned on the radio. Yes, ten o'clock. She told Imahn for the umpteenth time what to buy and sent her out the door. Once she was alone, Hanan began to pace from room to room. She started dusting and straightening, but the house was already immaculate. She soon gave up any pretense of normality and just paced and prayed. Everything would be normal when Yusef came home. Over and over she repeated to herself that it was *when* he came home and not *if* he came home.

At last she heard the shrill sound of the door buzzer. "Please, let it be Yusef. Please let it be Yusef," she said as she ran to answer. She unlocked the door and flung it open without even trying to see through the peephole. She was surprised and disappointed that a man she'd never seen before was at the door. She'd been so sure it was Yusef.

"Are you Yusef's mother?"

Hanan's moment of relief that the man knew Yusef was immediately replaced by an even worse fear. Her breath caught in her throat and she grabbed the door to steady herself. Why wasn't Yusef with him? What kind of bad news was he bringing? "Yes." Her voice quivered with fear.

"He's all right. He's all right," the man said as he reached out to steady her. "I'm sorry I frightened you. I just wanted to make sure someone was home before I brought him in. He's all right."

The man hurried toward the street, and it was only then that Hanan noticed the taxi sitting at the curb. The man opened the car door and Hanan saw Yusef in the back seat. The man helped him out of the car and supported him. Yusef held one foot up off the ground and tired to hop on the other foot. She rushed to support him from the other side.

"What happened? Were you shot? We were so worried. Thank God you're back. We've all been frantic." The words tumbled out of her mouth in a rush of relief.

"Mama, slow down. Say hello to Salah's father. I've been at their house."

"Thank you so much for taking care of him. I hope he wasn't a bother." Hanan hoped the man would understand her lapse of manners. "Please, come in." She blushed as she realized he had no choice. He was acting as Yusef's crutch. They guided Yusef to the nearest chair. "Won't you stay for a cup of coffee?" The invitation was pure ritual. No one had time for socializing during a two-hour break.

"Perhaps another time. My wife sent me out with a list of things I have to bring home with me. She said to make sure I told you that it was a pleasure having Yusef in the house." With that he gave a slight nod to Hanan, waved at Yusef, and left.

"Too bad he couldn't stay for coffee," said Hanan.

Yusef rolled his eyes. "Give me a break, Mama. The guy just wants to get all the stuff on his list so his wife won't yell at him the rest of the curfew. Not to mention I'm the one who was plopped in a chair. How come you're worried about him?"

"I'm sorry, Yusef." She rushed back to his side. "Tell me what happened. Are you in pain? Can I get you anything?"

Yusef blinked at the barrage of questions, but before he could begin to answer, the doorbell buzzed again.

Hanan hurried toward the door, calling over her shoulder, "Just wait there, Yusef. I'll be right back."

"Do you really think I should wait here? I was thinking of going for a jog, or maybe just a leisurely walk to town to visit Uncle Layth. Oops! I forgot I can't even stand up by myself. I guess I'll just wait here."

"Yusef, that is not amusing." She opened the door.

Imahn stood there holding plastic grocery bags in both hands. "Any news?" she asked before she stepped through the door.

Hanan smiled. "Yusef's home."

"Thank God. Is he all right?"

Hanan hesitated for an instant. "Yes, he's fine. He just hurt his foot."

"Hurt his foot? How?"

"I don't know yet. He just got home seconds ago." She saw the relief on Imahn's face.

"What happened to his foot? Is he all right?"

The doorbell buzzed again. Muhammad stood there, laden with bags.

"I'm fine," called Yusef from the living room. "Don't anyone worry about me. I've been gone for days and days, but no one seems to notice I'm back." Imahn dropped the bags she was carrying and ran toward his voice.

"Sounds like the same old Yusef." Muhammad grinned at Hanan. "I guess the experience didn't take much of the sarcasm out of him." He picked up the bags Imahn had dropped, added them to his own, and walked toward the kitchen, winking at Yusef as he passed.

"Just leave them on the counter. We still haven't heard what happened," said Hanan.

"Are you sure you're all right?" asked Imahn.

"Oh yeah, I'm fine. I just blew my ankle up like a balloon because I didn't have anything else to do. I thought it might be fun not to be able to walk for a while."

"Why didn't you come home?"

"I couldn't walk, it was too late to find a taxi, and it hurt really bad. It got all puffed up, and I still can't put any weight on my foot."

"How did it happen?" asked his mother.

"I was walking home and talking to Salah. Then the soldiers came and started shouting at us to hurry. They were very scary and began to wave their guns around while they shouted. One of them fired a shot at the ground behind us and we started to run. The soldiers laughed, and fired another shot behind us." Yusef paused and looked down. "I guess I just panicked and didn't look where I was going."

Imahn laughed. "So your usual clumsy self fell on your face in front of the soldiers."

"Imahn, don't make fun of your brother's misfortune. You wouldn't be graceful either if you were being harassed by soldiers using guns and bullets." She sent Imahn to make tea.

Muhammad knelt in front of Yusef and gently moved his foot. Yusef gave a sharp intake of breath. "There isn't any bruising, and I don't hear any bone-against-bone noise. I'm fairly sure it's just a sprain. If it isn't better by the time the curfew is over, take him to the doctor. I don't think it's broken, but you can't always tell."

Hanan nodded as she wrapped the ankle tightly. "I'll make him keep the foot elevated. That might help the swelling." She watched Muhammad help Yusef toward his bedroom. By the time Muhammad came back, she had three bags ready for him to take home. "I know Deena can't go shopping now—especially with those boys hanging on to her skirts every time she moves." Neither one mentioned the fact that lack of money was also an issue.

That night Hanan sighed as she pulled the covers tight around her. She never wanted to go through that again. What would she do next year when Yusef was in high school and he had to go into Ramallah every day? And the year after that when Imahn joined him? No, she could not stay in the camp. She had to be near her family, near enough for Ali and the children to come home at night. When they were first married, they'd agreed that they needed to live in Kalandia. Ali felt he needed to be near his family; Muhammad was still very young and needed him. He'd also felt strongly that the camp needed role models. Ever year the best people moved out of the camp, leaving the adult population drained of the most able among them. Hanan savored the memory of how very young and idealistic they'd been.

34

But that was a long time ago, and Muhammad now had a family of his own. She smiled as she thought of Deena. It was amazing, really. Muhammad couldn't even put enough food on the table with all the curfews, yet Deena was as happy as the day they married. She worked so hard raising her young family, but she never complained. Hanan hoped she meant it when she said this would be the last child. Their house was already bursting at the seams.

She snuggled deeper under the quilt. Deena would need help when the baby came. Hopefully Muhammad would find a decent job before next school year. Hanan tried to think about how she or Ali could help, but after spending two sleepless nights worrying about Yusef, she fell asleep almost before she completed the thought.

Three days later, the sound trucks began their street by street trek before dawn, announcing that the curfew had been lifted. Muhammad began rooting through the wardrobe to find clothes that weren't paint spattered or torn from protruding nails.

"What are you looking for?"

"Something to wear that doesn't scream construction site."

"Your good pants are in the back." Deena pushed him aside with a smile. She reached her hand in and pulled out the garment in question without even looking. "Here they are."

"But if I go job hunting in good pants, I'll put off the people who want floor scrubbers or garbage collectors."

"Don't worry about impressing anybody in these pants." Deena gave him a quick hug as she handed him the pants. "Where are you going?"

"I'm going to every store and business in Ramallah. I'm bound to find something." His words sounded more confident than he felt, but he was determined to find work. He'd do anything—anything that was not on the other side of the checkpoint.

Chapter III
❧ KAREEMA'S SECRET ❧

Israel raids Palestinian village ahead of US talks
                    Reuter News Agency; January 4, 2002

Israelis kill 5 in West Bank clash
                    The Evening Standard (London); January 22, 2002

50 Israeli reservists refuse to serve in territories
                    The Times (London); January 30, 2002

The Council of Jewish Settlements demanded the recall of US Ambassador to Israel Daniel Kurtzer
He urged students at the Jewish-Arab Center for Peace to pressure the Israeli government to reach 'reconciliation' and 'reasonable compromise' with the Palestinians.
                    The Washington Times; January 25, 2002

Kareema's hands shook with cold as she wrapped the kafiya around her head. Leaving the house at dawn every morning was not her idea of fun. She buttoned her long coat and settled her bag firmly on her shoulder. She'd started using a shoulder bag rather than a backpack because the shoulder bag made her look less like a student. As long as she kept her coat buttoned, her school uniform was not visible, and she didn't attract any attention walking around during school hours. And as long as she wore her school uniform everyday, her parents didn't suspect she wasn't going to school. A cold wind blew icy tendrils down her neck and she pulled her kafiya tighter. Head down against the wind, she walked toward the bus terminal.

She'd been doing this for almost a month—ever since she happened to meet her younger cousins on their way to school. Then that blasted curfew caught her still in camp when she should have been miles away in school. When she came home and told her father that she'd missed the bus, he'd given her another lecture on how dangerous it was to commute to school, what with curfews and checkpoints and soldiers wandering the streets. How long could she keep this up?

When she started leaving early, she'd told her mother she was meeting with a friend in the mornings to do some extra studying. She grimaced at the thought. Once you told one lie it seemed that you had to tell another ... and another. She resolved, yet again, to tell them what she was doing. Surely they'd understand how important her work was; surely they'd be proud of her. Kareema went through the same conversation with herself several times a day. Her sigh came out as a small white cloud in the cold air. The chances were very small indeed that her parents would understand. What would her father do? Would he keep her at home by force? Would he disown her? If he forced her to stop working, which she had to admit he probably would, she couldn't endure it. No way could her story have a happy ending.

Her father's religious views might be in line with those of the militant Hamas party, but his politics were as different as they could possibly be. It wasn't that he didn't want a free Palestine, but he thought he could just sit on his fat behind until it was handed to him on a silver platter. Anger put energy in her steps. He'd never let her work for the YFP. He saw the Youth for Palestine organization as part of the problem.

She pushed her hands deeper into her pockets. It wasn't just who she worked for, the real insult would be that she'd made the decision herself. He had to be the one in the family to make all the decisions. He was absolute dictator of the family. It wasn't that he thought of her as a child; it would be the same at any age. He hadn't thought her mother was a child when he married her and made her pregnant by the time she was Kareema's age.

Kareema found her bus and boarded. Her hands were so numb she dropped her fare and had to scrabble around the floor of the bus to find it. Mentally cursing her young cousins again for her early start, she dropped into an empty seat and leaned her head against the window. Why was she blaming them for her problem? Amal spent so much of her time trying to keep her little brothers out of trouble that she probably didn't have time to think unkind thoughts. Kareema almost smiled at that. She loved her little cousin, but sometimes it was hard to believe that Amal's almost cloying sweetness was genuine. Imahn was only a year older but a lifetime wiser. At first glance, she was as sweet and uncomplicated as Amal, but she was already able to converse logically about what was nearest to Kareema's heart — politics.

Tonight she'd talk to the girls. If they agreed to keep her secret, she could stop this pre-dawn stuff anyway. Last night she'd mentioned that her mother hadn't visited her brothers in ages. Wonder of wonders, her father had agreed that it was a good idea and said he'd go, too. He *said* he'd enjoy visiting with his wife's brothers. Kareema snorted. What he meant was he'd enjoy telling them why everything they said was wrong. She wondered how her uncles managed to be so unfailingly polite to her father.

The bus neared the city and Kareema's thoughts turned once more toward her work. She sat straighter in the seat and smiled with anticipation. The bus stopped, and she got off and bought two warm sesame rolls from a street vendor. If she was lucky, she'd get to the office before the cleaning lady left. She was too far down the ladder to have her own key. This was the best time to use the internet anyway.

Luck was with her and the woman was still cleaning the bathroom at the end of the hall. "Good morning, Um Jamil. Any chance I can get in the office?"

"Anything for you, Kareema." She hurried down the hall and opened the door. "You know, if our politicians were as dedicated as you and the other young people that work here, we'd be flying the Palestinian flag already."

Kareema laughed. "From your mouth to the ears of God, Um Jamil." She walked in and turned on her computer. While it booted, she took the battered electric kettle down to the bathroom and filled it with water. Um Jamil was still mopping the floor. "If you finish before the others get here, come in and have a glass of tea and sesame roll." The woman nodded her thanks.

Back at her desk, she began her first internet search for news about Palestine and had navigated to the first of the major English language newspapers before the water boiled. She reached for one of the thick glasses on the shelf but put it back and grabbed a different one when she saw the chipped rim.

The press was full of references to Ariel Sharon's campaign promises to protect the settlements and build even more of them—nothing new there. She warmed up the printer and captured the single reference she found about the closure of the Gaza airport and the crossings into Jordan.

She was swearing quietly at the first paper jam of the day when Um Jamil spoke. "Didn't your mother teach you not to say things like that?" The old woman displayed a gap-toothed smile at Kareema's embarrassment.

"I didn't hear you come in."

"That's no excuse. He can still hear you." She pointed at the ceiling.

"Oh, Um Jamil, He doesn't listen to me. If he did, this world would be a different place." She gave the printer stand a kick. "The printer would work for one thing."

"So what else has you upset today? That thing never works for you, but you never swore at it before."

Kareema wanted to share her problems with Um Jamil, but she didn't. The woman had her own problems or she wouldn't be working at her age. "They shut off every way out of Palestine, leaving us here like fish in a barrel — but no one else knows because the press chooses not to report it. It's not news worthy." At least knowing what *wasn't* being reported gave the leadership an idea of what they needed to include in their own press releases.

"If the barrel has water, it might not be too bad."

It took Kareema a few seconds to connect that to what she'd just said. "It depends on what they do with the barrel." She got out the sesame rolls and sat to enjoy her breakfast. "You always make me smile, Um Jamil."

"That's what life's all about, child. If you can't smile, there's no point to it."

That evening, Kareema, in preparation for the cold walk to her uncle's house, again wrapped her kafiya over the white scarf that covered her hair.

"Why do you have to wear that thing?" asked her father crossly. "It is not ladylike and it's certainly not becoming."

Kareema clenched her fists inside her pockets. Her father objected to the kafiya for the same reason she wore it — because it was a symbol of Palestine and worn by the freedom fighters. "It keeps me warm," she replied. She'd long since stopped trying to talk to her father about anything having to do with Palestine, or any topic that really mattered to her. She stepped outside onto the sidewalk, preferring to stand in the cold until everyone else was ready than to give her father an opportunity to tell her to remove the kafiya.

"Why *do* you wear it?" The voice in the darkness startled Kareema. She hadn't noticed Bilal as he slipped out of the house behind her. Bilal was a year older than Kareema, the third of her four brothers. Only Kareema and Bilal still lived at home. "You know it would make him happy if you stopped wearing it."

"Well it makes me happy to wear it. The way I see it, if only one of us can be happy, it might as well be me."

Bilal held up his hands. "Hey, don't bite my head off. If this is you doing what makes you happy, I'm glad you left it on."

Kareema bit back an angry response. She took a few steps away from him and ground her teeth in frustration. Bilal should be able to figure it out for himself. People like Bilal were part of the bigger problem. He just went along from day to day with his nose buried in his books or talking with his friends about whatever it was boys talked about for hours at a time as they hung around on street corners. If the world was ever going to pay attention to

42

Palestine and try to get a real peace process going, they had to make themselves visible. That meant everyone had to get involved. Taking a few deep breaths of the cold night air calmed her anger. She turned back toward Bilal to apologize for her attitude and to see if she could make another gentle attempt to talk to him about ways to help the cause. Too late. Her parents came out of the house, and they all started walking.

Kareema was pleasantly surprised when her father stopped a passing taxi. It was too cold tonight for a long walk. He directed the driver to Uncle Ali's house. Uncle Muhammad's house faced an alley that was too narrow for a car. It was also too small for comfort with so many people. By the time Kareema got out of the taxi, her father was already ringing Ali's doorbell.

"What happened to you?" her father's voice echoed in the nearly empty street.

Kareema looked up to see Yusef standing in the doorway, propped up on crutches. Hanan came up behind him. "Yusef, the story can wait until they come in from the cold. Go sit down in the living room and let everybody come in and take off their coats."

After a flurry of hugs, kisses and handshakes, everyone made their way to the living room. Yusef gestured with his crutches and held his injured leg out as though putting it on display. Hanan went to the kitchen to make tea, and Yusef launched into the story almost before everyone found seats. He somehow managed to make himself the hero of the tale with his injury the trophy. Hanan came in with tea as he finished.

"Imahn, where are you?" Kareema cringed; her father's voice seemed to shake the small house. "Get your coat on, I have an errand for you."

"Ziad, she's not your daughter. You can't tell her what to do." Ferial's soft-voiced objection made no impact on her husband. Imahn appeared in the doorway. "Go next door and tell Muhammad and Deena to come over."

"I'll go with Imahn and visit with the girls," said Kareema. Even though she was pleased by the perfect opportunity to talk to her cousins without anyone else around, she still ground her teeth in anger at the way her father thought he could make decisions for everyone else. She followed Imahn out into the cold for the short walk to Uncle Muhammad's house.

"My family's over at Uncle Ali's, and they wanted you and Aunt Deena to join them," said Kareema when Muhammad opened the outer door. "Imahn and I came to visit with Amal."

Deena apologized for greeting them in her nightgown. "Clothes are getting very uncomfortable." She patted her protruding pregnancy. "I'll be ready in a minute."

Imahn disappeared into the back room, leaving Kareema alone with her uncle. Should she ask him not to mention their early morning encounter? Maybe he forgot and it would be better not to remind him. Deena took the decision out of her hands when she emerged from the bathroom, ready to go.

As soon as their parents left, the boys asked if they could watch television. "I have a better idea." Kareema hugged them. "We can make you a play house in the back room."

"Build a play house in our bedroom?" Mustafa frowned.

Omar shook his head. "We don't have any wood or cement."

Kareema laughed and grabbed Imahn's hand. "Come on, Imahn. We can build a mattress house with a quilt roof for them while Amal makes us some tea."

With the boys playing happily in the back room, the girls settled down with glasses of hot tea. Amal had added a few of her mother's dried mint leaves to the tea. After a few seconds of inhaling the wonderful mint aroma, Imahn and Kareema put their glasses down and started talking at the same time.

"About the other morning …"

"The other morning …" They laughed and Imahn told Kareema to go first.

"No one has said anything about my not being in school the other day, so I'm guessing that you girls didn't tell anyone you saw me."

"Imahn said it should be a Sister Secret," said Amal shyly, "so we didn't tell anyone."

"What's a Sister Secret?"

"A long time ago when I was little," Amal blushed slightly, "I told Imahn that I really wished I had a sister. She asked me why and the only thing I could think of was that we could share secrets."

"Then I told Amal we could share secrets just like sisters. We vowed never to tell anyone anything we made a Sister Secret," said Imahn.

"That's great." Kareema wondered if she'd looked guilty. Why else would Imahn have decided it should be a secret? "Amal, did your father say anything about seeing me?"

"He's been so worried about losing his job because of the curfew that he probably forgot all about it. What *were* you doing there? It was too late for you to be going to school, and you were going the wrong way."

That was a relief. Now if she could enlist the girls as co-conspiritors, she could stop the pre-dawn madness. The idea of keeping secrets already entranced them. "If you want me to tell you, it'll have to be another Sister Secret." The younger girls nodded in unison. They linked little fingers and shook them as their secret sign of sisterhood, laughing as they did so. Kareema laughingly repeated the act with each of them.

"You both know why we're refugees, don't you?" Kareema said.

"Of course," Amal shrugged. "Even the twins know that. The UN took our land away and gave it to Israel."

"We all know why we're here," Imahn said. "What we want to know is why you weren't in school that morning."

Kareema took another sip of tea. All the misery in their young lives came out of Amal's simple sentence, yet neither girl seemed touched by it. It frightened her that anyone could be numb in the face of so much injustice. It happened all around her, even her own family had no thoughts of fighting for their rights. Unless she could open their eyes, Imahn and Amal wouldn't be any more understanding about her predicament than her parents. She didn't want to turn them into activists, but they needed a better understanding of her beliefs. She had to try.

"Our grandparents were young when they became refugees. Our parents have lived their entire lives as refugees. Do you want to spend the rest of your life like this?"

Amal spoke first. "It wouldn't be too bad without the curfews and checkpoints. I mean, if Papa could get to work each day, and we didn't have to stay in the house for days at a time. Papa says it wasn't always this bad. It used to be they just had curfews sometimes, and things were better."

Kareema reached over and put her arm around Amal's shoulders. She spoke gently. "He's right. They just had curfews sometimes; they just got shot sometimes; they just got beaten sometimes; they just got jailed sometimes. Maybe they did have longer periods of relative calm where life went on, but all the same things happened. No matter how calm it was, there was always a chance that the next day something would happen, and it would all blow up again. That's the reality of living under military occupation." She squeezed Amal's slender shoulders. "Asking for occupation without curfews and checkpoints is like asking for a pomegranate without seeds. It isn't possible. Instead of being a Palestinian refugee, wouldn't it be nice to be a Palestinian—without the refugee part?"

"I guess so," said Amal doubtfully, "but ..." her voice trailed off. At least she was thinking about it. The occupation hit Amal harder than Imahn because her father was usually on the wrong side of the fifty percent unemployment rate. In fact, he seemed to have his own fifty percent unemployment.

"It would be nice to be able to fly, too," said Imahn, "but it's not going to happen, no matter how many times I flap my arms and want it to work."

"I believe it will happen, but not until a lot more people flap their arms and want it to work," Kareema said.

"How often do you think people in the rest of the world think about us and our problem? I'll tell you—the vast majority of them only think about us when we make international news. One small thing we can do is to keep our problem visible. We make things happen. This won't win a war, but it's something we can do besides just sitting and hoping. We just sat, and hoped, and waited for decades; and the longer we waited, the worse things became for us."

"Maybe it will, and maybe it won't," said Imahn, "but you're still not answering our question. What were you doing the other morning?"

"I don't want to spend the rest of my life in a refugee camp. I don't want you to spend the rest of your lives in a refugee camp. I don't want anyone to live like this, but nothing's going to change if we just sit and wait. So, I joined the YFP—the Youth for Palestine movement."

"We know what the YFP is. Some of the girls in my class say they belong." Kareema wasn't surprised that Imahn knew about it, nor was she surprised by the questioning look on Amal's face.

"Think about it. Our fathers have to work, and our mothers can't go out and demonstrate."

"If Mama went, the twins would have to go too."

"My brothers would have to learn to cook."

Kareema joined their laughter. "Not to mention what our fathers would say about it." She looked from one girl to the other. "So the only people left are the young people who don't have families depending on them. We're the ones who have to do it." Kareema took a deep breath before blurting out the next sentence. "I have a job working full time for the YFP."

"But you can't do that *instead* of school." Imahn was horrified. "Education is important—essential!"

"What good is an education here? I know at least three guys with university educations who can't get jobs. Their entire families—aunts, uncles, cousins—all contributed so these boys could get their precious education. Now the only way they can get a job is to leave the country. But if they do go outside and get a job, their identity cards expire in six months, and they can't come back. How many men want to make that choice? What kind of a choice is that: get a job and leave your family forever or stay with your family and have no job? That's why this is so important. Our position gets worse all the time."

"Some people stay, like teachers and doctors. There are lots of educated people still here. Just because it's difficult doesn't mean it can't be done," said Imahn.

Kareema paused and looked at her audience. This wasn't what she needed to say. As usual, she let her patriotic fervor pull her away from her original path. All she needed from them is a promise to look the other way if they saw her again in the mornings. This was getting her no closer to a solution to the underlying problem. "Amal, is there any more tea?" She closed her eyes for a few seconds. Her tears were dangerously close. Amal went to the kitchen to heat the tea, and Imahn's hand clasped her own.

"There's more, isn't there? What else is the matter?" Imahn's pitched her voice for her ears only. Imahn's sympathy broke Kareema's last defense, and she started sobbing.

"I haven't been to school for almost a month. I can't concentrate on schoolwork … it just doesn't seem important anymore. But I'd rather face an Israeli tank than tell my father what I'm doing. I can't live like this, and they're sure to find out sooner or later. You can't keep secrets in the camp."

"What're you going to do?"

"What *can* I do? I really believe in what we're doing, and I'm not willing to give it up. I just know Father won't let me do this. You know how he is."

"Yes, I do." Imahn shuddered.

"Father never listens to the other side of a story. I'm not sure he ever listens to anything except his own voice. Even when he watches the news on television, he runs his own commentary, and you know he can't be listening to that either. Oh, what can I do?"

Imahn got up to get a tissue for Kareema and looked in the back room. Kareema heard the murmur of voices, and Imahn came back with a tissue and fresh tea. "Amal's in the other room with the boys. She left the tea on a low flame."

Kareema's sobs subsided. "Thanks."

"Kareema, I have the beginnings of a thought."

"That's more than I can say."

"You know not everyone in the family agrees about things like demonstrations and resistance."

"That might be the understatement of the year."

Kareema wondered if Imahn knew how active her father had been when he was in high school. It had been a major issue between him and Uncle Layth. He might be a good ally, unless he wanted to keep his past from his children. There was only one way to find out. "I've heard some wild stories about Uncle Ali."

Imahn laughed. "They're probably all true. Anyway, my idea is that you might never have a better opportunity to tell your parents what you're doing. You know you have to tell them before they hear it from someone else." Kareema moaned and clutched her tea glass so hard her knuckles turned white. "Go now and tell them that you have an important adult decision to make, and you want advice. That will get their attention."

"My father will be furious."

"Then you tell them that you're leaving school to do this work for the YFP because you believe that Palestine will never be free as long as we're a forgotten people and we need to make waves. Or maybe you start by telling them that you wanted to have their opinion about your feelings that we need to make a bit of trouble to grab some headlines. Hopefully that will get them all arguing and the politics will boil over."

"Father will turn red in the face and turn up the volume."

"At some point you'll get a chance to say you believe this so strongly that you've decided to quit school to work for YFP. The whole thing is very iffy, and I have no idea if it'll work. You just sit it out as long as you can. If it looks like your father is about to make some drastic decision, you jump in and offer a compromise."

"Compromise? I can't compromise my ideals. I can't be half-way committed to my work."

"Well, you could say you'll stay in school if they let you continue your work after school and when school is closed. Promise to study twice as hard to make up for lost time and, most important, promise not to deceive them again."

Kareema thought for a moment. "And if that doesn't work, what will happen? You said yourself it's risky."

"I know," said Imahn, "but would you be any worse off than if you told him when you were alone with them? Or, worse yet, if someone else told them before you did? Then they'd never believe you. The longer you put this off, the greater the chances that that's exactly what'll happen."

"I know. I had the same conversation with myself this morning—and this afternoon, and yesterday, and the day before, and the day before that. It's pretty much all I can think about now. I guess a bad plan is better than no plan. I have to do something." Kareema shuddered at the thought of the possible consequences. She had a very slender thread of hope that she could get through this night without some dire fate crashing down around her.

"At least this way you'll have your uncles to protect you from the worst of your father's anger," said Imahn with a shrug.

Kareema hugged her cousin. "All right, I'll do it. In any case, it'll be over—one way or the other. One thing I know for sure is that I can't go on like this. I'd better hurry before Father decides the visit has lasted long enough." She poked her head in the back room to say good-by to Amal and found her telling a story to two heavy-eyed boys.

Kareema stepped out into the cold of the alley and heard the door lock behind her. She wanted to turn around and beg the girls to let her back in the house. It was ridiculous to be less afraid of armed soldiers in the streets than of her own father, but she was. She squared her shoulders. If she expected to be treated as an adult, then had to act like one and take responsibility for her own actions. She tried to put confidence in her step as she moved forward, but it took all of her courage to ring the bell when she reached Imahn's house.

She was surprised when Jehad opened the door. He must have come home after she left. Was this a good thing or a bad thing? Which side would he take in the argument she was about to start? His opinion would carry weight, whichever side he chose. He was only a year ahead of her in school, but no one considered him a child. Just one more unknown thrown into the pot. She slipped quietly into a chair.

"So there are more opportunities for scholarships than I had thought." Jehad was obviously concluding a conversation. Kareema was proud of Jehad's hard working determination to attend university, as was everyone else in the family. She kept her own views on the choices that would be open to him after graduation to herself. Not so long ago she'd harbored thoughts of being the first girl in the family to go to university, but now she accepted that her options would be even more limited than Jehad's. When the conversation paused, Imahn's mother poured a glass of tea and put it in front of her with a simple welcome.

"I thought you wanted to visit with Imahn and Amal," said Kareema's mother.

This was it. The conversation around her paused, and she felt as though everyone was staring at her. She clasped her hands together in her lap to keep them from shaking. "We had a nice visit, but I came back to discuss something of an adult nature. I wanted to take advantage of the family gathering to get some advice."

Kareema saw her father's brows come together in the beginnings of a frown. She had only taken the first step, and already she was going in the wrong direction. Her father was already annoyed because she called this evening a family gathering. To him it was a visit to the in-laws. She took a sip of tea; everyone looked at her expectantly. There was no road back—she'd just blown up her bridges behind her.

She spoke slowly and carefully. "I've done a lot of thinking, and I decided to join the YFP." She paused, taking time to look at the faces around her. Her father was getting red in the face, and she could see he was ready to speak. To Kareema's relief, Jehad hurried to speak first.

"Congratulations, Kareema, that's a big decision to make. I admire your patriotism. I know it has to take up a lot of your spare time."

Kareema looked at Jehad and nodded gratefully. She glanced at her uncles before she replied. She wanted them to speak quickly and head off an explosion by her father. They did not disappoint her.

"The YFP is doing really good work these days," said Uncle Ali. "I don't know if I would do it in your place, but I certainly understand your decision. Things aren't what they were when we were your age. The YFP didn't exist then, and there was no organization to direct the youth activists that tried to keep the occupation forces aware of our feelings and keep the name of Palestine alive."

When her father finally found his tongue, as she had hoped, he directed it at his brother-in-law and not at her.

"You hit the nail on the head." Ziad's voice reverberated like thunder in the small room. "Things are NOT what they were—and one of the reasons for this is the young people stirring up trouble all the time. If they just stayed home and minded their own business the soldiers would stay out of the camp, and we could get on with our lives. Things would be better."

"Wait a minute," broke in Uncle Muhammad, "don't you ever watch the news? Palestine's been on the news and people are continuing to take us seriously—even after the Oslo Accords seem to have petered out. Maybe it isn't all the YFP, but they're certainly pulling their weight."

Relief flooded through Kareema. She relaxed her hands and sent a silent thought of gratitude to Imahn. However this finished, her uncles had taken the initial brunt of anger.

"I can't believe that you, of all people, would feel that way." Her father did not lower his voice. "You're a day laborer and you probably haven't earned a full week's wages in months—or doesn't that bother you?"

Kareema felt her face grow hot with embarrassment and anger. That was a personal attack, and totally out of place. Before either of her uncles could get over the shock of Ziad's rude remark, she spoke directly to her father. Anger loosened her tongue and made it easier for her to blurt out the rest of what she had to say.

"I've already joined the YFP, *and* I decided to leave school and work for them full time. Not only have I made the decision, I did it weeks ago and have been working ever since." She turned to her mother, pained by the expression of shock and dismay on her face. "I'm sorry, Mother, that I didn't tell you sooner, but I knew Father would never agree, and I'm at a point in my life when I need to make my own decisions."

Before she even finished that sentence, everyone else seemed to have come out of their shock and started talking at once.

"Of course it bothers me." Muhammad ignored Kareema's announcement and responded to Ziad's earlier remark. "I spend hours worrying about it, and sleepless nights are the norm. However, unlike some people, I realize that there are things in this world that are more important than my own personal comfort."

"Ziad, aren't you missing something here? It wasn't so long ago that we were sitting in this same room trying to convince you that Kareema should be allowed to go to high school, and now you're ready to explode because she decided to quit?" Ali made a good save, redirecting the thrust of the conversation.

"You're the one who's missing something," said her father, "or have you all forgotten that people get hurt, or jailed, or even killed when they go out on these useless demonstrations? Are your memories that short, or do you consider members of your family expendable?"

Kareema caught her breath at that remark. There had been a brother between Ali and Muhammad who was killed in a demonstration years before she was born. Her mother had told her how hard the death had been on the family, especially Muhammad. She looked around the room at the reactions. Jehad's jaw dropped and Muhammad's face paled. Kareema was sure her own face clearly showed her distress at having caused this conversation.

"Stop it, all of you!" Her mother's voice cut through the altercation with authority. Kareema was shocked to see her mother standing up, literally and figuratively. Even her father was staring at her in disbelief. Her mother had never stood up to her father—at least she didn't think she ever had. "Ziad …" She stopped in mid sentence, and Kareema didn't know what to expect.

"Ferial, it's—" Ali recovered his voice, but he was stopped by a look from his sister.

"I believe my daughter has more to say. Whether or not you agree with what she believes, she deserves to be heard."

"Thank you, Mama." Kareema whispered, amazed and grateful for the intervention. Her father's face had turned to stone, but Ali and Jehad were smiling encouragement. Muhammad's head was bowed, and Deena was holding his hand.

Kareema took a deep breath. "I am truly sorry that I didn't tell you the truth, but I'm not sorry I made the decision to act in accordance with my beliefs." She continued to tell how, in spite of her unwavering belief in the work of YFP, she now realized that she may have been hasty in quitting school. She presented the idea that she could do both—if she worked hard enough. She was confident that she could do it, and she fully intended to bend all of her efforts toward making it happen.

As she spoke, she watched her uncles regain control of their emotions. She heard herself repeating some of the same things she'd said earlier, but she wanted to hammer home her point of view—and she wanted to give everyone time to come back from their personal thoughts. Her father's scowl never left his face, but he finally sat back in his chair. She finished talking and sent a silent prayer that she had not caused this argument for nothing.

"I had an offer for you last week," said her father, "and I should have taken it. I can't believe I told them you were in school—and you were already out of school. Just look what you have done with your selfish thoughtless actions. You made a liar of me in front of my friends."

Unbelievable. Her father's first thought was for himself. She swallowed her angry retort and forced herself to answer in a calm voice. "But if you take my suggestion, it will be true—I will still be in school. I can do it."

Ziad was not ready to concede. "I should have made you marry Abu Mustafa's youngest son."

"Made her?" said Deena, speaking for the first time. "You can't *make* her marry someone." Kareema's heart sank. Of course he could. Half of her classmates from junior high were already married, and most had at least one child. She wanted to tell her aunt to rephrase the question. She meant he shouldn't. She just hoped her father didn't take the remark as a challenge.

Jehad jumped in and deflected the conversation back to education. "A lot of people talk about freedom and the need for us to gain our independence, but far fewer are willing to do anything about it. Almost no one shows the strength of character that Kareema has shown. She also showed incredible courage and good sense by coming here to work out a solution." His speech may not have convinced the men, but Kareema was impressed and grateful. It gave everyone else time to calm down.

Kareema watched her father closely. He was still scowling and ready to explode.

Her mother spoke first. "The boy makes sense, Ziad. Kareema may not have done what we would have wanted, but she has come forward to make things right." Following her lead, the two uncles and their wives all spoke in favor of the plan. Their words blended seamlessly, and they left no gap for her father to insert a comment.

By the end of the evening, Kareema's father grudgingly accepted the arrangement, with certain provisions. He made no secret of his displeasure at her activities, and he argued that she had deceived him once, and words alone could not convince him she wouldn't do so again. She would be closely supervised at all times. The other provision was really an ultimatum. If Kareema's grades did not maintain their previous level of excellence, she was to accept gracefully the marriage her father proposed.

Kareema was terrified. What if she was promising something she couldn't do? She'd be committed to a marriage that she might or might not find acceptable. She didn't know who the person was her father had in mind, but it was unlikely that his ideas of the "right" man would coincide with hers. She glanced at her mother but could read nothing in her expression. She looked at Uncle Ali and saw a suggestion of a smile on his face. Jehad gave her a thumbs up sign, shielded from her father's view. They were showing her that they had confidence in her — but they had no idea how hard it would be to make up weeks of school and work at the same time.

Finally they all agreed. It wasn't what Kareema had hoped for, but it was better than any alternative she'd been able to imagine before this evening began. The very thought of not being able to manage work and school made her blood run cold.

Chapter IV
❧ EMERGENCY ❧

No to Palestinian State
Emmanuel A Winston, Middle East analyst & commentator
USA Today; February 22, 2002

Tanks go in after pledge of action [by Ariel Sharon, Israeli Prime Minister]; Blitz kills 22 Palestinians
The Herald (Glasgow); February 21, 2002

High hopes for unseen peace plan
It may be a measure of the desperation in the Middle East that world leaders are swarming around an unseen peace initiative which remains in the drawer of a Saudi prince's desk.
The Guardian; February 26, 2002

Hanan lay in bed and went over the plan in her head. God, she was sick of curfews! She was sick of having no control over her own life. She was sick of worrying about her family whenever they were out of her sight. She swung her feet over the edge of the bed. Muhammad was right. Curfews were coming faster and lasting longer. There was always too much to cram into the infrequent two-hour breaks. Today she absolutely *had* to get Deena to the clinic—and there weren't enough hands and feet to get all the shopping done, too.

How had her mother and grandmother done it? Hanan sat straighter as she thought of the strong women she'd taken as role models many years ago. She pulled a heavy sweater on over her nightgown and slid her feet into her slippers. Her first job was lighting the two kerosene heaters to take the chill out of the air. One she placed in the wide hallway that served as a common area, near the door to the "children's" room, and the other inside the bathroom where it would stay until everyone had washed and dressed. No matter how cold it got or how much the boys complained, they never left the heaters on during the night. Each morning when she woke up with her breath making white clouds, she had to remind herself that people in the camps died every year of carbon monoxide poisoning from the kerosene heaters. Closing the bathroom door, she moved to the kitchen and lit the gas under the two tea kettles. She leaned back against the counter, savoring the early morning peace, and waited for the water to warm enough for her to wash comfortably.

Her grandmother's image floated in her mind, the way she always pictured her, sitting cross-legged on a mat, telling stories to her grandchildren. She'd been a great storyteller. In the village, storytelling was just about the only entertainment around. Even radios had been few and far between.

"How did you know it was a lie? By its huge size." Her grandmother always started her story of the Nakba with that old Arab proverb. That was what her husband had said to her when she told him about the terrifying rumor that the English were giving all their land to the Zionist Jews for a new country. He had laughed at the absurdity of the idea. "How can they give our land away? It belongs to us. Our family has farmed it for generations." She'd still been frightened, so he took out the little metal box where he kept important papers and pulled out one that he said was the deed to the land. "Look. We have a deed. It belongs to us. Rumors are just that," her grandfather had said, "stories to frighten ignorant women. Maybe the English were talking about the land nobody owns, like the useless rocks on the top of the mountains. What do the English know about us and our land?" Unfortunately, the rumors had turned out to be true.

Hanan's thoughts came back to the present as the steam rose from the kettle. She snatched it up and started toward the bathroom. On the way, she stuck her head in her children's room and gave a cheerful greeting. She felt guilty about complaining, even if she didn't say it out loud. No matter how sick she was of everything that was happening, it had to be ten times worse for her little sister.

Poor Deena was having a difficult pregnancy. Muhammad had given up trying to find a job in town, and had finally found another construction job. It was just his bad luck that another curfew came up so soon, and he was at work when it was announced. He was safe enough because this curfew only affected Kalandia, but Deena was having a hard time without him. At least he wouldn't lose his job over this one. He'd stay with Ali, at their older brother's house. She knew it was hard for him to leave Deena, but it was even harder for him to sit at home and let his brothers buy food for his family.

"Do you want me to go to town and get Uncle Muhammad?" Yousef asked when they were having breakfast.

"No, I'll wait and hear what the clinic doctor says when he sees her today. No sense in spreading panic." Hanan looked at the clock. "Besides, I need your help today. Let's go over the plan again."

"Yes, General," said Yusef with a mock salute. "At exactly ten hundred hours, Officer Yusef will head toward the market and the taxi stand with all possible speed and dispatch, with hopes of finding a car as soon as possible. Said car, when found, will be commandeered by Officer

Yusef. Meanwhile, General Mama and her aide, Imahn, will head for the house where Aunt Deena and her family are bivouacked. The General and her aide will assist DC (that's distressed civilian) Aunt Deena to the street and will begin to walk toward the clinic, watching for the return of Officer Yusef with a car. As soon as the car appears, the aide will proceed to the market and purchase supplies for the troops. After delivering the General and the DC to the clinic, Officer Yusef will proceed to the market and assist in the purchase of supplies. He will bring another car to the clinic before twelve hundred hours to collect the General and the DC."

By the time he finished, Hanan was laughing along with the youngsters, her earlier complaints shelved. "And what will the supplies be, Officer Yusef?" she asked.

Yusef saluted again and read off the items on his list. "Those items have been assigned to me because they are far flung and I am fleet of foot—also because I am not likely to trip over my own feet, and thus will not have to be brought home on my shield with a twice sprained ankle. An ankle," he added in a stage whisper, "that was honorably sprained while under enemy fire in a previous mission." Still laughing, they synchronized watches and set out on their various missions.

The plan started well. Deena was in good spirits on the way to the clinic, but when they arrived, the front of the clinic was already crowded with people jockeying for position. "How did all these people get here before us? We headed out as soon as the curfew lifted."

"I don't know, Hanan, but we'll never get through. I can't work my way through that. Maybe we should just go home."

Hanan looked at the jostling people and agreed that Deena had no chance of getting to the front of the line, but she was not willing to admit defeat yet. "You wait here. I'll get through." Hanan was still at the edge of the crowd when two staff members came out and shouted for quiet.

"We're going to go around and write down each person's name and the nature of the illness or problem. The doctor will see people in order of the seriousness of the complaint. Please spread out and let us through. Being near the door will not result in you being seen any sooner. Remember, we have less than two hours and only one doctor. The nurses will handle as many cases as they can on their own. Please be considerate of those who are more in need."

Hanan grabbed Deena's hand and maneuvered for a place in the path of one staff member. "He said there's only one doctor, which means the part timers from town didn't bother to come — and it looks like everyone in camp has a problem today."

"Let's go home," said Deena. "I am just a pregnant woman retaining water. They won't have time for me. Besides, I can't stand up that long."

"Wait here," commanded Hanan. She strode off toward the clinic door. A few minutes later, she reappeared with a chair. "Here," she said, "sit and wait for your turn. I already put your name on the list and convinced the nurse that you should be seen." Deena flashed a weak smile and sat down. Hanan looked around and listened to the people near her, trying to assess their chances of seeing the doctor in the small window of time they were allowed.

"My little boy was trying to climb up the wardrobe shelves two days ago while I was busy in the kitchen. The

64

shelves came down and he broke his arm. I kept telling him to sit still and not to act like a monkey. What can a mother do? It's not natural for a small boy to sit still for days at a time. He hasn't slept for two days now from the pain." The woman held a small boy who whimpered constantly. A kafiya tied his arm to his body so it wouldn't move.

A woman's voice shrilled from another direction. She needed insulin for her husband. She told someone he could die without his needles, and that, no, she didn't give them to him; he had learned to do it himself.

Someone else had a bad heart and brought her empty medicine bottles. "This one is for the little white ones," she explained, "and this one has tiny blue pills, and this one has big white ones. The doctor at this clinic is very good. He gives me three kinds of medicine. The last doctor only gave me one kind."

The two hours of break had almost ended, and they were getting anxious when at last Deena's name was called. They worked their way to the door and were shown into an exam room. Hanan was still helping Deena take off her coat when the doctor came in. Hanan recognized the exhaustion on the young man's face and was almost embarrassed to bother him, but her sister really needed help. They hadn't exchanged a word before a nurse burst into the room.

"Doctor, we have two casualties. One is bleeding profusely; we can't stop the flow. We need you."

"Sorry." The doctor stood and started out the door. He glanced at Deena. "Probably fluid retention. Keep your feet elevated. No salt diet." He began to run after the nurse, and then stopped in mid stride. "Could be preeclampsia." He whirled and began walking backward after the nurse, shouting to the startled women as he walked. "Go to the hospital the next time the curfew lifts. If you see any signs of seizures, call an ambulance immediately—no matter what. You got that?" When he saw Hanan nod, he whirled once again and ran through the door where the nurse had just disappeared.

Why had she nodded? Her answer should have been no. She didn't get it at all. Whatever he meant, it sounded serious. She looked around for someone to ask.

"Hurry, Hanan. Time's almost up." Deena tugged at her sleeve.

"You go out and look for Yusef. I'll catch up in a minute." She gave her sister a small push toward the door. She barely registered the sight of her sister shuffling like an old woman as she moved. Hanan's gaze darted from one side to the other, searching for anyone who might be able to explain the doctor's words. Everywhere she looked, she saw anxious faces. The distant sound of a burst of fire from machine guns caused an instant escalation in the volume of voices around her. That was the warning signal. Break was over and people needed to scurry back to their shelters like insects running for cover.

Trying to stay out of the way of people hurrying, she backed against a wall and stood up on her tiptoes. At last she spotted a staff member she'd seen earlier. She started across the crowded lobby as fast as she could, uttering a nonstop series of apologies. "Excuse me … Sorry ... Pardon me ..." She almost bumped into the man in the white coat and grabbed his arm. "What are seizures? The doctor said to look for signs of seizures. What did he mean?"

"Seizures aren't always the same thing, but they are usually uncontrollable muscle contractions. Sometime it looks like shaking and sometimes it's just clenching muscles. It could be part of the body or all over."

"If my sister has seizures, we're supposed to call an ambulance, but you know how long that takes. Is there anything we can do before they arrive?"

"Keep her from hurting herself."

She still wasn't sure she understood what a seizure was, but time was short. She asked a few more short questions and listened carefully to the answers before running to catch up with Deena.

When they reached the street, Hanan was overjoyed to see Yusef frantically waving at her with one hand while keeping the other hand on the door of a cab.

"Hurry!" he shouted, "the driver says he needs to leave *right now* because he has to get his cab off the streets." They raced home with the driver muttering about getting home before the soldiers shot holes in his car. The taxi dropped them at the mouth of the alley and raced off in a cloud of dust.

Together Hanan and Imahn helped Deena to walk the short distance to her house, while Yusef struggled with all the groceries. Amal ran to help him. "I've been standing in the doorway, looking for you. I was so afraid you wouldn't get back on time. What did the doctor say?" Hanan didn't answer until they were all inside and the door closed behind them.

"Yusef was a real hero today," said Hanan. "He managed the cars and made sure everyone was in the right place and the right time. Without Imahn and Yusef we'd all be eating rice and dried beans this week." Yusef gave them a grin and an elaborate bow.

"What a ham," said his sister.

"I'll just get you settled down before I leave." Hanan lowered Deena into a chair. "Life is easier now that we can get over the wall." They had cut it really close this time. The sound trucks and machine guns were already on their street. Hanan made Deena as comfortable as possible and told Amal to put the kettle on before telling them what she learned at the clinic. Deena was to have total bed rest, according to the doctor. It was their responsibility to make sure she got it.

They all worked to rearrange things so that Deena would be sleeping in Amal's bed in the back room. Amal would sleep on a mattress in the same room in case she needed something at night, and the boys would have the front room to themselves until their father came home. When Muhammad was home, Amal would join her little brothers. Hanan said she'd handle the cooking until things got better. "Thank God and Muhammad for the ladders," she said. It was only when she heard Amal's smothered giggle that she realized how that sounded. "Not *that* Muhammad, may God's peace be upon him. I meant *our* Muhammad." That made Amal giggle even harder.

The next day passed with no change in Deena's condition. Staying in bed with her feet up helped with the pain. Hanan spent her time between the two houses, cooking and sitting with her sister. Long after they'd turned off the lights and the heaters, Hanan's eyes flew open and instantly she was wide awake. What was it? Had she heard something, or had she just had a dream? Her heart beat so hard she could feel it. She threw back the covers and slipped her feet into her slippers. Moving silently, she tiptoed toward the living room. There it was again.

"Yusef!" She did her best to scream in a whisper. "Yusef, wake up." Oh, God, why couldn't Ali be here when she needed him?

"Yusef," she heard Imahn's voice echo her call. "Quick, Mama's calling you."

"What is it?" Yusef came out of the bedroom with Imahn right behind him.

"I heard something at the door." Hanan ran to the kitchen and came back with the biggest knife she owned. There was no doubt in her mind that she would use it, if necessary. She'd protect her family by any means available.

"Who is it?" Yusef asked. Whoever it was, it was not a patrol of Israeli soldiers. The soldiers often raided houses in the middle of the night, but they were never quiet about it.

"Okay." She hadn't heard an answer, but it seemed that Yusef was confident enough to open the door. She kept a firm grip on the knife and stepped closer. Yusef unlocked the door and began to open it cautiously. The door was forced wider, knocking him off balance. Hanan jumped forward with the knife. A man in a black hooded sweatshirt slipped in and slammed the door shut as he leaned against it. Hanan was still moving with the knife upraised.

"Hanan, it's me!" The man grabbed her hand. She recognized his voice, and the knife clattered to the floor.

"Muhammad." Her forward momentum carried her into his arms, and they held each other up while relief replaced fear and terror. It took almost a minute for her to calm down enough to speak. "Imahn, turn on a light and put the kettle on." She picked up the knife and handed it to Imahn. "Muhammad, are you insane? You know there's a curfew, don't you? You could've been jailed, or beaten, or shot, not to mention that I could have stabbed you. You *are* insane. Have you eaten? Imahn, heat some food for your uncle."

Muhammad held up his hand and Hanan sputtered to a stop. "Yes, I probably am insane. Yes, I know there's a curfew and I could've been shot, but I never imagined that you might stab me with your knife. No, I haven't eaten and that sounds wonderful. Hot tea would also be nice. I think I'm half frozen."

Yusef had already lit the kerosene heaters and placed one by his uncle. Imahn came out of the kitchen with the tea tray and put the kettle on top of the heater.

"The food will be hot in a minute, Uncle," she said.

Muhammad thanked them both and turned back to Hanan. "Tell me about Deena. How is my wife? I wanted to go home, but I was afraid no one would wake up to open the door because of the courtyard. If I started pounding on the door, the patrols would hear me from a mile away. I'll go over the wall as soon as I stop shivering."

"No, you won't. Do you want her to die of fright with you showing up in the middle of curfew? Look how afraid we were, and we have a man in the house. I nearly killed you."

Muhammad laughed softly. "That 'man' would sleep through a major invasion if you didn't wake him up."

"Whatever. You aren't going anywhere until morning. Your wife needs her sleep." She poured tea for everyone. Imahn came out of the kitchen with a plate of food.

"I guess I owe you an explanation," said Muhammad.

"I guess so."

"They extended the area under curfew. When I heard the warning announcement, something happened in my head. I can't put it in words. We were all sitting there complaining and I just looked up and said, 'I have to go home. Deena needs me.' Of course, Ali and Layth were upset. They tried to stop me. I told them I wasn't a little boy anymore, and I knew where I had to be. I promised to be careful, but I had to get out of town while people were still scurrying around trying to get home for the curfew. I had to hurry. In the end they had to let me go." He paused for a few mouthfuls of food.

"That was so dangerous, Uncle," said Imahn.

Muhammad shrugged. "It was already too late to go through the center of town, so I made a wide circle and stayed off the roads. Thank God it's winter and clouds covered the moon most of the time. It was perfect. Most of the time I had enough moonlight to see, but enough darkness to conceal, not that I didn't have my share of missteps and stumbles. I've walked from town before in about two hours. Tonight it must have taken me at least six hours, maybe more. I even avoided the small roads, and I tried to stay away from houses. The scariest part was right here in front of your door. I was terrified no one would wake up, and I was on the street, totally exposed to any passing patrols."

"Look." Iman pointed to Yusef and giggled. "I think he's asleep in the chair."

"There he is—your knight in striped pajamas, defender of your castle." Yusef sat up with a jerk, awakened by their laughter. He gave a jaw-cracking yawn and said good night. Imahn said she, too, was going back to sleep as she took the dirty dishes to the kitchen.

Muhammad thanked Imahn and watched her leave the room. He took another sip of tea before speaking softly to Hanan. "Now tell me about Deena. I assume because you insist that I stay here until morning that her problem is more about discomfort than danger." Hanan didn't answer right away. Muhammad grasped the arms of his chair until his fingers hurt. "Is she worse? What happened since the curfew?"

"I took her to the clinic today. She's not supposed to get out of bed except for trips to the bathroom." Hanan poured more tea. She described the new sleeping arrangements and what they were doing to keep the household running.

"So as long as she stays in bed, she'll be all right?"

"Maybe."

Muhammad's fear increased. "Maybe? You saw the doctor, right? How come you don't know?"

Hanan took a deep breath. She started at the beginning and told Muhammad everything. "The doctor didn't even have time to look at her. He was already running to save the other person when he thought of the new thing it could be. I didn't understand all of it"

"Can you remember the exact words? I won't understand them any better than you did, but I want to hear them anyway."

Hanan nodded and closed her eyes. "There isn't much to tell." She recited the conversations. "That's what I remember. But the doctor was so tired and overworked …"

Muhammad wished he could see the expression on the doctor's face or hear the tone of his voice. He was looking for some clue as to what the doctor thought was the right answer. "If he really thought it was that pre-whatever, he would have kept her in the clinic, right?"

"I'm sure he would." Hanan's words didn't sound any more sincere than his, but he clung to them. "Hey, you must be tired. Bring a mattress from the rack. I'll move the heater and get the bedding."

"Is there any more tea?" asked Muhammad.

Hanan's eyebrows rose. "You must be exhausted. It'll be dawn in a few hours."

"Yeah." He brought out the mattress and went to the bathroom with a pair of Ali's pajamas, leaving Hanan arranging the bedclothes. By the time he returned, she was sipping tea and a full glass sat near his chair.

"Okay, Muhammad, what's so important that it can't wait until morning?"

"I just thought I ought to tell you what's been happening. We, Ali and I, think that we're moving into a new phase of the occupation. Like they say, 'just when you think things can't get worse, they do.' We think that may be what's happening now. There are signs that Israel is moving a lot of troops and tanks toward the West Bank. We think there'll be major trouble." He reached in his pocket and pulled out a wad of money. He handed it to Hanan.

"What's this?"

"Once Ali knew he couldn't stop me from coming home, and he might not be able to get back for some time, he sent you his month's pay." Muhammad watched Hanan's face pale as she took the money.

"How long does he think it might be? He knows we have a reserve fund in the house. Oh, dear God, this sounds serious." Hanan blinked rapidly and soon recovered her composure.

Muhammad continued. "As far as we can tell, curfew's been extended to all populated areas of the West Bank. Of course, there's a lot of rumor and speculation, but none of it's good. Gaza is being openly attacked. Nothing too violent in the West Bank yet, but they're moving tanks and armored vehicles into the cities. I didn't want to say anything in front of Imahn because I don't want her to get upset, but things are pretty bad."

"Imahn might surprise you. She understands more about politics and what's going on than many adults. She keeps her mouth shut about it most of the time, but she listens and puts the pieces together. Sometimes I ask her about things when I don't think they make sense. She sees the big picture."

"She's so young."

Hanan shrugged. "If you don't grow up fast in a refugee camp, you don't grow up at all."

Muhammad wondered where he'd heard that phrase. He passed his hand over his face as he thought back to the harsh lessons of his own childhood. His father's death had been lumped in with so many others and casually dismissed as "collateral damage" from the 1967 war. He had no recollection of his father, but the loss of his brother when they were only children would be with him forever. He took a deep breath before continuing. "Some of what we think we know is flat out rumor, but some of it comes from the BBC and other stations we can get on Layth's short wave. The only good thing I can see is that things are finally so bad that a whole group of Israeli soldiers have refused to serve in the Occupied Territories. They issued a statement that was published in one of the big Israeli newspapers. More important, it's been picked up by all the

74

foreign new services *and* there was a big demonstration in Tel Aviv in support of their position. They say there were over ten thousand people there. That's bound to have an effect. The government has to pay attention to that kind of reaction and ease up their actions." He drained his glass. "I guess that's it." Suddenly his body felt too heavy to support. The effects of the long walk in the dark over uneven terrain and the repeated spurts of adrenaline that kicked in during his near-miss encounters with patrols had depleted his energy reserves and sleep was his uppermost thought. He stood up and placed his glass on the tray.

"Not quite," said Hanan seriously. "I have a question. What really made you come home?" When he didn't answer, she continued. "I mean, you knew it wouldn't be an easy thing. You risked your life to get here, and you knew it was a gamble."

A cold shiver ran down Muhammad's spine. "I don't know," he said softly. "I just knew I had to come." They sat in silence for several minutes.

Finally, Hanan stood and turned off the heater, and Muhammad moved it into the hall. As they said good night, she put her hand on his cheek. "You know your mother would have said that God had a hand in that decision." Muhammad smiled and nodded.

The next morning, Muhammad scaled the wall at first light. He opened the door and tiptoed into the house. The boys looked small and angelic sprawled across the big mattress. He stepped over them and gently tapped on the door to the back room before opening it.

Amal sat up when he opened the door. She opened her mouth in surprise but closed it again when he put his hand on his lips to signal silence. She clamored out from under the heavy quilt and ran to hug him. "Papa, I'm so happy you're here," she whispered. The circles under her eyes overshadowed her smile.

"Amal." They both turned to the bed. "Amal, I need to get up." Deena's eyelids fluttered and her hands scrabbled at the quilt.

"Coming, Mama."

Muhammad shook his head and moved toward the bed. He gently helped his wife to sit and swing her legs over the side of the bed. His breath caught in his throat. He wanted to cry out in pain at the sight of his beautiful Deena. Her face was so swollen she looked like a stranger. She tried to grasp his hand, but her fingers were so puffy she couldn't bend them. He put his arm around her. "I've got you, sweetheart."

"Muhammad, you're home." Even her wonderful smile was distorted by the puffiness of her face. Only her voice was still Deena.

"Yes, I'm home. I'll be here for you always." His eyes stung with tears as she slipped her swollen feet into his old slippers. Even her dancing curls lay limp and lank on her shoulders.

He pulled another big mattress down from the rack and told Amal and the boys they could sleep on them. Not only that, he said they could jump around and play on them as much as they liked as long as they didn't make noise that might disturb their mother. The boys were delighted.

Muhammad spent the day with his fear buried and ignored. He sat on the mattress next to Deena's bed and talked. He talked about the early days of their marriage; he reminisced about waiting for Amal to be born and their joy at her birth. When Deena dozed, he watched her sleep, storing up anecdotes to talk about when she woke up again. The boys were allowed to watch television as much as they liked, as long as the volume was low. Amal, freed from constantly trying to entertain them and keep them quiet, took advantage of the time to wash some clothes.

Night fell and silence embraced the house and the camp around them, broken only by an occasional shot or short burst of shots. Muhammad wondered if the soldiers were reminding them the curfew was still in place, or if they were trying to keep themselves awake during the long night. Deena stirred in the bed beside him, and he whispered a few words. Her breathing seemed slow and even, so he didn't switch on the light. If only he could do something to make her more comfortable. He wished the curfew would end soon. That was not likely. They wouldn't have given a break if they were going to end the curfew the next day. He slept lightly, jumping in fear at the slightest move from the bed.

The next day passed very much like the last one. No change in Deena's discomfort. Muhammad continued his cheerful patter of stories and memories when she woke and watched over her while she slept. Hanan brought over the main meal of the day and whispered with Muhammad as Deena slept. The news was not good. Not only was Ramallah under curfew, but tanks had entered the city. Yusef had picked up BBC on the radio, and they reported major gunfire in all cities in the West Bank. Muhammad and Ali had guessed right. Things were definitely getting worse.

By the time Hanan left, Muhammad wanted to scream in anger and frustration. If the political unrest kept escalating, there was little chance of the curfew ending soon. He couldn't even vent his anger by pounding nails this time. All he could do was sit and hope Deena didn't get any worse. He focused all his efforts on making Deena as comfortable as possible. He helped her sit and spooned food into her mouth because her swollen fingers had trouble holding the silverware. When night came, the camp again sank into silence, and confusing dreams of tanks and soldiers filled his sleep.

Muhammad sat up on his mattress, every muscle tense. What had he heard? Was it a sound in the house or part of his dreams? Everything was deathly quiet. Then a small sound came from his wife's bed. "Deena, my love, do you want me to help you to the bathroom?" he asked softly. He didn't want to wake the children. She didn't answer. He stood and felt for the string that turned on the overhead bulb. The light revealed a sight that made the blood drain from his face, his wife's eyes were barely open and only the whites showed. Even under the heavy quilt he could see her swollen body making spasmodic movements.

"Amal!" he shouted.

"Coming, Papa," Amal replied. She appeared in the room immediately, like an echo to the voice. "Get an ambulance — *now!*"

"How? There's a curfew."

"Damn the curfew! The Camp Director's house has a telephone. Run as fast as you can!" His daughter quailed in the face of his fury, but she ran to obey, grabbing her winter jacket and putting it on over her pajamas. He hadn't meant to yell at her. He tried to smooth his voice. "The doctor said to get her to the hospital as soon as the curfew lifted, and to get an ambulance if she started having

78

seizures." He babbled the explanation while Amal zipped her jacket and thrust her feet into the cheap plastic shoes. She raced out the door before he finished talking. He found himself muttering prayers. Anger rose in his throat, so thick he nearly choked on it. Why was he praying? No one was listening. *If God listened, we wouldn't be in this miserable situation.* He watched in helpless horror as the seizure played itself out. His wife's tortured breathing stopped, and all thoughts of God left his mind. Fear took over ever fiber of his body.

"No, Deena. No! Don't leave me." He put his arm under his wife, pulled her into a clumsy embrace, and took a deep breath, preparing to push air into her now limp body, but she gasped and took a series of short, rapid breaths.

"Thank God," he whispered. He held his wife and rocked slowly back and forth, listening to her breathe.

"It's over," he said, weak with relief.

"What's over?" Omar asked from the doorway. Predictably, Mustafa was right behind him, looking over his shoulder.

"Mama's very sick and you two need to be quiet so she can rest. Go back and sit still." He spoke quietly, both his rage and his terror swallowed by relief that the seizure was over and his wife seemed to be breathing normally.

"Where's Amal?" asked Mustafa.

Muhammad thought briefly of lying and saying she went next door to stay with her cousin. No, it was the middle of the night and they would know better. They were young; they weren't stupid. "She went to get an ambulance," he said after a long pause.

"There's a curfew. She could be shot," whispered Omar, his eyes wide with fright.

"They won't shoot Amal. She's only a little girl," said Muhammad.

Cold fear gripped Muhammad's heart. The boys were right, and they all knew it. The soldiers of the Israeli Defense Force were as varied as he thought their population must be—Jews from the four corners of the earth, many of them not even able to speak Hebrew. In his rational moments, he had to admit he knew almost nothing about the population of Israel, but this was far from a rational moment. He knew that some of the soldiers who patrolled the camp during curfew were little more than frightened boys, shooting at anything that moved. There were stories of soldiers shooting at stray cats, or even their own shadows. No one could separate the reality from the myth. Other soldiers had been known to look the other way, or even distract their patrol when they saw someone breaking curfew.

"Dear God, I've just bet my own child's life on meeting the right soldiers."

"Fly like the wind ... fly like the wind ... they can't see the wind," Amal told herself as she slipped out of their door into the alleyway. She ran to the left, away from her cousin's house, wondering if she should run through the streets or try to stick to the alleys. Advantage of the street: she could run faster on the pavement. There would be little danger of tripping over things in the dark. Disadvantage: the soldiers, if they saw her, had jeeps, and she couldn't outrun a jeep. They only patrolled the alleys on foot because they were too narrow for the jeeps. Foot patrols always consisted of several soldiers, and she'd probably hear them coming. She decided to stick to the alleys whenever possible.

She reached the end of her own alley and paused to listen. All she could hear was the thudding of her own heart. She raced across the open street, the sound of her shoes on the pavement louder than gunshots to her ears. She entered the next alley and froze at the sound of men's voices. Soldiers! She looked around in the dim light of the moon. This should be near Abu Samir's house, she thought. Yes, there it was—Abu Samir's cart, the flat handcart that he loaded with vegetables from the market each morning and pushed along the streets, calling out his wares so the women could buy at their front door. The cart was propped against the wall of his house. Amal wriggled into the space between the wall and the cart, certain the soldiers could hear her beating heart. She opened her mouth wide to get the most air into her lungs with the least noise. One of the soldiers thunked the cart with his rifle butt as the patrol passed, and Amal barely stifled a startled scream.

She didn't move until the soldiers' voices faded. The sound of panic she'd heard in her father's voice drove her to creep from her hiding place and move toward her destination even before the patrol had left the alley. She hugged the wall and moved slowly, watching for garbage cans and stray bits of junk. Her foot caught on some wire, invisible in the dimness of the night and she nearly tripped. Finally, the soldiers reached the end of the alley and turned onto the street. Amal counted to ten before she began to run again.

At the end of the next alley, she had to cross another street. She looked to the left—nothing. To the right she saw a jeep in the distance, its headlights too far to pick up her movement. "I can make it," she whispered to herself. "Run like the wind." She sprinted across the street and paused in the dark shadows of the next alley. Then she heard a patrol in front of her. Fear paralyzed her. She could not go back to the street because the jeep was surely near enough that the soldiers in the jeep would see her! She flattened herself against the wall, painfully aware of her white pajama pants sticking out under her jacket like a flag waving for attention.

Amal inched her way along the wall aiming for a recessed doorway in front of her. Maybe she could stand sideways in the doorway facing the same way as the soldiers. They would see the other side of the recessed area and only see her if they looked directly at her. It was not a good plan, but it was the best she had. She reached the doorway, closed her eyes, and listened as the thud of the combat boots got closer. She held her breath. No, she had to breathe now so she could hold her breath as they passed. Air shuddered into her lungs. She didn't know if she was shaking with fear or with cold. She clamped her teeth together to keep them from chattering.

Amal gasped as the door behind her opened. A hand clamped over her mouth and another grabbed her arm and pulled her inside. She felt a trickle of urine run down her leg; fear overpowered embarrassment. She fought for breath, and her eyes grew wide with fright. The hand over her mouth and nose lifted slowly, and her captor spun her around and held her face pressed into his shirt. She twisted her head to breathe. The hand that had been covering her mouth pushed the door gently closed until it met the frame but did not latch.

The two stood frozen in a strange embrace while the sounds of the soldiers grew louder and then faded once more. Amal breathed a sigh of relief. If the man had meant her harm he would have shut the door, heedless of any noise the latch might make, and pulled her into the house.

"What are you doing out?" he said in an angry voice.

"My mother needs an ambulance. I'm going to the Camp Director's house to call one."

"Follow me." His voice softened, and Amal didn't know what else to do, so she followed. He led her through the house to the narrow space behind, motioned her to stay there, then climbed a ladder to the roof. Amal heard a short whistle and a head appeared on the roof of the next house. The two men exchanged words in a low voice that drifted down to Amal as an indistinguishable murmur. The man came back down.

"I'm going to hand you over the wall to the next house. His house faces the street that runs straight to the Director's house. Listen for whistles and watch the rooftops. If a patrol is coming someone will signal and show you an unlocked door. Understand?"

Amal nodded and began to thank the man, but he stopped her in mid-sentence and told her to forget she ever saw him. "You are forgotten, Uncle," she whispered. He'd already moved the ladder and was motioning her up. When she reached the top he was right behind her. He grabbed her arms and told her to swing her feet over the wall. Strong arms took her weight, and a man with a kafiya wrapped around the lower half of his face lowered her to the ground. Wordlessly he led her through his house. They stepped carefully over sleeping children. A pair of big brown eyes stared at them over the top of a quilt.

When they reached the door, he held her back and slowly opened the door, looking up and then to each side. He pointed in the direction she should go, then pointed up to remind her of the men who would be watching. She grabbed his hand for an instant and, remembering the concern of the other man, whispered, "Thanks. You are forgotten, Uncle." The corners of his eyes wrinkled and Amal knew he had smiled under the kafiya.

Amal ran on, feeling much safer. When she heard a soft whistle she froze, her heart thumping with fear. "Wait," came a disembodied voice from over her head. She flattened herself against a wall and waited. She heard distant sounds and then they receded. "Go," said the same voice. She gave a final wave to whoever might be watching, sprinted to the door of the Director's house and rang the bell. She told herself to count to ten, but she rang again after five.

What if they don't come to the door? What if they don't wake up? Amal shifted from foot to foot. She rang again. "Break a damn window!" the idea came to her in her father's voice. Look for a rock. A light went on in the house. Thank God.

The ambulance took a small eternity to arrive, and it had no headlights. "They won't stop an ambulance, will they?" Amal asked the Camp Director.

"Good luck, child. I wish your mother well," he said and opened the door for her.

Chapter V
❧CHECKPOINT❧

Israeli tank shell kills two children
> The Evening Standard (London); March 4, 2002

Palestinian ambulance driver killed in Tulkarm; death toll now 26
> Voice of Palestine in BBC Worldwide Monitoring; March 7, 2002

High hopes for unseen peace plan
> *It may be a measure of the desperation in the Middle East that world leaders are swarming around an unseen peace initiative which remains in the drawer of a Saudi prince's desk.*
> The Guardian; February 26, 2002

Muhammad heard the footsteps in the alley moments before Amal burst through the door. His relief that she was all right made him almost light-headed. "Thank God ..." Thank God no one shot you; thank God you're safe; thank God you brought help. All the words got tangled in his mind as the ambulance driver arrived with a canvas stretcher. His thoughts moved to Deena.

The driver headed straight for the back room. He dropped the canvas stretcher on Muhammad's mattress, bent over the bed and tucked the covers around Deena's legs. "Let's get her on the stretcher with the quilt tucked around her. It's cold out there." He motioned Muhammad to the head of the bed. Deena groaned as they lifted her onto the stretcher. "Ready?" Muhammad nodded. Together they lifted the stretcher and moved toward the door.

Amal stood with an arm around each of her brothers, making sure they stayed out of the path of the men. He wanted to tell her how proud he was of her and how much he loved her, but there was no time. He'd tell her later. "Take care of your brothers," was all he could manage.

The ambulance driver led the way as the two men quick-marched down the alley, trying to keep the stretcher steady. "The baby's not due until next month. She had a seizure and stopped breathing then started again." Muhammad had no idea what information the ambulance driver needed. He helped the driver secure his wife, and barely managed to sit before the ambulance moved.

"If she has trouble breathing, the oxygen mask is over there." The driver waved one hand and Muhammad located the mask. He'd seen them on television. Would it help her if she stopped breathing altogether? He started to ask, but the driver kept talking. "Let me know if anything else happens. I can pull over and help. I usually drive with another paramedic, but he didn't show up for work tonight. Hell, if I hadn't slept at the hospital the last few nights, I wouldn't have been there either. Looks like the whole damned West Bank is under curfew. Soldiers are thick as fleas on a dog's back."

Muhammad heard the words, but his attention focused on Deena. He watched his wife anxiously as they moved through the deserted streets. "We're on our way," he whispered. "We'll get to the hospital soon." He looked up at the driver's curses and the ambulance slowed to a stop.

"Why are we stopping?" The words had barely left his mouth when the rear doors of the ambulance flew open, and Muhammad found himself staring down the muzzles of two Uzi submachine guns. Behind him, he heard the driver's door opening and a harsh command to the driver to get out. The driver's words echoed in his head. Soldiers thick as fleas meant more checkpoints.

"Papers!" demanded one of the soldiers pointing a gun at him.

"Papers?" echoed Muhammad, his mind suddenly blank. Where were his identity papers? Did he have them? Yes, in his jacket pocket. He reached for his identity card.

"Papers!" the soldier said again, louder. He jiggled the stretcher with the barrel of his gun. Deena moaned softly.

"I have them!" said Muhammad quickly. "I have them both." He silently thanked Amal for reminding him to take both identity cards. With shaking fingers he found the papers and held them out to the soldier. The soldier took the two identity cards, and the ambulance door slammed shut.

Muhammad waited. It began to get cold in the ambulance without the engine running the heater. He tucked the quilt around his wife and talked to her. He told her how much he loved her; he told her how beautiful she was; he told her what wonderful children she gave him; he talked and talked, hoping to get a response. Her eyelids flickered a few times, and he believed she heard him. He poured his love into every word, willing her to hear. He concentrated on his own words. Thinking about love helped him not think about soldiers.

Muhammad tried to gauge the time. It must have been more than an hour. What was happening? He wanted to go and check on the driver, but what would Deena think if she woke up and she was alone? He waited some more. He kept talking. He jumped when her eyes opened, and a low moan escaped her lips. She seemed to be trying to say something. Relief filled his whole being. She was back with him. That must be a good sign.

"Yes, my love." He put his ear near her mouth, trying to hear her.

"The baby's coming," she said weakly.

"It's all right. We're in the ambulance on the way to the hospital. Everything will be fine. I'm going to see why we haven't moved yet. Wait here." He grinned at his inane remark. Of course she'd wait—she was still strapped to the stretcher. The important thing is, she was back.

Muhammad got out of the ambulance and looked around. He knew exactly where they were. This was the little building that was next to the road to Ramallah. He knew it was an army building because it had an Israeli flag flying in front. He'd often seen a jeep or two parked outside it, but he'd never been stopped there. He'd assumed it had facilities like a bathroom and hot coffee or maybe vending machines for patrolling soldiers. A lone light post added to the light from the building itself. The road was dark in both directions. Only the ambulance and two jeeps were parked there.

Whatever purpose the building normally served, it was a checkpoint tonight. Muhammad started toward the building. A soldier came toward him. When they met, the soldier handed him the two identity cards.

"Where's our driver? My wife needs to get to a hospital."

"Aha! Well, your driver has a record of prior offenses." The soldier spoke Arabic very well. "He has broken curfew before, and we've been forced to detain him for questioning."

"He's an ambulance driver. It stands to reason he'd have to be out whenever there's a medical emergency — even during curfew. It's his job." Muhammad managed to keep his tone conversational. Always remember who's holding the gun.

"I am sorry, but our regulations state that he must be detained here until an officer can come to interrogate him."

"How long will that be? My wife is in urgent need of medical attention."

"In that case, you shouldn't leave her unattended. Return to the ambulance at once."

"But ..." He had to keep trying. He couldn't give up trying. "Her life is at stake."

"NOW. Do *not* leave the ambulance again." The soldier placed his hand lightly on his gun. There was no mistaking the threat behind the words. Muhammad had no choice.

"I'm sorry, Deena. The driver is being held." He sat by his wife's side.

"I love you." The words were mere wisps of sound, but they filled Muhammad with a fierce mix of emotions that roared in his ears ... love, protectiveness, frustration and helplessness. He knelt in the small space by the stretcher and bowed his head to rest next to hers. He murmured words of encouragement and gave her assurances that were more wishes than statements. "Soon," he whispered, "soon." He took her hand in his.

Did he doze? Perhaps. He sat up and knew time had passed. What had jerked him awake? He listened but heard only silence. White puffs of his breath reflected the weak light coming through the small back windows.

The hand he held in his own, swollen with the sickness, gripped his fingers with surprising strength. "What,

Sweetheart?" he asked and peered at his wife. His heart sank as he saw that the grip was involuntary and other muscles began to spasm beneath the quilt. No, not another seizure. What if she stopped breathing again? Oxygen. The driver said there was oxygen.

Muhammad grabbed the oxygen mask and put it over his wife's face. Should he hear something? Was it working? Did it need the engine running to work? He put the mask on his own face. Nothing. He fought the panic building inside him. Stay calm. Think.

There it is — a tank. He opened the valve at the top of the tank and put the mask over his wife's face. He tried to hold it in place as she moved convulsively, straining against the restraints. Maybe he should loosen them; after all, they weren't going around any sharp corners. He loosened the straps and saw bruises beginning to form on her arms. He tried to comfort her and keep her from hurting herself, and he watched her breathe.

She stopped breathing. "Breathe," he begged. "Breathe." He pushed down on her chest, trying to push air out; he put the oxygen mask over his own face and drew it into his lungs; putting his mouth over hers, he pushed air as hard as he could. Was this right? He had no idea, but that was all he had. He tried again ... and again. Their teeth knocked as she spasmed again, cutting his lip. His mouth filled with the salty metallic tang of his own blood. Never mind.

At last he felt her body go limp. The seizure was over; she should breathe now. He pushed more oxygen into her lungs — at least that is what he hoped he was doing. This one was worse than the first one. "Breathe," he begged again. He held his own breath as he waited for her to respond. As before, she gasped and took short rapid breaths before settling into what looked like a natural sleep.

"I'll be back," he promised, even though he was sure she couldn't hear him.

He opened the back doors of the ambulance. The cold air hit his sweat-covered face.

"Hey!" he called to the soldiers at the door of the guardhouse and ran toward them. They looked in his direction and raised their rifles.

"STOP!" The shout froze Muhammad in his tracks.

"My wife is dying. Please. She must get to the hospital."

"Your driver hasn't been interrogated yet. Get back in the ambulance."

Desperation made him grasp at another idea. "I'll drive the ambulance. Just let us go. Please." How hard could it be? He'd sat next to drivers hundreds of times. It couldn't be that hard to keep the ambulance on the road, especially tonight with no other traffic.

"We haven't searched the vehicle. Any vehicle out during curfew must be searched thoroughly."

"Then search it and let us go. For the love of God, let us go. She's dying."

"We must follow our orders. The orders are very clear."

"Can't you just search us and let us go?"

"Enough talk," said the other soldier in understandable but broken Arabic. "Get back in the ambulance or your sick wife will have a dead husband." The soldier raised his rifle until Muhammad was looking straight down the barrel. He heard a click from the rifle.

"You'd better do as he says." Did Muhammad hear a spark of sympathy in the Arabic-speaking soldier's voice?

He tried again. "Please, sir, I'm begging you."

91

"We're not joking." The sympathy he thought he heard was gone now. The soldier lifted his own rifle and released the safety.

Fear turned his stomach to a ball of ice, but the fear was for Deena. If the soldiers shot him, Deena would be alone. Who would help her breathe if she had another seizure? Defeated, Muhammad returned to the ambulance. Relieved to see his wife still breathing normally, he settled in the small space beside her and let his mind wander back to the soldiers.

He'd never known life without soldiers. He wondered why the soldiers outside had caused him no discomfort, only fear of what would happen to Deena. Had he always felt suffocated by them? Surely not, but his childhood memories had great gaps in them. In the quiet darkness, with Deena sleeping beside him, he hugged his knees and thought about that time in his life. Suddenly, a memory surfaced. He remembered screaming and kicking at a soldier. He must have been very young, because the soldier held him at arm's length. He remembered the anger, or maybe the rage that gave strength to his arms and legs. Anger overcame fear.

Deena moaned and her arm fell off the edge of the stretcher. He took her hand between his own and blew on it to warm it; then he tucked it under the quilt again. But tonight there was no anger, no rage, no panic — there was only fear for Deena. Tonight fear overcame anger.

"Oh, my love, my soul, please hold on. We'll get there. The doctors will help you." He had to believe his own words. If they had no meaning, then nothing had meaning anymore.

Memories fled and he lived minute by minute, instant by instant. Time had no measure. Each moment stretched to infinity. Muhammad was grateful for each breath his wife took. Each time she exhaled, he held his own breath until she inhaled once more. He continued his litany of love and hope. His eyes burned and his head throbbed, but they were less than minor annoyances.

Then what he most feared happened. Deena's body moved uncontrollably in another, stronger seizure. He fought to keep his wife from hurting herself. Part of him was sorry he had unfastened her restraints because it was difficult to keep her on the stretcher, but the rest of him was grateful that the straps no longer held her. The seizure was so strong that he thought she might have broken her bones. When her body finally relaxed, blood was trickling out of her mouth, and he was as bruised as Deena. As before, she didn't breathe. Muhammad grabbed the oxygen mask and tried what had worked the last time.

Again and again he tried to force oxygen into her lungs and push air out. She didn't respond, and the longer he worked, the more desperate he became. Sweat rolled down his face and mingled with tears. He tried to share his breath with her, but still she did not respond. He put his hand on her neck and, felt for a heartbeat. Nothing. Fear changed to terror. He didn't know what else to do, so he kept trying to force air into her lungs. He had no idea how long he worked, but the oxygen ran out and still he kept trying to breathe for her.

How long was it before he admitted defeat? It felt like a lifetime, and, like a lifetime, he felt it end in death—his as well as hers. A cold void grew within him, eating his soul, until there was nothing left but a shell. He held his wife's lifeless body and stroked her hair.

Sound came back into Muhammad's world with the slam of the ambulance door and a steady stream of curses.

"You all right?"

Muhammad struggled to make sense of the sounds.

"Are you all right?"

He blinked and eventually the meaning came to him. It was the ambulance driver.

Was he all right? No. He would never be all right again.

"They said we could go." The driver turned and looked at his passengers. Muhammad was sitting with vacant eyes, clutching his wife to his chest. After a short silence, the cursing resumed, louder and more vehement than before. The engine started. The ambulance pulled away from the checkpoint.

At the hospital, the driver and a staff member took the stretcher inside. Muhammad trailed along behind, not because he wanted to move, but because he was unwilling to let his wife out of his sight. The doctor led him from the examination room and handed him to a nurse, who took his hand and led him like a child to a chair, pushing him gently into it. He sat, unseeing and unthinking.

A woman sat in the chair next to him. "What is your name?"

The sound reached his ears but his mind refused them. What did it matter? What did anything matter now? Tears flowed unheeded from his eyes.

The woman went away and left him alone. Alone. People came and went like shadows. He got up and walked back to the room where they'd taken Deena. He had to see her again, to touch her face one more time.

There was a curtain around the bed. Voices. Who was in there? What were they doing? Were they treating her? Had he mistaken unconsciousness for death? His heart began to beat faster. Could it be? He paused with his hand on the curtain. He didn't want to interrupt.

"The preeclampsia became eclampsia at the onset of labor—or perhaps the labor was triggered by the eclampsia. Damn!" Muhammad jerked back, startled by the explosive shout. "No one should die of eclampsia in this day and age. It's so damned frustrating. If they'd only come a few hours earlier, she'd be alive now. God damn it to hell." Muhammad turned away, blinded by tears, as the curtain was yanked open.

A woman was running toward him.

"They lifted the curfew this morning. I came as soon as I could." She looked at his face and cried out. "NO! Oh, God, no! Not Deena!" Her wail penetrated the fog in his mind.

Deena. Muhammad focused his eyes on the woman who looked so much like his Deena. But she wasn't Deena. Deena was gone. The thought exploded inside his brain. Deena was gone! A cry of agony wrenched itself out of his very soul and sent cold shivers through the people who heard it. He pulled his hand away from his sister-in-law and fled through the ambulance bay door.

Muhammad didn't stop running until his legs gave out and he collapsed, too exhausted to think. He emerged slowly from oblivion, as though coming back to life bit by bit. His first awareness was cold—cold that reached his inner depths. He floated in cold. No, he wasn't floating; he was lying down. Sharp stones under his cheek. He forced his eyelids to move. Bright sunlight, dirt, rocks. He moved first one stiff limb then another. Cold and stiff like ... Oh God! Deena! He sat, drew his legs in to form a ball, rested his forehead on his knees and sobbed. Great wracking sobs tore from his soul, interspersed with screams of denial, refusal, rejection of what he knew to be his new reality — life without Deena. It was a contradiction. There could be no life without Deena. But Deena was gone. She left him here without her.

No, *he* was the one who left. He ran out on her. He ran out of the hospital when she ... when the ... He couldn't finish the thought. He had to finish the thought, didn't he? He had to face it. Deena was gone, and what time was it? Muhammad looked around. He must have walked for hours. He had to go home, but where was home? He needed to find a landmark. He stood and turned in slow circles.

There — the mosque at the outskirts of the camp. He lurched into an unsteady jog. He had to say good-bye to Deena. He couldn't let them bury her before he saw her one more time. He vaguely remembered seeing Hanan. She said curfew had been lifted. They'd bring Deena home, and he had to get there. He glanced at the sky. Morning was well advanced. He began to run. He *had* to get home before the noon prayer.

The closer he got to home, the harder he had to force his legs to carry him forward. How could he step into his house without Deena? How could he live without Deena? He turned into the alley and again forced his feet to move.

"Muhammad." An arm went around his shoulders. "Come with me."

"Layth." Recognition came with relief. Layth was here. His big brother would help him now, as he always had in the past. Layth steered him away from his own door.

"Muhammad, answer me."

"I'm sorry, Layth, what did you say?"

"You haven't heard a word I said. Are you all right?"

He made an inarticulate sound. No, of course he wasn't all right. Deena was gone. He'd never be all right again.

Layth's voice was too low to carry beyond Ali and Hanan's kitchen. "Muhammad, what happened? Where were you today?"

"I ... I'm not sure. The doctor said Deena was gone, and I couldn't stand being in the closed room. That's about all I remember." He had other memories, but none he was willing to share. His throat was still raw from his screams of rage and sorrow. He'd tried to vent his grief through sound, but the fire under it was too great. Grief boiled out faster than he could vent it. His legs were still shaky and his hands shook.

"Here." Layth thrust a bowl at him. "Eat. You have to be strong for Amal and the boys. People are already coming to give their condolences."

Muhammad looked at the spoon in his hand. Tears rolled down his face. "Deena." The single word felt like a tear falling from his lips. He watched tears make crooked tracks down Layth's face. It shook Muhammad to see Layth cry. Layth never cried. Muhammad was three when they lost their father. Layth had been the man of the house as long as he could remember.

"Please, Muhammad, eat." Layth nudged the hand with the spoon. Dutifully, Muhammad lifted it to his mouth. The bowl seemed to empty itself, and his hands stopped shaking as the warm stew did its job. Layth handed him a stack of clean clothes and led him toward Ali's bathroom.

"I have to go home. I have to see Deena one more time."

"You will, Muhammad, you will. But you don't want to see Deena looking like this. The women are in your house now, getting Deena ready." He nodded and stumbled toward the bathroom. A dull buzz of conversation came from the room full of men who'd come to give him condolences—as though he could ever be consoled.

And then it was time. Time for the final good-bye. Layth and Ali helped him up. Somehow his legs held him up and he walked.

The world turned into a blur of sight and sound. He wanted to open the coffin and carry Deena in his arms one last time. Ali was talking to him. He heard the comfort and love, but not the words. He felt the weight of the wooden box on his shoulder. He tried to imprint that feeling on his mind. He felt it every step of the way to the small mosque. The words of the prayer held no meaning for him, but there was some comfort in the good wishes and sympathy of those around him. He felt no need to pray to God. God never listened.

His mother had prayed constantly and sincerely. What good had it done? She died with only her sons near her. Her prayers hadn't stopped her being widowed when he was still a toddler. Her prayers hadn't prevented his brother from being shot, spilling his blood and last breath on top of him, leaving him with haunting nightmares that only Deena chased away. God never listened.

He let his brothers guide him. He had no will of his own. He watched in agony as Deena was lowered into the earth. They moved as a group back to Ali's house, with Muhammad following their gestures and whispered words mechanically. Men came and said the standard words. Some shook his hand, some embraced him, some with tears, all acknowledging his loss.

Coffee appeared in his hand. Not the thick sweet coffee, but a thinner bitter brew, reserved for gatherings such as this. A sip or two and return the cup for the next mourner. Nothing escaped the fog of grief. Time droned on.

Large trays of food were brought from somewhere. He stared at it with no desire to eat. His soul was empty, what did his stomach matter? He was vaguely thankful for his friends and neighbors. The women must have been cooking since word first reached them. Ali took him into the bedroom and gave him a dish. He ate because Ali cajoled him into taking just one more bite. Like speaking to a baby, but his baby had gone with Deena. At least she had her baby with her.

Ali took the empty plate and led him back to a seat next to Layth. Jehad came with a large glass of hot tea. "Thank you." The words came out in a whispered croak.

"Are you okay?" Layth looked anxious.

"The tea helps." He *had* to pay attention, to live in this room at this time. People were here because of Deena. He had obligations. He took another gulp of tea and tried to blink the room into focus. His children. "How's Amal? And the twins?"

"Ferial is with them."

"That's good." Relieved that they were safe, the room began to fade. No, don't go there. Think of Ferial, the older sister who was more like an aunt than a sister. He didn't even remember her living at home. Her husband didn't make it easy for them to be closer. As he thought of Ziad, he heard his voice, and the room wavered into near-focus.

Ziad leaned toward the man next to him as though to whisper, but even then his voice carried to every corner of the room. Unlike the other quiet voices, it invaded Muhammad's head, filling it with noise. "It's a damned shame, you know. People die at checkpoints all the time. I was reading about it the other day. I don't remember the number, but well into three digits. It's all documented. Damned shame." Was Ziad talking about Deena? That's all he has to say? Damned shame? Anger boiled within him like thick Arabic coffee that foamed and overflowed the pot, sizzling onto the flame beneath. Ziad cocked his head to one side. "I wonder if they'll count this as one or two deaths. She died in childbirth, you know."

Muhammad's head exploded in white hot rage. He jumped up, shaking off Layth's restraining hand. He closed the space between his chair and Ziad in two strides. "Count her? You can't count a universe. Deena was the world." The room was too small to hold his grief. Tears filled his head and his heart, leaking out to run down his face. The gray fog of grief expanded yet again, crushing him with its pressure. He had to have more space. Almost blinded with tears, he moved to the door. He had to get out before it crushed him. He ran into the cold night air, only vaguely aware of Layth's voice calling him and footsteps behind him. He ran, stumbling through the dark night with no destination in mind. The footsteps faded behind him. He ran until his feet slowed of their own accord. His eyes, now accustomed to the pale light of the crescent moon, looked around and recognized the cemetery. He found Deena's freshly covered grave and sank down to sit at her feet.

"Muhammad, you're needed at home." Layth sat next to his brother and pulled a blanket over their shoulders.

"How did you know where to find me?"

Layth blinked away tears and put his arm around Muhammad. "We've done this before," he said softly and pulled his brother close. Minutes later, or maybe hours later, he spoke again. "Let's go home."

Chapter VI
❧KAREEMA'S VISIT❧

SP gives blood to help the Palestinian People
> Turkish Daily News; March 15, 2002

Peace in a body bag
> Sydney Morning Herald; March 29, 2002

Make me a martyr; As Israel storms Arafat's stronghold and the Palestinian leader vows defiance, a teenage girl joins the ranks of the suicide bombers
> Daily Mail (London); March 30, 2002

Amal and the boys were moved into the back room again, and Layth slept by Muhammad's side. He made him eat when it was time to eat, and led him to Ali's house when the first mourners of the day were expected. Muhammad had to leave because his house was where Amal and Hanan would receive the women mourners. It all made sense when he could free enough of his mind to focus on what was happening around him. The day passed in a blur of faces and words. Some of the words floated to the surface and he understood. Ferial packed the boys' things and took them to her house. At the mention of their sister, Muhammad scanned the room. Ziad was conspicuous by his absence. Without the responsibility of the twins, Amal could return to school. Other things didn't exactly float to the surface, but seeped in around the edges of his grief. Hanan was much better. Better than what? The thought floated away before he could ask.

Layth walked him home after all the mourners had left. "Amal, would you make us a glass of tea? I'd like to sit and relax for a few minutes before we pull out the mattresses." Within minutes Amal set a tray with two glasses in front of the men. "One more glass, sweetheart. Come and sit with us."

Muhammad looked at his daughter. Her eyes looked too large in her pale pinched little face. He blinked and turned away. How much pain could fit in one human being? When she returned with the third glass of tea, he patted the mat beside him. He put his arm around her thin shoulders. She had lost her mother two days ago, and this was the first time he had thought of her grief. He searched for words to comfort her, but found none. All he had was pain. Perhaps shared pain would be a comfort of sorts. Her shoulders shook and she buried her face in his shirt, soaking it with tears. He was helpless. What could he say? His own tears flowed silently down his face, and their tea grew cold.

Layth made fresh tea and began talking. The words were irrelevant. He was calling them back from their grief. "Here, take the tea."

Amal nodded. "I need to wash my face." She got up and went to the bathroom.

"Muhammad, she needs you now. Her world has crumbled just as much as yours has, and she's going to need a lot of support to get through this. I have to go home tomorrow. I've been away from the shop too long. There are things I have to do. Before I go, I need to know you'll be here for her. I'll send food every couple of days. If you need anything, you know where I am."

"Yes. Thank you." Layth was still looking at him. He wanted him to say something else. Muhammad made an effort to remember. "I'll take care of Amal." Satisfied, Layth picked up his tea.

As expected, the third and last day they would receive mourners was quiet. The three brothers were often alone in the house. It was a relief not to have to listen or respond. Ali and Layth talked. Muhammad paced. He did everything they asked of him. That night he stared at the blackness of the ceiling and felt the emptiness of the room. No, it was the emptiness of life. He felt cold inside — cold like death. The night passed slowly.

"Papa, have some breakfast with me. Aunt Hanan says I have to go to school today." Breakfast? He'd been awake until the dawn call to prayer soothed him into sleep. He opened his eyes. Amal sat cross-legged on a mat looking at him. A tray with bread and cheese sat on the floor between the mat and his mattress. Two glasses of tea sat, one on either side. "I'm heating water for you." The hiss of the kerosene burner seconded her words.

"Thank you." His vocal cords protested their first use of the morning. She waited until he sat up before starting her own breakfast. She ate in silence, and he was grateful for the time to gather his courage to face another day. He broke off some bread and picked up a piece of cheese, aware that she was watching. He took a swallow of tea. "Thank you for breakfast."

"Papa" she said with slow deliberation, "I don't think I should go back to school. You need me here."

"No, you go to school. You need to keep up with your schoolwork." He didn't want her in the house all day. He

104

didn't want a witness to his grief, nor did he want to see his pain mirrored in her eyes.

"If I stay home, we can bring back Omar and Mustafa. I'll be able to take care of them." Her eyes filled with tears and her voice broke. He could barely understand her words between sobs. "I can't do anything to bring back Mama, but if I stay home I *can* bring back Omar and Mustafa. We can't let them take everyone away."

"I …" He didn't know what to say. He'd been pleased that they boys were taken care of. It never crossed his mind that Amal might be unhappy about her brothers going to stay with Ferial. "I think you should do what Uncle Ali and Aunt Hanan say." The doorbell rang.

"Please, Papa." Her face twisted with her effort to stem her tears. "Please."

"We'll talk about it later. Today you go to school. Now open the door for Imahn." Suddenly, he couldn't wait for her to leave. His need to be alone almost overwhelmed him. The doorbell rang again, and with a quick kiss she was gone. When the door closed behind her, he released his own tears.

Eventually, he put his mattress away, dressed and left the house. He had no particular destination. His mind shied away from the idea of getting on a bus. He could barely control his panic in the best of times—and this was as far as he could get from the best of times. It was too late to pick up a day's work, anyway. He walked for hours, lost in his grief. When the sun began to wane, he turned and started for home. It was full dark before he arrived, and opening the door was like opening the wound again. Deena's smile would never again greet his return. Pain fogged his sight. He stumbled through the courtyard, and, holding the doorframe for support, struggled for sanity. He could do this; he knew he could. Think of Amal. Concentrate.

"Amal, I'm home." No answer. "Amal? Did you hear me?" He opened the door to the back room. Empty. Panic cleared his mind like a bucket of ice water. Of course, Amal must be next door with Imahn. In the bathroom, he splashed water on his face to clear the rest of the cobwebs and caught sight of himself in the mirror. How long had it been since he'd shaved or combed his hair? He ran a comb through his hair—no time to shave now, he had to go to Ali's. Deciding against using the ladders, he ran next door and rang the bell.

"Papa! We were so worried." Amal threw herself at him, her hug surprisingly strong.

"Hanan's waiting supper for you." Ali threw his arm around Muhammad's shoulders.

"Sorry I'm late." The smell of the food made his mouth water. He couldn't remember his last meal. He must have eaten, but he couldn't remember.

"Jehad, don't bolt your food down. What's your hurry?"

"Sorry, Mama, I have to study a few more hours tonight."

"The dreaded tawjihi exam," said Hanan with an exaggerated shudder. "I don't understand the logic of the system. It's not right that one examination should determine a young person's entire future. What happens if you're sick that day? Or just too nervous to focus?"

"Don't worry, Mom. Everyone else will be just as nervous."

Muhammad's conscience poked him. "Amal, you must have homework to do." The tears that followed caught him off guard. He stared at his daughter, bewildered. He didn't know how to deal with the sudden emotion. Deena had left him with a task he didn't know how to accomplish.

"I don't want to go to school. I want to stay home so we can get Omar and Mustafa back and have a family again." Hanan put down the dishes she was carrying and put her arms around Amal. "I'm going to fail anyway, so why make things any harder?"

"You have a family. We're your family, and your brothers are still your family. They'll come back. Next year they'll go to school when you do, and they can come back and live with you. Meanwhile, you can visit them." She motioned the men toward the living room. Muhammad didn't move. Maybe he could learn how to raise a daughter. "And you're not going to fail. Whatever gave you that dreadful idea?"

"I got a zero on the test today. The miss explained fractions when I was gone because of ..." She couldn't finish the sentence, but the meaning was clear.

"I can help you with fractions," said Imahn.

"I don't want help with fractions. Why do I have to learn fractions anyway?" Hanan led the tearful girl into the bedroom, closing the door behind them.

Hanan climbed up on the big bed and pulled Amal up beside her. She fussed with the pillows and pulled the spare blanket up over their shoulders. The room was chilly, but the real reason for her actions was to gain time to organize her thoughts.

107

Deena was not only her sister but also her best friend. The pain of her loss was almost unbearable, so strong and raw that she couldn't sit still for two minutes without tears. Yet through it all, she'd had to keep the two households going. The neighbors brought food, but she had to make sure it was hot and served on time. She had to make sure there was bread and the dishes were always clean. She couldn't say that to Amal because it would sound like complaining. She had to teach by example. Maybe Amal didn't need a teacher right now. Maybe her more urgent need was for comfort and understanding.

How could she console Amal when she needed consoling herself? Amal was her sister's little girl. She had to do this, for Amal and for Deena, no matter how hard it was. The only thing she could do is get on with it.

She pulled Amal close and tucked the blanket around them both. "Amal, sweetheart, it's just the two of us, and I have all the time in the world. Now tell me all about what's upsetting you so much. Is it really fractions?" Hanan's body tensed as the answer hit her with overwhelming intensity, as though she'd lanced an emotional boil. How could one small girl hold in so much emotion? The pain rushed out of Amal as though some internal dam had cracked. Hanan cried with her, letting the silent tears flow. She held Amal close, rocked her, and handed her tissue after tissue.

Eventually the well ran dry, and Amal stopped talking and sobbing. Hanan felt as emotionally spent as she imagined Amal was. They sat for several minutes before Hanan spoke. "Amal, you've had to do a lot of growing up in the last few days, and you've managed better than I could have imagined. I'm incredibly proud of you."

"Honest?"

"Yes, and I know your papa's proud of you, too. He's lucky to have you to help him through this. I'm sure you can do it, but it isn't easy growing up in a few days. You've done really well, but you need time to get your balance."

"Maybe that's what wrong with Papa. Maybe he can't get his balance."

"That's one way of looking at it, but now we have to talk about you. We need to make a plan to help you while you get where you need to be. Are you willing to listen and work with me on the plan?"

The change in Amal was enough to make Hanan smile for the first time in days. Hope overlaid the sorrow. "Can you really help us get the boys back?"

"I think so, but not before the summer. In the meantime, you let Imahn help you make good grades in school. I won't cook until you get home from school, and you can help me and learn to cook. By the time school closes for summer vacation, you should be able to cook for your Papa and your brothers."

"Oh, Aunt Hanan, you always know what to do." Amal threw her arms around Hanan's neck and squeezed her hard. "You're the smartest, bravest, strongest woman in the whole wide world."

"You're doing pretty well yourself, young lady. Now go get your jacket on. Your house will be quieter for studying." Hanan stuck her head in the children's bedroom. She'd probably still be thinking of it as the children's bedroom when her grandchildren came to visit. "Imahn, would you go next door with Amal and help her get caught up with her schoolwork?"

"I'll go with them," said Jehad.

"It's only a few steps, Ali."

"That's more than enough for a passing patrol to decide to have some fun. Besides, it'll be quieter there for me, too, without the TV in the next room."

That night, as she had the previous few nights, Hanan stayed awake long after the house had fallen quiet—only tonight she wasn't crying. With Ali spooned behind her, and safe within the circle of his arms, she thought about Amal. She wasn't sure how long Amal would be able to keep up her spirits if Muhammad didn't help. If only her mother-in-law were still with them. Her strength and wisdom had always been an inspiration to Hanan. She'd always been there to provide support.

She suddenly twisted to face her husband. "Ali, wake up."

"Huh? What's wrong?"

"Nothing's wrong. I need to talk to you for a minute." She sat up.

Ali struggled upright and put his arm around her. "What is it, love? Did you have a bad dream?"

"Did you ever meet any members of your father's family? Or your mother's?"

"Layth said an uncle came with them from the village, but he went to Kuwait to work as a mechanic before I was born. He's probably dead by now."

"So Layth's the head of the family?" Ali nodded. Hanan rushed to speak before he could interrupt. "But his wife has never really tried to be part of it."

"She's always opened her house to us when we couldn't come home."

"She has no choice. Layth would never let her turn you away." Ali shrugged. "In all the years we've been married, she never came to visit—not once. She didn't even pay her

110

respects to Deena. She never set foot in this house. Layth loves you, and does whatever he can for both you and Muhammad, but she is merely polite when you're there."

"You woke me up in the middle of the night to tell me this? It's not news."

"Ali, I'm the new anchor. Your mother left it to me, and I never realized it."

Ali grinned and scooted down in the bed, pulling her down with him. "And a damned fine job you're doing of it, too."

"You knew?"

"Goodnight, Madame Matriarch, my love."

Kareema slung her bag over her shoulder and tried to contain the active twins while they waited for a car. Her mother gave some last minute instructions to Bilal before closing the front door and joining them on the sidewalk. The boys were too excited about seeing their father and Amal to stand still. She shivered and tucked her kafiya tighter around her neck. A passing car hit a pothole and splashed muddy water onto the sidewalk. She grabbed the boys and pulled them out of the way.

The taxi dropped them at the mouth of the alley, and Kareema left her mother and the twins at Muhammad's house and walked on to Ali's. She had her fingers crossed that Jehad would be home. She had nowhere else to turn. He was her last hope.

"I'm sorry, Kareema, he's working all day. Yusef's home, if that helps."

"No, Aunt Hanan, I need help with math. I've talked to the teacher and my friends tried, but I just can't seem to get it. I don't know what else to do." Her words ended with a half-suppressed sob. She had promised to make up her schoolwork before the marks came out, and the deadline was getting closer.

Hanan pulled her into the kitchen. "Have some tea. Imahn and I were just preparing stuffed squash for everyone. Maybe you can stay the night. You can eat with us, and Jehad can help you after supper."

"I'll have to get permission, but that would be wonderful." More than the prospect of Jehad's help made Kareema smile; she looked forward to a night without her father's sullen silence. She was convinced he hoped she would fail so he could get her married and out of his house. She took a deep breath and renewed her vow to succeed or die trying.

The doorbell rang. "I'll get it. It must be Mother."

Ferial joined them. "I wanted to give them some time alone," she said. She washed her hands and picked up a squash. Imahn handed her a corer, and she started hollowing it out for the stuffing. "It was like pulling teeth to get Muhammad to say anything when I talked to him, so I figured I'd disappear for a while." She shrugged. "Maybe now that I'm gone, the boys will come out of the back room and climb all over him. That might help."

"Amal misses them a lot," said Hanan.

Ferial nodded. "Once they were in the back room, I tried to talk seriously to Muhammad. I want to get him to stop looking at Deena's death as his own personal tragedy and realize it was a tragedy for his children as well. I don't know if he even heard me."

Hanan stacked the last of the stuffed squash into the large pot and hefted it up onto the stove. "The food should be ready in an hour, and Ali should be home by then. He doesn't usually work on Friday, but with all the days he's been ..." Kareema watched Hanan's eyes fill with tears. Everyone was so concerned over Muhammad's loss, she sometimes forgot that Hanan had lost her sister. Hanan blinked back her tears and found a smile somewhere inside her. "I'd love to see the boys, too, and I'd love to have you all stay and eat with us."

"Jehad won't be here?"

"No, he'll probably come later. Speaking of which, can Kareema stay the night? She said she's having a tough time with some of her homework, and she hoped Jehad could help."

Kareema held her breath at her mother's hesitation. Didn't anyone understand what this meant to her? If she didn't do well on her next math exam, her father was sure to force her into a marriage she didn't want. "Please, Mama, I've tried for hours to understand it on my own. I've asked the teacher, but she only repeats what the book says."

"Of course you can stay." Ferial's hands clasped and unclasped on her lap, betraying her anxiety. "Your father isn't here to object, so I decide." She looked up and smiled. "There are some advantages to not having telephones."

"Thanks, Mama." Kareema hoped her father wouldn't be too upset about the arrangement. She didn't want her mother to bear the brunt of her father's anger that was meant for her.

Kareema enjoyed the delicious meal and reveled in the easy play of conversation. Even the twins were allowed to talk about what they were doing in the new pre-kindergarten school Ferial had found for them. Kareema was glad to see her mother laugh with genuine humor over her explanation that it had taken less than a day to realize she wasn't up to chasing after two active little boys anymore.

After they'd cleaned the kitchen and Ferial left with the boys, Kareema sat with her aunt and uncles watching television. The program held little interest for her, and she soon began worrying about her school problems. She should be studying, and not sitting and watching television. This was valuable study time, and she was wasting it. After what seemed like hours, Jehad came home. She followed him into the kitchen and explained her desperation while he ate.

"I'm overwhelmed trying to make up three weeks of work and keep my job and keep current assignments. I try to do the current assignments first, and then go back and make up the work I missed. I prioritize the subjects by the patience of the teacher. You know, the squeaky wheel method."

"And your math teacher's one of the patient ones."

"How did you know?"

"Think about it." Jehad took his plate to the sink. "Come on. Get your books and we'll go over to Uncle Muhammad's. I promised I'd keep the girls on task with homework."

"Why not here?"

"Mama says it's to keep me from listening to the television while I study, but I think it's more about keeping Uncle Muhammad from going home. If he goes home, he just sits and broods. Here he can sit and brood, but at least he's warm and safe."

"He's not safe at home?"

"Sometimes it gets too much for him, and he goes out walking."

"At night? In winter?" Kareema pulled her coat extra tight and wrapped her scarf around her neck. She picked up her bag and followed Jehad and the two girls into the cold. "You know you look like the pied piper of Hamelin leading us all down a dark alley." The girls may not have gotten the reference, but they giggled nonetheless.

"I want you to open your math book to the last lesson you took before you went off to save the world," said Jehad as soon as they closed the door behind them. She threw her coat over a chair. By the time she looked up, everyone had disappeared. Jehad reappeared with the kerosene heater, which he lit. Amal came out of the kitchen carrying a tea kettle. She put the kettle on the heater and set out the little table, just in time for Imahn to put down a tray of glasses, spoons, and sugar. It looked like a well-rehearsed play.

"Let's see what you have," said Jehad, folding his legs and sitting on a mat next to her. "Do you have a problem with any of this?" She shook her head and reached for the book to show him the lesson that stumped her. "Good. Read the section after this and work one or two problems while I organize my own work."

Kareema shrugged. Jehad was very methodical about his studying, and she didn't want to upset him. After all, she was asking him for a big favor. She blocked out the sounds of books and paper as the others settled down to work. She read rapidly through the explanation and sample problems and did a couple of random exercises at the end. "That wasn't too hard. Now what?"

"Keep going with the next section. Let me know when you get to whatever it was that got you stuck." His eyes never left his book.

Kareema nodded. This wasn't the section she needed help with, but she didn't trust her words to come out without shouting. She couldn't risk getting him angry; he was her last resort. With nowhere else to turn for help, she did as she was told and buried herself in the work. Surprisingly, the next section wasn't as hard as she'd thought it would be, nor the next. She wondered about that for a few seconds, then went on to the next problem. After a while, the noise pattern in the room changed, and she lifted her head to find the kettle boiling and Amal spooning sugar into the glasses.

"Break time." Jehad looked at her with a mischievous grin. "Now it's time to pay for your lesson."

"Pay for what lesson? You haven't done anything yet."

"Really? You don't seem to be having any problems."

"That's because—" She was going to say it was because she was working on stuff she already knew, but it wasn't.

"Because you didn't try to skip a month of foundation. I think that's a very good lesson."

"Maybe." Kareema wasn't ready to concede yet. "What do you want?"

"I want to know what's really going on."

"Nothing." What was he talking about? Did he think math was just a cover story? "I really have been trying desperately to get this math under control. You remember my bargain. My father's just looking for an excuse to yank me out of school to marry."

"No about that. You work in the office. You must know things the rest of us don't know."

116

His expression appeared so earnest, that she only just managed to swallow her tea before choking with laughter. "Oh, sorry. My thoughts were on my own problems. Do you think I'm Arafat's personal secretary? I'm so busy with my shorter hours I barely have time to talk to anyone. I probably know less than you do. I don't even have time to watch the news." She made a face. "It's been so gloomy, I haven't wanted to ask. You can't imagine how long it takes to recover from the chaos. You walk through town and see the torn up streets from the tanks and the crushed cars and broken windows, but you don't see what happens in an office when computers are smashed and file cabinets have their drawers forced open and papers scattered, walked on, peed on, and in some cases used for kindling. We were lucky. The YFP office is so small and dingy they didn't think we were worth the effort."

"I'm sorry." Jehad's expression had gone from earnest to curious to shocked and finally disappointed—and all within a handful of seconds.

Kareema dredged up the only bit of good news she could remember. "I'm sure you already know about the fifty-two Israeli reserve soldiers who refused to serve in the West Bank or Gaza."

"No, I didn't, but that's not much to brag about. What's fifty-two soldiers against the thousands who are more than happy to use their guns and grenades?"

"It's not the number. What matters is that it's public, and half of them are officers. This has tremendous potential. It shows that Israel isn't as united in their draconian methods as they want the world to believe." He shrugged. Why couldn't Jehad, the smartest guy in the family, see the importance of this? "Jehad, neither one of us

117

thinks that we're going to win a war with rocks. Against tanks? But we still go out there and risk our lives because we desperately want the world to look at us—to see what we see."

"Maybe we should get back to math."

"Wait, let me read this to you." She pulled a paper out of her bag. "It's from *The Washington Post*."

"All right."

She began to read: "We will no longer fight beyond the Green Line for the purpose of occupying, deporting, destroying, blockading, killing, starving and humiliating an entire people." With the help of a dictionary, they translated the sentence. "There's one more sentence you should hear. "You can be the best officer, always be first … and suddenly you are asked to do things that should not be asked of you—to shoot people, to stop ambulances, to destroy houses in which you don't know if there are people living." Jehad was able to supply a running translation for that one.

"It's too late now." The vehemence in Amal's usually quiet voice startled Kareema. "They shouldn't have refused. They should have been here to let the ambulance through, but it's too late now." They could barely understand the last words. Amal ran to the back room and closed the door behind her.

"Should I go after her?" Imahn started to get up.

"No. Sometimes people need to be alone to cry. If she doesn't come out soon, you can go. I should have had better sense than to read that part."

"Tea break is over. Let's get back to work."

"Wait," said Imahn, "can I ask a question first?" Kareema nodded. "What exactly do you do?"

118

"My *office* job is searching foreign media for mentions of what's going on here. We try to find out which papers are sympathetic, where we need to focus or attention, what public opinion is outside. I started working as an organizer last year, and I still do that as well."

"It seems to me there are a lot of grown men organizing and ordering things around with no great hope of getting results. No offense, but you're still a girl. What do you organize?"

"People."

"People? You organize people?"

"I recruit young people who're willing to help, usually by taking to the streets when there's a call for action, but sometimes by running errands and delivering food to the fighters on duty. I organize what are called cells; they're like the branches of a tree. When I need to pass the word, I tell the three to six leaders under me. Each of them passes the word to three or four others, and that's the way it works."

"You're an organizer *and* you work in the office?"

"Yes, and often the computer's in use and I do a lot of filing and fetching and carrying." She gave a short laugh. "Now I really do have to get back to algebra. The teacher's been patient, but I still have a deadline." The three went back to work.

Amal rejoined them after a few minutes. Her eyes were red from crying, and she kept dabbing at her nose.

Jehad yawned and raised his arms in a spine-cracking stretch. "Are we ready?"

"I've *been* ready," said Imahn. Amal nodded her agreement.

"I think I am, thanks to you, Jehad." Kareema's back ached from bending over the short table so long, but she felt happier than she had in weeks. They said good night to Amal, and trooped back next door. They found Muhammad and Ali moving the living room furniture to make room for two mattresses for Imahn and Kareema.

The house gradually settled down to sleep, but Kareema's head still whirled with algebraic symbols and problems. "Kareema." The whisper came from the next mattress.

"Yes," she whispered back.

"Can I be in one of your cells?"

Kareema's breath caught. That was the last thing she expected Imahn to say. Her aunt and uncle would never forgive her if their only daughter got hurt because of her. Why was she hesitating? She asked girls to join every day. They all knew the risks. Imahn knew them, too. Why should Imahn be any different?

"Kareema, did you hear me?"

"Yes. Let me ask you a question. Why are you asking this in a whisper in the middle of the night?"

"Because, uhm ..."

"We both know the answer. Your parents would never let you do it. What did you tell me when I came to you with a problem dealing with the YFP and my family? You told me I had to come clean and make some sort of compromise. Now compare my situation to what you are proposing. What you want to do is exactly the same thing I did, but on a smaller scale. Do you see that parallel?" There was a long silence. Kareema used the time to develop her idea.

"I guess so," Imahn finally admitted. "So can you think of a compromise for this?"

"See how this sounds to you. You can be a special cell all by yourself under me. I won't put your name on any official lists and no one else will know. I'll try to let you know when something's about to happen."

"That sounds all right, if I can help."

"Of course you'll be a help, every warm body helps. But telling you where to be and when is only the first part of the agreement. The other part is that you must promise to leave immediately at the first hint of danger. If a shot is fired, or you get even a whiff of tear gas, you run like a rabbit for home."

"Don't treat me like a child." Her whisper sounded like an angry hiss.

"I'm treating you as a very beloved cousin. I could never live with myself, let alone with the family, if anything bad happened to you because of me." Imahn's silence proved she wasn't convinced. "You didn't bring this up in front of Amal, did you? Could that be because you understood it was not a conversation for children?" Did Imahn's answering grunt sound a touch smug? "Imahn."

"Hmmm?"

"I need to hear you say you promise to run at the first sign of danger, any kind of danger. Promise."

"Hmm hmmm."

"Say it."

"All right, I promise."

Days later, Kareema wrote a short note to Imahn and prayed that she'd made the right decision. She read it one more time, then slipped it into an envelope.

Dear Imahn,
Keeping my promise. Land Day after school.
(Sister secret)
Remember to keep your promise.
Love, Kareema

As an afterthought, she picked up a couple of the twins' drawings from school and added them to the envelope. She put a scarf on her head and reached for her coat.

"Where do you think you're going?" Bilal's tone sounded like a pale echo of his father's. He had the belligerence, but not the depth or volume.

"Sorry, I forgot you need to report my every move to Papa. Isn't it enough escorting me to and from school and picking me up from work? You need this information to include in your daily secret service report to Papa, too?" Bilal didn't even blink at her sarcasm. "I'm going next door to give some of Omar and Mustafa's drawings to Rula to give to Amal when she goes to school tomorrow." She unfolded the drawings and displayed them before yanking the door open. The March air was still chilly, but her anger kept her warm on the short walk.

Chapter VII
❧LAND DAY☙

In the night, Israeli tanks enter and re-occupy Bethlehem and Beit Jala.
> PASSIA, Palestine Chronology 2002; March 30, 2002

The United Nations Security Council passes Res. 1402 calling for Israeli withdrawal from Palestinian cities
> PASSIA, Palestine Chronology 2002; March 30, 2002

The Israeli army declares Ramallah a closed military area, banning journalists from the city; soldiers also seize local TV channels and replace normal programming with pornographic films.
> PASSIA, Palestine Chronology 2002; March 31, 2002

PM Sharon addresses the nation, saying "We are at war, and it is a war for our home"
> PASSIA, Palestine Chronology 2002; March 31, 2002
> **PASSIA** - Palestinian Academic Society for the Study of International Affairs

Crisp and cool, a perfect spring day. It was Land Day and, wonder of wonders, there was no curfew. They'd been planning this demonstration for days. Kareema had told all of her cells and asked them to pass the word to as many girls as possible, even those not in the YFP. This was going to be huge. Kareema shivered in anticipation. She wondered how many of the protesters even knew that the Arabs who lived inside the borders of Israel started Land Day with an organized protest over an Israeli land grab in 1976. Today it didn't matter where you were—if you were Palestinian, you observed Land Day, and this year's demonstration might be the best one yet. Kalandia was just one of the many planned demonstrations. Even Bilal's sullen face at her side as they walked toward the buses couldn't dull the anticipation. She only hoped the television crews were on hand.

"Oh, damn!" Bilal's unexpected expletive startled Kareema. She looked up and saw what caused it. Patrols loitered on either side of the street, and a troop carrier passed them going deeper into the camp. Kareema's heart beat faster. This did not bode well. "Maybe I should take you home."

"Bilal, for heaven's sake, you know I can't afford to miss any more school." Not to mention once she'd never get out of that house again in time for the demonstration. The closer they got to the bus terminal, the more evident it became that things were far from normal. The buses parked in their usual spots, but the doors remained closed. Students milled around aimlessly; soldiers watched from all angles; military vehicles moved slowly up and down the street. She spotted a group of men sitting on a bench, flanked by soldiers. They looked vaguely familiar. The flame from a lighter caught her eye, and she recognized the man on the bench as one of the bus drivers. No wonder they looked familiar. Kareema surveyed the scene and realized that their plans were slipping down the drain. If the buses didn't load soon, students would go back home. A girl beckoned to her. She recognized her, but she didn't know her well.

"Bilal, I'm going to talk to a friend. I'll meet you on the bus—if the buses ever decided to move. She walked quickly toward the girl before Bilal had time to protest.

"Hey, what's up?"

The girl pointed out one of the boys that Kareema had seen in the YFP office. "He's looking for you."

"Can you come with me? My brother's watching, and he'll freak out if he sees me talking to a boy." The girl laughed and together they moved toward the YFP boy.

"I think we need to move the schedule up before something happens here and we miss our chance." The boy didn't waste time with a preamble. Kareema nodded, pleased that he seemed to have a plan. "Can you and your friend pass the word and have the girls gather at the school? Move them out in groups of two or three. I'll see if I can't find some volunteers to light the tires and block the other entrances to the camp. The boys'll come to the girls' school through the alleys."

Kareema felt almost light-headed with excitement and anticipation. Their plans wouldn't be wasted after all. She hoped the television cameras arrived in time to catch the demonstration.

Kareema looked around at the sheer numbers of people now milling around. "Can you manage all this?"

"Nothing could be easier," he said with a grin. "All I have to do is tell them the girls are already organized and demonstrating in front of the school while we stand here with our hands in our pockets."

"I'll try to make you into an honest man." Kareema gave him a wink, grinning to think it would scandalize her father. "Willing to lend a hand?" she asked the girl who'd given her the message.

"Wouldn't miss it for the world." Excitement lit the girl's eyes, and Kareema made a mental note to try recruiting her for a new cell. Now all she had to do was slip away without Bilal charging after her like a bulldog and dragging her back.

Kareema held out the kafiya she had draped over her shoulders. "If you start with 'Kareema says' and wear this, the girls who know me will follow your instructions without question." Kareema lowered her voice, "Can you keep your back to the bus and stay in sight for a few minutes? One girl in a school uniform with a white head scarf and a kafiya on her shoulders looks pretty much like any other. When my brother starts looking for me, he'll zero in on you first."

"Must be tough having a built-in guard."

"Sometimes." She didn't have any idea how tough. Kareema laughed and they separated to spread the word among the high school girls waiting for the bus. Kareema worked her way toward the far end of the terminal, trying to stay out of sight of Bilal, trusting the other girl to stay within sight of the bus as long as possible.

She imagined the area as a grid, and as she met members of her cells, she gave them areas to cover. She watched as excitement replaced disappointment on their faces. This was what it was all about—organizing made things like this easy. Little by little, the girls melted back into the camp. Satisfied, Kareema scanned the area one last time for green school uniforms. Was it her imagination, or were there fewer soldiers standing around? Maybe they were already patting themselves on the back for dispersing the students before they demonstrated. She started for the elementary school, putting as much distance between herself and the buses as she could before Bilal pushed his panic button.

Girls crowded the area around the school. Some of her cell leaders rushed toward her, speaking at once. Kareema's excitement crowded out the less pleasant thoughts of what Bilal would do when he discovered her absence.

"This was brilliant, changing the time. We have all the elementary girls here because it's time for them to get to school. It was a stroke of genius." Kareema agreed that it was perfect and wished she could take credit for the new plan.

"I think the boys have tires at the main entrances to the camp, ready to burn."

"Yes, they're going to start the fires now."

"Do you think the television cameras will still be here?"

"Your cousin was looking for you. She's over there." The girl pointed. Kareema followed her direction and waved at Imahn. She hadn't expected to see Amal, but there she was, tugging on Imahn's sleeve. Of course, because of the time change, Amal would be here too. Oh, well, one more person in the crowd. She wanted to remind Imahn of her promise, but she had no time now.

The chanting began near the center of the crowd and spread outward like spilled water. Within minutes, the milling crowd of girls became a demonstration. Even the youngest girls, who minutes before had been bewildered by the presence of high schoolers in front of their school, joined their voices to the familiar chants.

NO JUSTICE—NO PEACE

NO JUSTICE—NO PEACE

The words got louder and louder as the chant spread throughout the crowd. Kareema worked her way to the center, feeling like a general reviewing her troops. This was going to be the best demonstration ever. She'd been going to demonstrations ever since junior high, and none of them had measured up to this one. She was so proud of all her girls, even the little ones she'd never seen before. She wanted to run up to the little girls with bows on their pigtails and tell them how proud she was of them.

She patted the ones she passed on the back or the shoulder, keeping up a constant patter of praise. "Good job." "You tell them." "Keep it up."

Bits and pieces of conversations floated through the air as the girls passed information through the shifting mass of students. "The fires are lit." "The boys will come soon." "Soldiers are everywhere." "Yeah, we know that." "They're looking for people." "I heard they're making arrests already." "Did you hear about the list?"

"Look at all of us," one of the older girls said proudly. "They won't get through here, at least they won't get any vehicles through." Kareema couldn't contain her pride. She gave the girl a quick hug as she passed. Here they were, just simple school girls, and they were effectively blocking entrance to the camp by a well armed and well trained army. It was a glorious feeling. She neared what she thought was the center of the crowd, and two of her cell leaders linked arms with her, leading her forward. They formed a line across the street and up the sidewalks on either side. Some of the younger girls slipped past them, moving toward the rear. Were they just letting the older girls lead, or was there something up ahead?

As the ranks of the younger girls moved, Kareema caught sight of the tanks that stood facing them. A shiver raced down her spine at the view of the enormous guns. She thought of the soldiers inside the tanks and tried to imagine how it must feel to have such big guns pointed at a large crowd of school girls. Did the men inside think of them as simple school girls? Or did they, too, think that when the girls were all together they really turned into something strong and powerful? And did the strong and powerful thing need to be destroyed? She wasn't sure she wanted to know the answer. Somewhere above the general noise, she heard the chanting begin again. It grew louder, more purposeful. Kareema raised her voices with the others.

PALESTINE IS OUR COUNTRY
PALESTINE IS OUR COUNTRY

Suddenly the entire crowd became one chanting entity. Kareema felt the rush of excitement return as her voice became a full-throated part of the cry.

PALESTINE IS OUR COUNTRY
PALESTINE IS OUR COUNTRY

The line moved slowly forward. Kareema felt the power of the solid lines of girls.

"Look," shouted the girl on her right, "the tanks are moving backward!" Kareema advanced triumphantly, and her cell leaders led the way with her. The chanting and pride filled her to overflowing. She shouted the words, feeling the truth of each syllable. The chant intensified.

Kareema couldn't distinguish her own voice from the others. This was as it should be, they were one in the face of oppression.

NO JUSTICE—NO PEACE

Two tanks came down the street toward them and stopped far enough away from the girls that it could train the guns on them. Neither Kareema nor the other girls blocking the intersection moved. The chanting grew louder.

NO JUSTICE—NO PEACE

A few of the girls pointed and nudged the girls around them. Once again, the chanting grew louder. Kareema finally saw what the girls were showing each other as they pointed—television cameras! Her heart beat faster, and she shouted as loud as she could.

NO JUSTICE—NO PEACE

This was it! This was going to be broadcast all over the world and people would know what was happening—and she was part of it. The chant changed and Kareema's voice flowed into the new chant with ease. Jeeps drew up alongside the tanks. The soldiers wore face masks and carried shields.

PALESTINE IS ARAB

PALESTINE IS ARAB

Again the volume increased. She noticed a change in the pitch. Then she heard a new sound—rocks hitting the tanks.

PALESTINE IS ARAB

PALESTINE IS ARAB

She poured everything she had into the words. She wanted to show her soul through the words. Palestine. Every time she said the word, she felt a shock of emotion. Maybe love, maybe just excitement; it didn't matter. They were going to make it happen. At long last they were going to make their case heard, and the world would listen to them.

WITH MY SOUL AND BLOOD, I WILL FREE PALESTINE!

WITH MY SOUL AND BLOOD, I WILL FREE PALESTINE!

WITH MY SOUL AND BLOOD, I WILL FREE PALESTINE!

They were all together, one people in the face of the occupiers. The tanks didn't frighten her. The cameras were rolling, and she was fighting for her country. Together they could do anything. They were making a difference in the eyes of the world. She picked up a loose rock and threw it at the jeep nearest them. Maybe threw wasn't the right word, it was more of a toss. Her brothers were right, she threw like a girl. Never mind the rocks. The important thing was that the jeeps weren't coming any closer; they were backing away from the entrance to the camp. She looked left and right, and she thought her heart would burst with pride. Nothing broke the line of green school uniforms, except for the bits of blue.

She smelled burning rubber. Other students had rolled old tires into the roads. Once the tires caught fire, it was nearly impossible to put them out.

She looked around. At least as many boys as girls now surrounded her. The boys carried rocks in their arms and in kafiyas, and the girls were retreating slowly.

Suddenly a couple of shots rang out. Kareema scanned the sidewalks and rooftops, looking for the source. Shouts from the jeep moved her attention back to ground level. Rocks flew from all directions. More boys appeared. High school age students came out of the narrow walkways. Other boys appeared on rooftops and rained stones down on the tanks and jeeps. The students seemed to be everywhere! The YFP had outdone itself today. The days of planning had not been in vain.

Some carried bundles of stones and others carried thick pieces of wood. Clubs? What did they expect to do with those? Stones were for throwing, clubs only worked at close quarters. Kareema's chants died on her lips. She didn't remember anything about that in the plans. Many of the boys had kafiyas wrapped around their heads just like the resistance fighters. The volume of sound around her became almost unbearable. The girls chanted and the boys yelled. Kareema picked up the current chant and tried to take in what was happening all around her. Her throat felt raw, but she had never felt more alive.

A sound truck drove up the street behind the tanks, blaring that a curfew was going into effect immediately.

"Get the girls off the street," a boy shouted at her. "Get them home *now*." He was giving her an order, so he must know who she was. Was it an official order? Was it the guy from the bus terminal? His face was half covered by his kafiya, and then he was gone. Kareema saw other boys attempting to get the girls to retreat. She was still shouting, but she stopped when she realized the organized chant had dissolved into the same chaos as the girls' advance.

The sounds changed again. Over the din of voices and the blare of the speakers came a new sound—the sound of gunfire. Rapid bursts of machine gun fire erupted from different directions, followed by several single shots. A scream of pain rose above the general screaming and shouting of the crowd. Someone was hit. Kareema made an instant decision to follow the order and get the girls out of harms way. But where were the shots coming from?

Kareema looked up and saw a soldier on a rooftop. His machine gun was pointed up and he was firing in the air. The boys on the rooftops had gone. More soldiers with rifles appeared on other rooftops. Her heart pounded. Who were they trying to keep out with their pitiful little fires? The soldiers were already in the camp. The snipers were all around them, and the sheer number of them frightened her. There must be a whole battalion, or company, or whatever they were called—and every one held a rifle. Some of the rifles pointed up, shooting into the air, but others pointed down toward the crowd.

She looked up, directly into the muzzle of a rifle, and for just a second, the world seemed to stop. The moment froze in time— silent and unmoving. The soldier wore reflective sunglasses.

Kareema thought of the Terminator movie and how easy it would be for him to pull the trigger. She saw a flash of white teeth, and the rifle barrel swung skyward. Did he just smile at her? Kareema shuddered, and time reset. Girls were screaming; boys were yelling; the sound truck continued its blare, announcing the curfew. Gunshots, the thud of rocks and the sounds of smashing glass all mingled into a deafening roar.

All around them, girls ran. Her two cell leaders still stood on either side of her. "It's time to leave," she shouted at them. "Make sure all the girls leave now."

"We'll go when you do," said the girl on her right.

"Don't argue—just GO." She gave them each a shove, but they tried to pull her with them. A young man rushed toward them with his arms outstretched.

"Get back, Sisters," he yelled. Just as he reached them, his shout turned to a scream and he fell forward, clutching Kareema's uniform skirt as he fell. She saw blood blossom around a hole in his jacket. She knelt beside him. She had taken the YFP first aid courses. Maybe she could stop the bleeding. As she reached toward him, other boys appeared, picked him up, and ran.

"GO! GO!" they shouted as they ran with their burden. A sharp stab of guilt made Kareema turn toward home. If she'd left earlier, the boy might not have been shot. She pulled her companions off the road and told them to run home—fast. Pausing only to make sure they were on their way, she turned back and headed for a patch of green uniforms. She needed to get the girls out of harm's way. She moved around shepherding girls to side streets and yelling to others to get home. She couldn't see any more girls in the street.

Black smoke billow up from several piles of burning tires, one in front of her and the others farther away. In accordance to the plan, the boys had used tires to block all entrances to the camp wide enough for a vehicle to pass. Her eyes smarted from the acrid smoke.

What happened today? For a brief moment, she prayed that Imahn remembered her promise, then she caught sight of a girl in a blue uniform crouched down behind the school fence—much too young to be in the midst of this. The girl looked too frightened to move. Kareema ran over and helped her up. Half leading and half carrying the girl, she ran with her across the street and toward an alley that led to the interior of the camp. "Run home as fast as you can." The girl was already doing her best to set a new speed record.

"Hey, Kareema!" She heard her name called above the din of what had become a battle. Looking around, she saw the YFP boy she'd spoken to earlier that morning running toward her. He pulled her into the space between two buildings. "I heard your name is on the list."

"List?"

"Yeah, patrols are inside with a list of specific people to arrest." Soot smudged his face, and a little blood stained his trousers. He put his hands on his thighs and bent forward, catching his breath before he continued. "Mine's on it, too," he said ruefully. "Dammit. We thought we were so smart burning tires to keep them out of the camp. Not only were they already here, they stopped the buses and cars to keep us from getting out. It's a good bet everyone on the list is still inside the camp."

Thwoop. Thwoop. Kareema recognized the sound of tear gas canisters being launched.

"This might be a good time to leave," he said with a grin that she recognized from the morning conversation. "Get off the streets as soon as you can. It might also be a good time to visit a friend for a few days. Don't go home, and don't get caught." He gave her a gentle push. "Now run, that's an order!" She recognized the urgency in his tone and began to run. She heard him call "good luck," and kept running. Once the sounds of the conflict faded behind her, she slowed to a brisk walk, not wishing to attract attention.

Her mind raced as fast as her feet. How could she have missed the obvious? The boy was right. The army had deployed the troops before dawn—all of them, not just a bunch of vehicles at the bus station. The students had closed the barn door, but the horse was already gone. It was all so obvious now. How had she missed it? She'd been so caught up with the planning and the change of plans that she didn't look beyond what she saw in front of her nose.

Maybe it was all about the list after all. Her mouth went dry at the idea of her name on the list. It must be a rumor. She wasn't important enough for that. She caught sight of a jeep in front of her and ducked down an alley. Some alleys were dead ends, but others led from one street to another. The entire camp was a maze of alleys and walkways. She'd thread her way through them until she got home. Staying with a friend was out of the question.

No, as much as being on "the list" frightened her, her father's reaction frightened her even more. She might be able to talk her way out of getting separated from Bilal at the bus station, but spending the night away from home was not an option. Maybe the list didn't even exist. As fast as news spread from end to end of the camp, rumors spread even faster. Sometimes rumors were started by the wrong people and were intended to spread panic.

The camp had become eerily quiet. The sound trucks were barely audible in the distance, and the guns sounded like children's toys. She wove her way through the smallest alleys she knew, even when it meant walking three sides of a rectangle to avoid a street, and approached each intersection cautiously. She wanted to take no chances meeting a patrol—just in case the list did exist.

She froze at the clink of metal on metal. Boots crunched on the unpaved alley behind her. Her heart thumped like a drum, and she turned to the nearest doorway. She knocked on the door and called as loud as she dared.

"Auntie! Auntie, please let me in. The soldiers are coming." Kareema prayed there was someone listening on the other side of the door. She was thankful she was a girl. A woman was more likely to open the door for a woman's voice. She knocked again and looked around, judging her chances of trying another door.

The door opened a crack, then it opened wide enough for her to slip inside. She leaned against the door, her legs weak with relief, and looked around. Five sets of big brown eyes looked back at her from the worn sitting mats that furnished the room.

"Hello," she said to the children and managed to smile.

"Please sit," said the woman in a quiet voice. She'd been to the kitchen and returned with a glass of water which she offered to Kareema.

"Thank you." Surprisingly, she actually did feel calmer after drinking it. She'd always thought that idea a superstition. Five minutes later she was on her way again.

It took a long time for her to reach her house. She didn't know exactly how much time the soldiers allowed between calling a curfew and deciding everyone had been given enough time to reach shelter, but she knew she had far exceeded it. She was terrified to be out, but she made it home without meeting another patrol. She watched the street in front of her house for several minutes to be certain there was no one else on the street before she knocked.

Bilal opened the door. "Where have you been?"

"I got caught up in things and had trouble getting here." It was a lame answer, but at least it was true.

"Thank God you're home," said her mother, rushing to embrace her. "We were worried. Come in and eat something. We already ate." She took Kareema's hand and pulled her to the kitchen.

Breakfast seemed like a distant memory. She followed her mother into the kitchen. "Is Papa very angry?"

Her mother nodded. She didn't expect any other answer.

"Mother," she said, and then she hesitated. She loved her mother dearly, but she probably shouldn't tell her mother anything that she didn't want her father to hear later that night.

"Yes, Kareema?"

"Thanks, Mother. I love you." She walked over and gave her mother a hug.

Suddenly the house reverberated with the sound of banging on the door. Her mother's body stiffened and her arms froze around her. They were coming for her. The list wasn't rumor, and she was right where they knew she would be. Kareema felt as pale and frightened as her mother looked. She felt dizzy and unable to move. Her mother's frightened eyes filled with tears. Paralyzed by fear, Kareema remained frozen in a hug that had turned into a desperate clutching for support. The banging came again. It was the unmistakable sound of rifle butts against the door.

"Open the damn door before they knock it down!" yelled her father from the other room. The familiar surge of anger at her father's order broke the paralysis. Bilal and the twins came out of the bedroom as Kareema and her mother emerged from the kitchen holding hands.

"Sit down and look small," said her mother to the twins. Kareema had no idea what she meant, but the twins sank down where they stood, fear written clearly across their faces.

The rifle butts attacked the door again, this time accompanied by loud voices.

Bilal went toward the door; his hand shook as he turned the key in the lock. Kareema heard her father's footsteps behind her.

The door flew open forcefully as soon as Bilal turned the knob. He was thrust aside so hard that he lost his balance and landed on the floor with his feet spread in front of him. A stray thought made a cameo appearance in Kareema's head, "I hope we can laugh about that some day." A cold shiver betrayed the thought beneath it: if I live that long.

Two soldiers stood in the doorway with their rifles pointed at the family. The one who had pushed the door open took a paper out of his pocket.

"We're here for…Krema Al…Abo…Abdul…A…" Either the paper was so creased and dirty that the writing was not clear or the man was semi-literate in Hebrew. Kareema was too frightened to speak. Her mind, however, slotted the soldier neatly into a category: new immigrant, European, maybe speaks Yiddish, maybe not, just learning Hebrew. Anger released her from her fear. What right did a European have to come here and take her from her family? To take their land? It didn't make sense! It wasn't right!

"Look what you've done!" her father shouted at her.

What? Kareema turned her astonished attention to her father. He was shouting at her? He was standing there in his bare feet with his belly straining at his shirt buttons and his face red as a beet, ignoring the soldiers and shouting at her.

"You've brought soldiers into my home. This is all your fault. If you behaved yourself this would never have happened!"

Inconceivable! Disbelief turned to anger. Kareema wanted to scream at him that he was supposed to be protecting his family. What was he doing? She wanted to scream, but the short shallow gasps of her breathing kept the scream inside her head. Her father's face had begun to turn an even deeper color. Maybe he'd have a stroke or something. How *could* he blame this on her? How dare he shout at her?

Anger narrowed her vision. She'd almost forgotten the soldier when he grabbed her arm. She yanked her arm away and turned her fury on the soldier, screaming and lashing out with her hands and feet.

The soldier reacted instinctively and slammed her across the face with his rifle butt, knocking her to the ground. Pain exploded in her head and a boot connected with her abdomen. Kareema couldn't breathe, and all the fight went out of her. Her body begged for air, but she couldn't take a breath. She was going to die right here on the floor in front of her family.

The soldier grabbed her arms and yanked her roughly to her feet. Kareema gasped in pain. Air at last. Blood trickled from her nose. Two soldiers took her arms and pulled her toward the door. She had no more strength to resist.

Her mother, who had not moved a muscle since the soldiers entered, suddenly ran after them. At the door she grabbed a sweater and head scarf and thrust them into Kareema's hands. "Dear God, Mother." Kareema mouthed the words, but she barely managed a breathy mumble.

I'd laugh if I had the breath and strength. Hysteria bubbled up within her. She'd been shouted at by her father, had her face smashed and her stomach kicked by soldiers, was being led away to jail and God knows what else—and all her mother can think about is that she's going out without her hair covered.

Chapter VIII
❦LOST AND FOUND❧

Israelis Attack Arafat's Complex; Palestinian leader yards away as troops, security guards exchange fire
Seattle Post-Intelligencer; March 29, 2002

Israeli Army Bans Delivery of Relief Supplies to Qalqilya
RIA Novosti; April 24, 2002

Sharon plays cat and mouse with Arafat
The prospect of the Palestinian President, Yasser Arafat, attending the Arab summit in Beirut hung in the balance last night. Israel's Prime Minister, Ariel Sharon, has insisted that Mr Arafat must get a truce in place and arrest more Palestinian militants if he is to be freed to go to Beirut.
Sydney Morning Herald (Australia); March 27, 2002

Muhammad sat staring at the flickering pictures on the screen. The sound was muted, but it didn't make any difference. He neither watched nor listened. The set was only on because if he turned it off, he'd never know if he was sitting in the dark or if the darkness inside had finally swallowed him whole. Sometimes he woke up slumped in the chair with nothing but static and snow on the screen. He couldn't bear to take down the mattress. It was too hard to reach over in the night and have his hand meet nothing but emptiness—the same emptiness that filled his soul.

Damn these curfews! He'd barely pulled himself together enough to start looking for work when they clamped down another curfew? What purpose did they serve? So what if the students demonstrated on Land Day. Leave them alone and they'd go home after a few hours. Why call another curfew and leave him penned up in the house with nothing to do but think about the emptiness? Deena wasn't humming in the kitchen. Deena wasn't folding laundry in the evening as she watched television with him. Deena wasn't talking to the children. He heard a soft whimper from the other room. His heart, which he'd thought broken beyond feeling, proved him wrong. Poor Amal was trying so hard.

He stood and switched off the television. He realized he needed to shave — and bathe. He went to the bathroom and started the process of heating bath water. "I need to build a new life." Speaking the words aloud gave them more substance. "Even if it's a doughnut life." He was a man without a core. His life would always have a yawning gap in the middle, but he needed to put it back together again — for the children. When school got out for summer break, he'd bring the boys home and they could be something resembling a family once more.

"What're you doing, Papa?" Amal's voice startled him. He nearly tipped the water off the kerosene heater. He smiled at his too-small daughter in her even smaller pajamas. Her hair was tousled, and her eyes showed signs of recent tears.

"I'm taking a bath."

"It's the middle of the night."

"I know, but is that any reason to be dirty?" That coaxed a vestige of a smile to her lips.

"Can I get you anything?"

"How about you make me a sandwich to take with me tomorrow? I'll probably be on my way to work by the time you get up."

"Okay." Her shoulders straightened.

"And then go right back to bed."

She nodded.

The next morning, he silently got ready to meet the predawn gathering of construction workers hoping for jobs. He joined the group of men with various degrees of hopelessness written on their faces. The young ones, confident in their youthful strength, were the only ones who looked eager. As the trucks pulled up, men jostled for position. Muhammad stood and watched. The young were eager; the not-so-young were desperate. He was neither. He wasn't even sure he had the strength to handle a job yet. These men were hired for muscle, not for skill. However, it was a place to start. Once a foreman noticed his skill, he stood a chance of a regular job. Regular in the sense that he'd have work every day he could get there until the job finished, or the foreman got tired of his missed days during curfews.

"Hey, Muhammad!"

He looked up, as did half a dozen other men, presumably all named Muhammad. A man he vaguely recognized was motioning to him from the back of a truck.

"He says he can take one more. Get over here."

Grateful, Muhammad trotted to the truck and climbed on board. Once, he would have felt bad to be singled out over men whose naked desperation was so apparent. Once, he would have been embarrassed to be standing with the "donkey" laborers. Today he felt nothing. He sat, grateful for the damaged or missing muffler of the truck that made conversation impossible.

The truck slowed as it joined the long line of vehicles waiting to be searched at the first checkpoint of the route to the job site. Muhammad sat with his head bowed, staring at his hands clasped together on his lap. He could get

141

through this. He was in the back of a truck, not trapped on a bus with the soldiers. He tried to empty his mind of thoughts. Failing that, he focused on the thought that his hands would bring in money to feed his children. He tried to focus on the end of the day and pictured money in his pocket. He concentrated on his hands. He closed his eyes and took deep breaths. A drop of sweat trickled down the side of his face. He clasped his hands together so hard that pain ran up his arm.

The truck began to inch forward. Muhammad lost his ability to take deep breaths. He had an unreasonable feeling that he could not get enough air.

"Are you all right?" asked the man sitting next to him.

Muhammad heard the concern in the other man's voice. He should answer. He opened his eyes and turned his head. Right in front of his eyes was a soldier. The soldier seemed to look right through them. He looked bored. He'd look the same if the truck held a heap of turnips. For just a moment Muhammad wondered about his own existence. Did he exist at all? He had to exist. The pain was real. The suffering was real. But was he a person? Did turnips feel pain? The soldier didn't think he was a person. Muhammad could see it in his face. His only concern was getting home that night, or getting out of the sun, or being in bed with his girl friend. The men in the truck meant less to him than the gravel on the road.

Was this the soldier from the other checkpoint? No, he remembered the faces of the two soldiers who'd pointed their guns at him that night. He'd never forget those faces. Did it matter? Weren't they all alike? This soldier wouldn't have helped him either. Muhammad wanted the satisfying heft of a hammer in his hands. His empty hands curled into

142

something resembling the talons of a bird of prey. His vision darkened and his sole desire was to wipe the look of indifferent boredom off the face of the soldier. He pictured himself jumping from the truck and grabbing the rifle. The soldier wasn't paying attention. Who would pay attention to a truckload of turnips? He wanted to stand nose to nose with him and shout in his face that these were *men* on the truck — human beings. It would be easy to smash that look off his face with the rifle. Then the others would shoot him and it would end. He moved toward the tailgate of the truck.

Hands grabbed him from both sides and someone pulled his legs out from under him. The back of his head crashed into the truck bed with enough pain to bring him to his senses.

"I can't breathe," he tried to talk, but he had no breath. Someone was sitting on his chest. He heard men laughing.

"He'll be fine by the time we get to work. He had a little too much to drink last night and he isn't used to it." More laughter — strange, strained laughter.

Hands sat him upright. Hands held his arms and other arms crossed in front of his chest, preventing him from moving at all. Someone was sitting on his legs.

The man he almost recognized put his face inches from his own and shouted. "Stop being such a clown. The foreman won't let you work if you don't sober up quick." In a low voice he continued, "What the hell do you think you're doing? You nearly got us all shot. Sit still until we get past this checkpoint." Muhammad nodded his understanding. The man sat down. Abed. That was his name. Abed. "If you want to get yourself killed, that's your business. Just don't do it when we're in the same truck. I

143

have a family to feed."

Muhammad nodded miserably. "They killed my wife like a turnip." The whisper was lost in the roar of the missing muffler, and the truck inched forward. The rage ebbed and left exhaustion in its wake.

When their turn came to be searched, strong hands lifted him off the truck and did not release their hold when his feet were on the ground. He closed his eyes to shut out the sight of the soldiers. He didn't struggle, but the men took no chances. They gave the same excuse of drunkenness, swearing they'd sober him up before reaching the job site. He opened his eyes to climb back into the truck. The driver scowled in his direction.

They passed the checkpoint without further incident. Muhammad was surprised when the truck pulled to the side of the road and stopped as soon as they were out of sight of the checkpoint. The driver got out and walked around to the back of the truck. He told Muhammad to get out.

"I'm not having a labor crew with a drunk. I have a job to keep too, you know."

Muhammad nodded and Abed told the men to release him. He climbed out of the truck and gave a crooked smile of apology to the other men. With a wave of his hand, he jogged between two buildings and slipped behind one of them. He heard the truck resume its journey and sank down on the ground.

Now what? He was past the checkpoint. Maybe he should walk to the nearest construction sites. A new settlement was going up not many miles away. But by the time he got there, the work would be well underway. No one paid for less than a day's labor. Even if he got a job, they'd ask him to start tomorrow. He'd never make it through the checkpoint on the bus. He barely made it with a truck full of men covering for him.

What had he done? He'd ruined the first chance of a job he'd had in ages. How? Why? Was he insane? That's the only kind of man who can't control his own actions. He had little enough control over his life under occupation. He might truly be insane. No one else would attack an armed soldier — at a checkpoint — with his bare hands. Life was miserable, true. Each minute was a struggle; each hour was a struggle. But what had he hoped to accomplish? Suicide by soldier? There were better ways, if that was what he wanted.

He didn't have the energy to think. His rage had exhausted him. His body was content to lean against the building; his mind was unable to think beyond the question. Now what? He sat, staring at nothing.

Now what? He couldn't get the question out of his head.

He opened his eyes to a different time. The sun was on his face. Past noon. Had he slept? He was unaware of a break in his thoughts, but time had passed. He could either sit here until he starved, or he could get up and start home. His legs protested as he stood. Time had definitely passed. He stretched and shook like a stray dog. It would be a long walk home.

Next decision. He could go back the short way along the road and go through the checkpoint, or he could go a long way around and add miles to his walk. Going back into Kalandia was always easier than coming out of Kalandia. But no matter how much easier, it was still a checkpoint, and he wasn't sure he could face the soldiers again so soon. He started walking away from the road. Once he got out of sight of the houses and buildings that lined the street, he could turn toward home. It shouldn't be too hard to stay out of sight of houses, which meant out of sight of roads, which meant out of sight of jeeps with soldiers. Stretches of empty land weren't that big, but by walking around the hills he could keep the horizon close.

He walked for what he thought was a couple of hours. Unless he misjudged the time or his direction, he would soon be in sight of the camp. He walked another hour. Still no sight of the camp. Had he gone too far away from the road before turning? Had he overshot the camp entirely? If so, he should turn in the direction he thought would lead to the main road. He turned and resumed his walk.

He was tired. His legs were tired. He trudged on, eyes unfocused, his only thought was to take the next step. His feet barely cleared the ground with each step, occasionally catching on the scrubby plants that gripped the patches of hard dry soil with stubborn roots. The bright green of spring had faded into the dark green that would soon be coated with summer dust. If anything could grow here, the land would be farmed. Land was too precious to leave idle, but this land was good for nothing. The little hills had worn down to bare rock in most places, and what little soil was left had been sucked dry of nutrients millennia ago.

He walked on. The camp could be right over the next rise. But it wasn't. Was he even headed the right way? What if he'd been walking in circles? Rocky mounds of sameness surrounded him. He kept thinking he'd be able to see farther from the top of the next hill … but all he ever saw was the next hill. His head drooped with exhaustion. His feet appeared and disappeared as he watched them.

146

Left, right, left, right, in a hypnotic rhythm.

He could walk in circles until he died of hunger or thirst. It would be no great loss to the world. What good was he? He couldn't even find his way home. He was useless. Amal would get over it. The boys wouldn't even remember him when they grew up. The hole in the family would heal quickly. Deena's loss was a mortal wound, but his would be a pinprick, a scratch, easily healed.

Only the loss of light as the sun dipped below the horizon reminded Muhammad that he could tell direction from the sun. He really was useless if he didn't remember the simplest thing about direction. He scanned the landscape for a sheltered spot to spend the night. When he was a boy, he'd heard these hills had cave-like holes worn into the softer rock by wind swept sand, but he hadn't seen any. Maybe it was just a boy myth, like jinn and pirates. He sank into a depression between two hillocks where a small outcropping of rock provided a little shelter from the night wind.

He pulled the zipper of his jacket up for greater warmth and felt a bulge in the inside pocket—the sandwich Amal had made the night before. Wrapped in a scrap of plastic bag, it was almost blood warm. Stale bread and goat cheese had never tasted so good. It was one of the most delicious things he'd ever eaten.

He smiled as he thought of his daughter. They'd named her hope, and Deena had said that she was their hope for a better tomorrow. He leaned back, resting on the uneven hillside, and watched the stars. More stars sparkled in the sky than he'd ever seen before. Even if he couldn't make his mind believe in hope, he had to take care of Amal. In the morning he'd walk, keeping the morning sun on his left. Even if he missed the camp, he was bound to run into Ramallah or some other evidence of people. Too many people lived around here to walk all day without seeing anyone—unless he kept changing direction. He'd be cold, but he wasn't likely to freeze to death.

A boot nudged Muhammad in the ribs.

"Is he alive?"

Muhammad moved an arm, afraid the next nudge might be a kick.

"Yeah. You think he was dumped here?"

Muhammad blinked. His lips were cracked, his mouth tasted like dirt, and the ground under him had turned into sharp stones, artfully placed to inflict the most pain. He sat up slowly.

"Who are you? How did you get here?" Two men silhouetted against the rising sun looked down on him. They weren't wearing army helmets, but they still sounded very unfriendly.

"I walked." Muhammad's voice came out as a hoarse croak. He coughed and spat out dirt. He tried to get up, but his legs didn't hold his weight, and he sank back down. "I … I …" His teeth chattered too hard to form the right words. What were the words he wanted? Thirst, hunger, cold, lost. He shuddered convulsively and couldn't stop shivering.

"You walked alone? Here? At night?" The man wasn't convinced.

"Can't you see the man's freezing?" The larger man moved away from the rising sun as he spoke, and Muhammad saw him clearly for the first time. His unkempt hair hung below his ears, and his face hadn't seen

148

a razor in days. The kafiya wrapped around his neck looked more gray than black and white. "You're not going to get any answers like this. Let's get him inside. I could use some hot tea myself." Inside? Inside where?

"All right." The small man jerked his head to one side, pointing the direction he expected Muhammad to walk. Muhammad took the hand the large man extended and stood on shaky legs. The man grabbed his arm and half-led, half-pulled him around to the other side of the hill. They led him to a small door of weathered wood and covered with enough dust to match its surroundings perfectly. Muhammad must have walked right past it. The smaller man pulled out a key and unlocked the rusty padlock.

Muhammad blinked in the darkness. The air smelled comfortably of earth, cigarette smoke, and men. He took another breath. The smell of a bus full of laborers, the smell of men packed into tight spaces waiting to be searched—sweat with a tinge of fear mingled with other odors. He heard the scrape of a match, and the soft yellow light of a kerosene lantern lit the space. Was it a room? A cave? A door on the opposite wall indicated another room deeper in the hillside.

Wooden crates drawn up to a rickety table constructed from pieces of similar crates furnished the center of the room. The small man sat on one of the crates and pointed to another. Muhammad sat, and his eyes adjusted to the lighting. The large man lit a kerosene burner and filled a kettle from a battered jerry can. The kettle looked as if it had been rescued from service as a neighborhood soccer ball. Large sand bags lined the walls, and stacks of crates framed the exterior door.

149

"Now tell us why you're here." The smaller man started his questions again.

Muhammad sat on his hands, trying to warm them. At least his teeth had stopped chattering. "I got turned around and got lost. I'm looking for Kalandia. Can you point me in the right direction?"

"Why do you want Kalandia?"

"I live there. I was trying to get home, and I guess I overshot the camp." Who were these guys? What was going on here? "Just point me in the right direction, and I'll be on my way."

"Get home from where?"

"It's a long story."

"We've got all day."

"I have to get home. All I want is directions."

"Kalandia's under curfew."

"No, not again. They just lifted the curfew. What was it two or three days ago?" How could he face another curfew? At least getting lost saved him from more days in a house without Deena.

"As I said, we've got all day, maybe more." The words were cold. He wasn't going to avoid an explanation.

Muhammad opened his mouth and closed it again. He didn't know where to begin. He could say he got crazy when he saw soldiers. That probably wouldn't work—not here, not now. These men were hard. Their eyes looked hard. Understanding flooded Muhammad's thoughts. "You're ..." Should he finish the sentence, or pretend he didn't know?

The smaller man laughed. "That's us. Garden variety freedom fighters." He held out his hand. "Mazin, at your service."

150

"Muhammad." He grasped the man's hand.

"Abood." The larger man plunked three glasses on the table and poured hot strong tea in each glass before shaking hands. "Cheers."

Muhammad wasn't sure how it happened, but the men changed from suspicious strangers to friends in the blink of an eye. He put his hands around the hot glass and leaned forward to inhale the warm steam. He closed his eyes and enjoyed the feeling of warmth spreading from his hands and lungs. The tea was too hot to drink, but he slurped up a few drops before he spoke. "What just happened?"

Mazin chuckled again. "You should've seen your face when you realized where you were. There's no way you could've faked that expression. I wish I'd had a camera."

"So?"

"So it means you stumbled into us by accident—just like you said. It means you weren't looking for us. You had no idea we were here. So you weren't leading anyone here. We can also see that you're in pretty good shape, no bruises or broken bones. That means you weren't dumped here for us to take care of, which would mean our location was compromised."

"But you *are* taking care of me."

"Uh … not that way. Sometimes collaborators are beaten and dumped. We're pretty sure no one knows we're here, but I hear it's happened in other places."

Abood spread an old blanket and sat on the ground, leaning against the wall. "I think we're ready to listen to your long story now."

"I don't know where to begin."

"Begin by telling us why you want to avoid the checkpoint. It would've saved you a lot of miles if you'd just followed the road."

"I haven't been able to go through a checkpoint since …" Tears stung his eyes. He looked down at his glass until he had them under control. The tea was cool enough to drink. He drained half the glass. "… since my wife died." Once he managed to say those words, the rest was easier. It was the first time he talked to anyone about what happened at the checkpoint that night. He went through it all. He let the tears flow when he had to, and his audience accompanied them with a stream of low-voiced profanity. He didn't know why it was easier to talk to sympathetic strangers than to his brothers, but it was.

Abood got up and refilled the tea glasses. Mazin produced some bread and cheese from a bag Muhammad hadn't noticed before, then changed the subject and asked about Muhammad's children. He talked about his rambunctious boys, and his voice broke again when he spoke proudly of Amal. "She goes to her aunt's house every day and learns cooking. She keeps the house clean, too."

The conversation ran down, and Mazin turned on a small radio. They sat like old friends, drinking tea and commenting on the news and sports.

When they brought out the bread and cheese again, the talk turned to food. Mazin described the dishes his wife made, and Muhammad chimed in with praise of Deena and her cooking. Abood kept them laughing with tales of his bachelor misadventures in the kitchen.

When it was time for the evening news, they turned on the radio again. The curfew would be lifted at dawn.

The next morning, Mazin pointed out the direction to Kalandia. "Remember what I said about no one knowing we're here. We like to keep it that way. Forget where we are. Better yet, forget you ever saw us. You spent the night in the cold, and yesterday morning you saw some sheep on a hillside and found their shepherd."

"Of course. Thank you for everything. You gave me so much more than food and shelter for a day."

Mazin held him by both shoulders and stared into his eyes. "You take care of that little girl. Just remember that as cruel as her death was, your wife is now beyond pain. She and the unborn child she carried are at peace. Your daughter is struggling to take up household duties she's not ready for. Death is often cruel, but life can be even more cruel."

Muhammad nodded, not trusting himself to speak. He turned and began the long walk home. For the first time, he felt alive again. He looked forward to seeing Amal. He would show more interest in her cooking—and her homework.

Chapter IX
❧CONSEQUENCES❧

'Informants' meet death on Peace St.
National Post (Canada, Toronto); April 24, 2002
Hebron mob executes 'informants'
National Post (Canada, All but Toronto); April 24, 2002

5 Palestinian Police shot by Israeli Troops Near Hebron
Xinhua General News Service; April 25, 2002

Persecution of Palestinians
It seems ironic that Israelis, who have in the past quite rightly drawn the world's attention to the terrible atrocities inflicted on Jews during the Holocaust, could impose such suffering on another people. Palestinian deaths in the past six months number about 1200 to 400 Israeli casualties.
Waikato Times (Hamilton) New Zealand; April 26, 2002

Kareema opened her eyes and groaned. She huddled under her thin blanket on a cement floor in a cell with more women than bunks. She was cold and everything hurt. Her head hurt; her feet hurt; everything in between hurt. As the youngest and the newest resident of the cell, she didn't rate a bunk. She was sure she'd been here a week. It could have been more. She'd lost count of days.

Kareema tried to take comfort in the presence of the other women. Some of them were sullen; some of them were morose; not one of them was friendly. She kept telling herself that all of them were fellow human beings, fellow Palestinians. Kareema tried to cling to that thought, almost like a mantra as she watched them and followed their lead. Instinctively she tried to avoid calling attention to herself.

The nights were cold and the food was miserable. The guards came periodically and took one or two of the women away. They usually came back after a couple of hours, though sometimes it was longer, and sometimes they never came back. Transferred? Released? Held in isolation? The women who returned to the cell sat away from the others or huddled on a bunk. Kareema thought of all the horror stories she'd heard in the camp. She didn't see bruises, but that didn't mean much. The stories told of electric shocks, rape, beatings that wouldn't leave marks in visible places. She wanted to put her arms around them, to give some sympathy at least, but she didn't. She'd never seen so many women in one room that were as quiet as these were.

She'd expected to be interrogated right away, maybe even tortured or beaten, but that hadn't happened. Every time a guard came to get someone, she expected it to be her. She'd also expected camaraderie among the prisoners. Nothing except the terrible food was as she'd expected.

She'd asked a few questions the first day. Sometimes one of the women had answered with nod or a shrug, but more often she was ignored. After the second day, she stopped trying. That night Kareema wrapped herself in the thin blanket she'd been given and prepared to curl up for sleep.

"The floor's cold and the blanket's too small," said a woman she'd spoken to earlier. "If you don't move or snore you can share my bunk for a couple of hours. It gives us two blankets for cover." Kareema felt suddenly vulnerable. She'd seen other women squeezing themselves into one of the narrow bunks with another woman. What should she do? Had she passed some kind of test? Or was this something else?

"Don't be an ass! It's cold," hissed the woman, evidently understanding her hesitation. Kareema accepted the invitation, but with trepidation. They made themselves as comfortable as possible and tucked the two blankets around them. Kareema was sure she wouldn't be able to sleep. She was wrong. The warmth put her to sleep within minutes.

"Shhhh." Kareema's eyes flew open and her body stiffened with fear. The woman's hand was over her mouth. "Don't talk, just listen." Kareema nodded and the woman removed her hand from her mouth. She whispered directly into Kareema's ear.

"I don't know how it is in other places. Here we don't ask questions, and we don't give any information. There are collaborators planted among us who relay everything to the guards." She must have felt Kareema's surprised intake of breath. "Don't be naïve, and don't be too quick to judge others. Do you have brothers? A father? We all do, and some of us have husbands and children as well. Would you tell on us if they were threatening your father?" Kareema was glad she wasn't expected to answer. Informants? Collaborators? Weren't they were all in this together? She thought about Bilal. As annoying as he was, would she let harm come to him by not repeating a conversation between women she didn't know? She needed to think about that. It would be a terrible choice to have to make.

"I didn't know."

"Well, now you do. Off you go. I'm not as young as you are, and I need my sleep." Kareema hated leaving the warm bunk, but she didn't argue.

Two or three days passed in exactly the same way. Kareema began to understand the stories of prisoners who scratched marks on the walls to count days. She'd finally recovered enough to stand up straight without her stomach hurting. She hoped that meant nothing was damaged. She could breathe but it still hurt to take a deep breath.

Then one day Kareema's name was called. The guards came to the cell door and one stepped forward and opened the cell. He gestured with his rifle for her to come out. She followed the soldier and heard the boots of the others following her down a corridor. Her knees felt wobbly and her breath became ragged and uneven. She had no idea what to expect. She knew some of the stories she'd heard were exaggerated, but she also knew that hundreds of people had died in Israeli prisons.

The farther they walked, the more she thought about the possible terrors that might be waiting for her when they got to the interrogation room. After a series of twists and turns, the guard she was following stopped and opened a door. He gestured for her to enter. One soldier entered behind her. Three soldiers sat at a long table facing her. The smoke from their cigarettes curled upward and dissipated. The small empty or half-empty tea glasses and the larger water glasses in front of them made it look as though she was interrupting a casual conversation. One of them leaned back in his chair. The one in the middle spoke.

"What's your name?"

She answered. Her mouth was dry with fear, and her lips and tongue seemed to belong to someone else. She clasped her hands behind her to hide the shaking she felt.

"Where do you live?"

She answered.

"You work in the PLO office." It was a statement, not a question; it took all of her will power not to say anything. She'd been prepped. The YFP told all their members what to do when questioned. Only answer direct questions, and do it with as few words as possible. "What do you do at work?"

"I copy and file mostly. Sometimes I make coffee or tea."

"A smart girl like you is willing to quit school to make coffee and tea?" Their information was out of date. They didn't know as much as they thought they knew. She was no longer terrified, but she was still very afraid.

"I didn't quit school."

"Give me names." Kareema gave him names of people who worked in the office. Everyone knew the regular staff.

"Who else? Many more people go there."

"I only know the ones who work in the office every day. I don't get introduced to visitors."

As the questions continued, Kareema began to feel less fearful and was better able to focus on her answers. She answered every question regarding what she did in the office, focusing on the mundane tasks. There was nothing of interest. No, she did not read the documents as she copied them, not because it was of no interest to her, but because she had a job to do and no time to read other people's documents. Yes, she filed documents. No, she didn't read them. They had a title or keyword highlighted

158

and she used that to create the needed files. Yes, she remembered some of the key words. Many of the documents were filed by city or region. Others were filed by date. The more questions they asked, the less afraid she felt. This was going better than she had expected.

"You worked full time for weeks before returning to school. Surely you didn't do that just to file unread documents and make coffee and tea." That surprised her. She tried to keep her face expressionless. They obviously knew more than she'd thought earlier.

"One of my jobs is to read the English language newspapers published in Israel and mark all articles that might be of interest. There was a huge backlog."

"Why didn't you mention that earlier?"

"You must read the same papers every day. Why mention it?"

The soldier who had been asking the questions wrote something on a paper in front of him. Neither of the others had said a word. He made a small gesture with his hand and Kareema was escorted back to the cell. No one met her gaze when she returned. She followed the example of the other women and sat by herself.

No one had shouted at her or threatened her; no one had beaten her, or broken any bones, or put a bag over her head, or hurt her in any way. While she was grateful, she was also puzzled.

That night Kareema slept on the cold cement floor. The woman who had befriended her was gone. The next day the guards came to get Kareema from the cell again. She was escorted to a different room and one of the guards went in with her. The only things in the room, identical to one from the previous day, were several straight-back chairs on the far side of a long table.

Kareema found it almost impossible to stand still and not show her nervous fear by fidgeting or tapping her foot. Why were the officers late? She faced the empty table, waiting for others to enter. The guard behind her shuffled his feet every few seconds. After what seemed like an hour, but was probably closer to five minutes, the guard sat on the edge of the table a few feet from Kareema. He set his rifle on the table, keeping it within his reach, and started swinging his feet like a small boy in a too-tall chair. She smiled, and he smiled back.

They looked at each other for a few long seconds. He said something in Hebrew. She shrugged. "I don't understand Hebrew." He could have been saying anything, but he didn't look hostile.

He smiled again and patted his chest. "Moshe."

The smile was encouraging. She patted her own chest. "Kareema." After a pause, she added, "Why haven't they come to interrogate me? That *is* why I'm here, isn't it?"

It was Moshe's turn to shrug and say a few sentences to her. It wasn't a conversation, but rather two monologues punctuated by large gaps of silence. He started talking to her, even though she couldn't understand him.

She shifted from foot to foot, uncomfortable standing still. He moved a chair from the other side of the table and put it near her. "Thank you."

"You're welcome." So, he did know some Arabic. She laughed, and it embarrassed her. Why did she laugh? It certainly wasn't appropriate; she was his prisoner. Maybe it was because no one else had smiled at her since she'd been here. Eventually, she started talking to him.

160

She poured out her stories of the Nakba and the troubles that had befallen innocent families. She poured out her frustration with life under occupation. It was safe. He didn't speak Arabic. Even if he did, she wasn't giving any information. It just felt better to say these things and pretend she could convince him of the injustice of what he was doing. Aware of the possibility of surveillance equipment, she avoided any mention of the resistance, the YFP, or the work she was doing. If someone else was listening, so much the better.

He talked. He could have been complaining about army food; he could have been telling her about his family; he could have been telling her what he had for breakfast, or what his dreams were for his future. It didn't really matter. The words weren't hostile or angry—maybe a little sad. Maybe he needed someone to talk to as much as she did.

Eventually Moshe looked at his watch and shrugged. He gestured to Kareema and they left the room. They met other guards and Moshe spoke to them for several minutes. He escorted Kareema back to her cell. The women seemed even colder than before, but that could be her imagination. The relief of talking to someone after so many days of silence may have made the contrast all the more noticeable. Again, Kareema kept to herself and slept on the cold cement.

The next day Moshe came by himself and collected Kareema from her cell. That was strange. She'd never seen a single guard unlock a cell. She felt the eyes of the women follow her. She could feel her heart beating, and her hands felt sweaty, but her knees didn't wobble this time. She walked in front of him, guided by the rifle barrel that prodded her when she needed to turn. All the hallways looked alike, and she had no idea if they were retracing their steps of the previous day or not. He stopped her and opened a door, indicating she should enter. She took a couple of steps into the room before she realized it was not an interrogation room but a storage area.

No! He was going to rape her! What could she do? She turned to flee but Moshe had already closed the door behind them. She stopped, immobilized by fear, and found her face only inches from his.

Suddenly the enemy had a face. Even yesterday, she'd been talking to a uniform. The enemy had always been a gun and a uniform—never a face. In the time between one heartbeat and the next she realized that the face was extraordinarily handsome. He said something in a low, pleading voice. His face showed no anger and his movements bore no menace, but he reached out and pulled her toward him.

Alarm bells went off in her head. "Use your knee to hurt him," she told herself, but even if her knees had not been almost too weak to support her weight, he held her too close to try that. "Bite him," her head said when he forced her mouth open with his own. But her body betrayed her. It responded with a warmth that turned the alarm bells into a swarm of harmless buzzing gnats. Half of her said "This is wrong! Stop him! He will stop if you fight. You saw his face—he doesn't want to hurt you." But the other half of her thought wonderingly, "So this is what it's like." He released her mouth and she felt his breath hot on her neck. His hands began to fondle her clumsily, and he pressed his body to hers. Her own breathing quickened.

Finally, her mind snapped into panic mode and she began to struggle weakly.

162

The sharp bark of a command in Hebrew filled the small space, followed by the stifled sounds of male laughter. She yelped in surprise. Moshe snapped to attention and went pale. A sergeant who looked incredibly fierce and incredibly angry nearly blocked the doorway. Behind him stood two young guards. The sergeant's glance barely quelled their laughter.

The sergeant grabbed her arm and shoved her at the two guards. They walked on either side of her and followed Moshe and the angry sergeant. She couldn't see Moshe's face, and she couldn't understand the sergeant's harsh words, but she didn't need to. Moshe kept repeating, "Yes, sir." After a few minutes of tongue lashing, the sergeant turned into another corridor. Moshe flashed her a grin and blushed as he joined the braying laughter of the others. They kept up a steady patter of remarks Kareema was happy not to understand. She pulled her scarf back over her hair and straightened her clothes. When they reached the cell, one of the two guards opened the cell door and stood aside to let her enter.

"Until tomorrow, Kareema," said Moshe in Arabic, giving her behind a squeeze.

Kareema heard a collective gasp from her cellmates above her own exclamation of surprise. "I didn't …" She began to protest, but the women who had been facing in her direction pointedly turned away from her. "Please," she addressed them all, "please believe me. I did nothing. He did not dishonor me. I swear it."

"Collaborator, traitor," she heard the words hissed from more than one direction. Her knees grew weak and she sank to the floor. Tears coursed down her face.

"How could you believe them?" she said. "How could you believe an enemy soldier over a sister patriot? How could you?" She cried and begged and pleaded with the women to believe her.

Finally one woman turned to her with a look of disgust. "Do you know what day it was yesterday?"

Taken aback by the sudden question, Kareema shook her head. She'd long since lost track of the days.

"It was Saturday. They do not interrogate prisoners on Saturday. There was only one officer on duty. That's why we don't believe you. Today you weren't gone long enough for any kind of questioning. That's why we don't believe you." Kareema felt the cell begin to tilt. She reached for the solidity of the cell wall to steady herself. The woman looked her up and down before continuing. "You weren't taken for interrogation, and you don't seem to have suffered any injuries from a forced encounter. That is why we don't believe you." She spat at Kareema and turned her back on her.

Kareema again sank to the floor, too shocked to cry this time. She sat motionless until the second time a woman "accidentally" tripped over her outstretched legs, bruising her shins. She drew her legs up, crossed her arms over her knees and rested her head on her folded arms. With her face safely hidden from the other women, Kareema allowed her tears to flow. She did not shake with sobs; there were only tears. Self-pity overwhelmed her, and the echo of "collaborator" haunted her mind. How could they think she was a collaborator? She'd given up her dream of university education; she'd faced the wrath of her father; she'd worked herself to exhaustion for Palestine.

When she'd gone back to school, her immediate supervisor had been pleased and hinted they would groom her for greater responsibility. She'd begun to harbor dreams and ambitions again, dreaming of ways that she could earn an education and serve her country at the same time.

Now it would never happen. She'd been labeled a collaborator. Nothing she could do or say would prove that nothing had happened in that interrogation room, and she didn't even want to think about the storage room.

Kareema tried not to move. Maybe if she stayed still enough, the others would tire of looking at her or thinking about her. She tried desperately to stop thinking about them. She was living a nightmare, but she knew it was reality. Her thoughts spun in circles. She went over everything again and again, but of course, nothing changed. Her ears registered the usual sounds of women moving about the cell, but they became meaningless. Her thoughts dead ended in a funk of misery and self-pity.

Her back got cold from leaning on the concrete wall. She leaned forward and hugged her knees. Her body got stiff from lack of movement, and her behind went from cold and uncomfortable to painful to numb. Eventually the cell settled into the closest semblance of silence it ever reached. Soft snores drifted around her, punctuated by loud unpleasant ones, often interrupted abruptly when a cellmate prodded the offender. A few quiet moans and whimpers reminded Kareema that she was not alone in her unhappiness, but it was little comfort. She longed to stretch her legs, but she couldn't because a large woman was sleeping a few inches beyond her feet. The sleeping women covered the floor in a random pattern that hemmed her into her small space. Sleep was impossible.

Her thoughts gradually regained coherence. Why had they arrested her if they believed she was merely an office grunt? Why would they bother with someone who made coffee and tea? They knew she had worked full time, yet they had not pressed their questions. They had not insisted that she must have read some documents; they had not suggested that she make copies for them and avoid further trouble. In fact, they had not even suggested that there might be further trouble. It didn't make any sense. Everyone got asked for names. Some people were pushed to the point where they began to babble names, any names, just to make it stop. She hadn't even been asked, except in a casual way.

The second time, they had taken her out of the cell on a day when they never interrogated anyone. It couldn't have been a mistake. Three guards had stood at the door before they unlocked it. Two held guns aimed at the cell, and the third unlocked the door and relocked it after the person they wanted had exited. Moshe could not have taken her out on his own whim. The other two guards had to know there were no interrogations. The more she thought about it, the less sense it made.

Hours passed, and only the occasional thud of boots when the guards made their rounds broke the quasi-silence of the cell. Someone very close to her took the shuddering breaths of a woman crying. Under any other circumstances Kareema would have gone to the woman and tried to comfort her. But not now.

And then the pieces all came together in her mind.

This was not about her at all! She wasn't important enough for the soldiers to make up an elaborate plan to discredit her. The charade had more to do with breaking the morale of the prisoners than breaking Kareema.

Coming to her home to arrest her might also have been a message to the office: we know who you are to the smallest among you, and we know where you live. Kareema just happened to be the smallest of them all and, as such, made a good object lesson. No, that might be unimportant. Anyone could follow a person home from a regular place of work. It was more likely to be showing that they could find anyone, no matter how small, any time they wanted to arrest them. Having found what she felt was a reasonable explanation for what had seemed totally unreasonable, Kareema fell into an exhausted uncomfortable sleep.

It seemed like minutes later when the more religious of her cellmates spread their blankets and began their morning prayers. Her stiff body ached from sitting up in one position all night. The final bitter truth came to her, and her head fell back onto her folded arms. No one had pressed her for names because she didn't know any names worth telling. They had not tortured names out of her because they already knew the names she had. Pick any girl at random and she would be a sympathizer to the idea of a free Palestine. To totally discredit her, they had only to arrest one or two girls at random and say that Kareema gave their names. Everyone would believe she'd given their names. She could never prove she wasn't a collaborator.

Kareema had thought the fear and terror she felt when the soldiers burst into her home were the worst emotions she could ever feel. She was wrong. Now she felt a cold dread that started in the pit of her stomach and grew outward until it filled her entire being. A collaborator had a very short lifespan in the camps. Still numb with fear and shock, she heard breakfast arrive, but didn't look up until they called her name. The guards had come for her again. She looked at their boots, afraid their faces might show mocking laughter. They prodded her with their rifles, and she walked forward, barely aware of her surroundings.

As before, they led her to a door and motioned her inside. An officer sat at a small table. She stood in front of the table. What a difference from her first visit to an interrogation room. This time her mouth wasn't dry, her hands didn't shake, she wasn't afraid or nervous. It just didn't matter anymore. Nothing mattered—she'd been labeled.

The officer ignored her presence and continued reading the file in front of him. Finally, he lifted his head and looked at her. He verified her identity and told her she was free to go; one of the guards would escort her to the street.

"Thank you." It was an automatic response that she regretted as soon as she said it. She felt no joy at her release. She was probably safer in jail now. She kept her eyes down and numbly followed the guidance of the rifle behind her. The single set of footsteps behind her echoed in an empty corridor.

"Sorry, Kareema." She recognized the voice as Moshe's. Her humiliation was complete. They'd assigned Moshe to escort her out. In another time and place she might have laughed at the inadequacy of the words. She thought of turning around and telling him that he had pronounced

168

her death sentence and sorry wouldn't help, but she didn't have the will or the energy. Besides, his Arabic was so awful he probably wouldn't understand anyway. She walked in front of him.

They reached the door and she squinted her eyes against the glare of the sun, blinded after so many days inside with dim lighting. She heard Moshe follow her toward the street.

"You have money for car home?" She shook her head and kept walking. "Here, take this." She heard the rustle of bills and the clink of coins. She kept walking. She reached the street, turned left and recognized the street at once. The prison was only a couple of miles from town, and maybe another mile to the bus. But she didn't have money for a bus.

She felt weak from hunger and lack of sleep, so she turned around and returned to the prison. Even if Moshe didn't leave money, she could sit there until someone came by who would give her enough money to get home. People came and went all the time around a prison. To her surprise, the money sat on the top of the low stone fence that faced the street. She took it and began to walk toward the center of town to find a cab.

Her mind seemed cloudy, but she had to think. She was all out of options. She had to go home and let her father yell at her and finally submit to marry the unknown friend's son. With luck he didn't live in the camp, and she could escape the rumors and the consequences attached to them. Whoever the man was, could it be any worse than living with her father? It was a chance at life. Her step quickened.

169

The doorbell rang incessantly, interrupting Muhammad's thoughts. Amal ran to open the door, and he glanced up briefly. Kareema stood there in a rumpled school uniform. Although she'd pulled her not-so-white head scarf forward to cover as much of her face as possible, it didn't hide her tear-reddened eyes and a big bruise on her face that was turning green and yellow. So her father had finally turned violent. His brothers could take care of it. He shut out the voices and turned his head back to the television. He neither heard nor saw what was happening on the screen.

There had to be another door he could knock on, another avenue to explore. He'd spent days and days looking for a job, and nothing worked. Probably the only place he hadn't asked for a job was Layth's store, and he was still toying with the idea. Layth didn't need his help. How would that be any different from just sitting here and letting his brothers take care of him?

"Papa," Amal put her hand on his shoulder. "Papa, Kareema wants you." Reluctantly he brought his attention back to Kareema. He gestured to a seat. Amal disappeared into the kitchen.

"I'm sure Amal told you about the demonstration on Land Day." Muhammad wondered if Amal had told him. He gave a small nod. Kareema continued, "The soldiers had a list of people to arrest, and my name was on it. I made it home minutes before the soldiers arrived. Father never even protested." Tears rolled silently down her face. "I'm still not sure if I was more afraid of the soldiers or angry at my father. He just stood there yelling at me that it was my own fault as the soldiers took me away."

"Have some tea." Amal set down a tea tray and poured two glasses. She went back to the kitchen and returned with bread, cheese and fruit. Kareema ate hungrily. Through the open bathroom door, Muhammad saw Amal fire up the kerosene burner. Finally the burner hissed satisfactorily, and the large pot of water was heating. Cold water half-filled the larger tub, ready to have the boiling water added to make a comfortable temperature. Amal came out and poured herself a glass of tea.

Her initial hunger sated, Kareema related the terrible conditions in the cell, how unfriendly the women were, and why. Muhammad found himself unwillingly drawn into Kareema's story. When she started talking about the strange session with no interrogators, she started to cry and couldn't continue.

Amal took her hand. "The water should be hot by now. Why don't you go in and bathe?" Kareema fled to the bathroom. "Papa." Muhammad turned his attention to Amal. "I think something bad happened to Kareema that she can't tell you about."

"Maybe." Muhammad forced the word out. Part of him was disgusted at what he guessed might have happened, part of him was upset that his little girl knew enough to guess the same thing. Why had Kareema come to him?

"Papa." Amal waited for his eyes to meet hers.

It shamed Muhammad to realize that she knew he didn't always listen to her unless she got his attention first. He was trying, but every day was a struggle. "Yes."

"I need to get some clothes out of the wardrobe for her to wear."

"No! Those are …" He couldn't finish the sentence. How could she even think about it? How could anyone else ever wear Deena's clothes?

"Papa." Amal knelt in front of him. Her face looked so sad and serious. "Kareema needs something clean to wear. She can't wear my clothes." She held his eyes for a long moment. "She came to us for help."

"Why?"

"Because her clothes are filthy."

"Why did she come to us? Why didn't she go home to her mother and her own clothes? Why didn't she go to Ali's?"

"I don't know. Maybe she'll tell us later, but she's family and we need to help her."

At last he nodded. Amal was right. She was family, and he couldn't refuse if she needed help. Family is all that had kept him going. It still puzzled him that Kareema came to the least able member of the family for help. He couldn't even help himself, how could he help anyone else?

He walked out into the courtyard. Clothes are things. Clothes aren't part of the person they belong to — they're only things. No matter how many times he said it to himself, he still didn't want to see Amal taking clothes out of the wardrobe. And when did his little girl grow up?

He paced in small circles until Amal came out and began to hang the clothes Kareema had just washed. He took a deep breath and walked back into the house. The breath came out in a puff of relief. It was Kareema and not his beloved Deena. The clothes didn't even look familiar. He poured some more tea.

"You were released today?" asked Muhammad.

"Yes, about noon. And when I got home …" her voice broke and she struggled to get her words out, "my father wouldn't even open the door. He said a woman was released yesterday, and she told a neighbor about my scandalous behavior. I'd brought shame on the family. I tried to tell him it was all lies, but he asked why he should believe me." Tears began to run down her face again. "He told me to go back to my Israeli lover and let him feed and clothe me."

Muhammad glanced at Amal. She looked at Kareema with wide eyes. Maybe he should ask her to leave. No, maybe Kareema would feel better with Amal in the room. "I think you need to explain what did happen. What made her say your behavior was scandalous if it wasn't?"

Kareema told him exactly what happened up to the point where Moshe closed the storage room door behind them. "And when I realized we were in a storage room, I knew what he wanted, and I screamed. Some guards heard me and opened the door. They took me back to the cell."

"But the woman didn't know about the closet."

"No, but …" Kareema turned her head away from him, but he saw the blush creep up her neck to her hairline. She was hiding something. He didn't like the image that came to mind. He couldn't imagine the guards hearing her scream and just taking her back to her cell. From all the stories he'd heard, they'd be more likely to join in the fun. His anger began to rise.

"Kareema, what really happened? Would you be more comfortable talking to your Aunt Hanan?" Kareema shook her head. "Listen, bad things happen. Whatever it is, you don't have to feel guilty because it's not your fault."

"Nothing happened, I swear."

173

"Then why can't you tell me what happened? Why are you acting as though something dreadful happened?"

"Because something dreadful did happen — something even worse than rape."

"Worse than rape?" Amal's eyes widened.

"The women thought I went with the soldiers willingly. They called me a traitor and a collaborator." Kareema dissolved into tears again. It took a long time, but she finally managed to tell them the rest of the story. "I swore it wasn't true, and I begged them to believe me. What more could I do? I swear, Uncle, I have never been with a man — any man."

He saw the pleading in her eyes. She needed him to believe her. She needed him to help her. She was waiting for him to tell her what to do. The anger he'd felt only minutes earlier drained out of him. He was the wrong person to ask for help. He could do nothing. He was helpless.

Kareema's problems just added to the list of his failures. He'd tried so hard, but it was like fighting from the inside of a balloon. Nothing he did made more than a temporary dent on the surface. And outside the balloon was darkness. If he relaxed, the darkness would take him again. He mustn't relax. He had to keep fighting.

Long minutes passed, the silence of the room broken only by Kareema's occasional sniffles and stifled whimpers.

It took more long seconds for Muhammad to find his voice. "I believe you, Kareema." Did he believe her? She acted like something happened, but swore it didn't. He had to believe her words, but the story didn't make sense, unless … The only words that came to his mind were

174

words he didn't use in front of Amal. The bastards! How many birds did they kill with that stone? Would anyone believe her story? The women had a more logical argument. Any social support the women might have had in that prison was destroyed by the knowledge of internal collaborators. How easy it was to turn the same weapon on the YFP. His anger rekindled and turned to rage. He *would* fight the darkness. It wasn't only his darkness now. It was spreading like a cancer and destroying his whole world.

"I … I have to go. I'll be back tomorrow." He barely recognized his own words. He rushed from the house, only marginally aware of the two girls staring at him. His eyes guided his steps, but gave no meaning beyond the obstacles he must avoid. His ears heard only the chanting of his own mind, telling him that he must fight the darkness.

He ran. He ran through the streets of the camp. When he reached the end of the camp, he slowed, then jogged through fields and jumped over the low stone walls that separated one field from the next. His body only stopped jogging miles from the camp when his labored breath no longer fed his muscles with enough energy to do more than walk. His breaths came in shallow gasps. The sun had set long ago, but he walked on, dragging his feet. He sank down on the ground. He wanted to scream but didn't have the energy.

"Hey, what're you doing back here?" Muhammad looked at the man bending over him. He grasped Abood's outstretched hand and pulled himself upright. "You promised to forget this place. Why are you here?"

"I did forget. Until I needed you, I did forget."

"This isn't a joking matter."

"I'm not joking. I was running, but I didn't know I'd find you."

"Why were you running?" The man narrowed his eyes. "Who were you running from? Who was chasing you? Did you lead anyone here?"

"No one was chasing me."

"If no one was chasing, what were you running from?"

Muhammad looked down and scraped his toe across the dirt floor. "From life, I guess."

Chapter X
❧REARRANGING FAMILY❧

**Colin [General Colin Powell, US Secretary of State Jan, 2001 –
Jan, 2005] OKs chat with PLO head**
> Daily News (New York); April 10, 2002

The guns are silent, but cries for help go unheard
> Sydney Morning Herald (Australia); April 18, 2002

EU says Israeli refusal of UN probe into Jenin a "mistake"
> BBC Summary of World Broadcasts, April 30, 2002

War in Palestine
*So is Israel's war against Palestine a war against terrorism, or the
result of an unjust occupation of Palestinian land? To get an
overview of what's at stake, read this history published by the
United Nations -- which has recognised the inalienable rights of
the Palestinian people to self-determination.*
> Herald Sun (Melbourne, Australia); April 10, 2002

We usually go to Aunt Hanan's for supper." Amal's unspoken question hung in the air.

"I'm not up to explaining everything again." The thought of telling her story in front of her aunt and uncle made Kareema shudder. It was humiliating to tell it once, but twice in one day was more than she could bear.

"I'm not telling her." Amal disappeared into the kitchen. "I have some leftovers here."

"Perfect." Kareema decided she was more tired than hungry, but her stomach rumbled and reminded her that she'd be starving before morning.

"I'll run over and tell her my homework's done and we have leftovers."

Left alone in the house, Kareema didn't have the energy to move. She remembered how small the house had seemed on earlier visits. Tonight it looked spacious. She was safe.

The next morning Muhammad returned shortly after Amal left for school. "I'm taking you to the clinic. It occurred to me that we can settle the question of your so-called shameful behavior quite easily."

"But how could I? It wouldn't be proper." Her cheeks burned with shame, and she couldn't meet her uncle's eyes. She'd heard the women talk about examinations during pregnancy, and she couldn't imagine living through the embarrassment.

"Kareema, either you go through this embarrassment, or everyone believes you've done far worse. Think about it." She did think about it, and finally nodded.

"The nurse fit you in without an appointment because you said it was urgent. You all look fine to me, except for a rather nasty but fading bruise. What's this all about?"

Kareema knew her uncle expected her to speak. No. She couldn't. Her face got hot, and she shook her head. She heard him take a deep breath. "To put it bluntly, we need a certificate of virginity for my niece."

The doctor suddenly looked tired and older than he had a few minutes earlier. "What kind of stupid idiotic mating ritual is this? I'm sorry, sir. I work long hours for very little pay. I do my best to take care of people using inadequate supplies and outdated equipment." His voice changed from tired to angry. "I don't have time to cater to the antiquated whim of one family forcing a girl who is barely more than a child to marry into another family that already doesn't trust her. What kind of start to life is that?" The doctor stood.

178

"No, that's not what happened." Kareema couldn't let him refuse to examine her. Not now that she'd gathered up what little courage she had left. But it would be easier to let the doctor think it was her father. It was almost true. Her father *had* tried to force her into a marriage. She'd thought that was the worst thing that could ever happen to her. How wrong she'd been.

Muhammad remained seated. "Please, Doctor, give us another thirty seconds. It isn't that way at all. She was arrested after the Land Day demonstration. They released her yesterday after one of the guards made it clear to the other inmates that she'd granted him sexual favors. They called her a collaborator."

The doctor sat down again. "If the rape was recent, I can attest that it was not consensual, but I can't give a certificate of virginity."

"But I wasn't raped, I swear. Why doesn't anyone believe me?"

"So if nothing happened, what's the problem? You were lucky."

Muhammad nodded. "Go ahead, Kareema. Tell him."

Haltingly, she explained the situation to the doctor, including her father's very public refusal to let her back into the house. "My father is a hard man, and he's almost fanatical about his honor. If he accepts me, the rumors might die."

The doctor nodded. "It's a strange story, but you've convinced me. I wish I could spare you further embarrassment, but professional ethics won't allow me to give you a certificate without an examination." Kareema blushed even deeper. The doctor called for a nurse and asked Muhammad to wait in the hall.

"Just stare at the ceiling and pretend you're somewhere far away," the nurse advised. She tried, but it wasn't that easy. She wanted to be somewhere else—anywhere else, but her imagination couldn't overcome the reality. She closed her eyes, clamped her teeth together, and endured.

Muhammad rested his head on the cool window of the bus. A copy of the doctor's letter was in his inside pocket. Kareema's visit to the clinic had been hard on her, and it was too much to expect her to explain everything again. He hoped she was resting. The bus stopped a couple of blocks from Layth's store.

"Muhammad, what a great surprise!" Layth's face lit up as he came around the counter and gave his brother a hug and the ritual air kiss on each cheek. "Come into the back, and we can catch up." Muhammad could tell that Layth thought his unexpected visit was a sign of his healing. He hated to disappoint his brother, but Kareema's problem was too serious for him to ignore.

"Can you call Ali and see if he can get off work for an hour or so?"

"Sure." Layth's smile disappeared and he picked up the telephone. Muhammad went into the little space behind the store that Layth called his office. There had once been a full apartment behind the store, but the store had gradually expanded until there was nothing left of the apartment but this small room and the adjoining bathroom. Muhammad sank down on the stacked mattresses that served as a couch. He and Ali had spent a few curfews here. Sometimes all three of them stayed, along with Layth's helper.

"Are you all right, Muhammad?"

"Yeah, I'm okay." The dark emptiness was still inside him. No, he wasn't okay, and maybe he never would be, but at least he was managing.

Layth picked up the battered kettle and walked to the bathroom to fill it. "Want to tell me what's wrong?"

"Did you know Kareema was arrested on Land Day?"

"No." Layth's face paled. "How is she? Where's she being held? That was a month ago, why didn't we know?"

"Put the kettle on. She's in my house now. Ziad thinks her arrest brought shame on the family."

"What an idiot."

"It's worse than that, but I don't want to tell it twice. Can we wait for Ali?"

"Sure."

Kareema was making tea and Amal was finishing her homework when Muhammad got home. Kareema brought another glass from the kitchen.

"I talked to your uncles."

"You did?" Kareema's sounded noncommittal, and she kept her head down, concealing her expression. "We're going to see your father tomorrow evening. The certificate will convince him you're innocent." He still couldn't see her expression, but the hand holding her tea trembled. "Take the copy to school with you tomorrow in case anyone gives you a hard time. I'll keep the original to give to your father."

"Papa!" exclaimed Amal in a shocked voice. "No! You couldn't … she couldn't …"

"Why not?"

Amal blushed bright red. "Papa," her voice clearly said he was being unbelievably dull witted. "You know what she had to do to get that paper. It's bad enough to share that with family, but to wave it around in school!"

"Oh." Comprehension dawned, followed by anger that Kareema had been put in such a humiliating position.

"I can't go back to school now. It isn't only the shame of the rumors. I've missed too much time. Even if I could make up the work, between jail time and the time I missed when I went to work, I've missed too many days to pass." Tears filled her eyes.

Muhammad stifled a curse. He needed to move. There was no room to pace, no room to breathe. He went into the tiny courtyard and started swearing. He ran out of swear words and curses and started all over again. Eventually he cooled down enough to act civilized and returned to the house. The girls had disappeared into the back room, and his mattress lay on the floor ready for use. He grabbed his pajamas and went to the bathroom to change.

When he came out of the bathroom, Amal was sitting on his mattress. "I thought you and Kareema were in bed."

"I wanted to tell you how proud I am that you're helping Kareema." She stood up and rested her head on his chest. "When I was little I used to sit on your lap and listen to your heart beat. That was when I was happiest." He didn't know what to say, so he just put his arms around her. Her voice was almost inaudible, muffled against his chest, when she spoke again. "This is the first time since … It still makes me happy to hear your heart beat. My papa's back."

She was right. For the first time since his world collapsed, he'd gone a whole day without withdrawing into his grief. His breath caught with the pain of it. Was it healing? Or was it betrayal?

Muhammad left the house at dawn the next morning. He took a deep breath and smiled at the cloudless sky. He'd walked into the hills so many times since Deena's death that no one would question his whereabouts. He just had to be sure to get back in time for the appointment with Ziad.

When he returned in the afternoon, he stopped in the doorway. The house smelled different. It smelled of cooking and scrubbing. It shouldn't smell that way anymore. Deena made cooking smells and clean smells. He should be grateful to Kareema, but he resented it. "Looks like you've been busy." He forced a smile.

"I was too anxious to sit still. I'm so worried about how my father will react tonight."

"Doesn't it smell wonderful, Papa? Everything is so clean." Kareema was obviously pleased by Amal's praise.

Amal chattered through the meal and Muhammad listened. He complimented Kareema on her cooking, and surprised himself by the truth of his words. They had just cleared away the meal when the doorbell rang.

"Are you ready to go?" Ali asked from the doorway. "Hurry up. Layth is waiting with a car."

"I'll be with you in a minute." Muhammad saw Kareema's face pale. He put his hands on her shoulders. "Kareema, I just want you to know," Muhammad paused, searching for the right words; "I'm glad you came to us. Whatever happens tonight, you're welcome here." The words were inadequate, but it was the best he could do right now.

"Thank you," Kareema said barely above a whisper.

When he got in the car, Layth turned and looked into his eyes. "Just remember that the hardest thing we may have to do tonight is to control our anger. You know how violent Ziad's temper is. We must not answer his temper with our own, no matter what he says. Can you promise?"

"I'll try," answered Muhammad. Ali merely nodded.

When they arrived, Kareema's father opened the door and greeted them each with a short handshake before leading them to the living room. The lack of any welcome set the tone before they even sat down.

"I've been expecting you. I assumed my willful daughter showed up on one of your doorsteps," he said without preamble once they were seated. "Why didn't you bring her with you?"

"She was under the impression she would not be welcome."

"She's my daughter, and it is my duty to provide for her."

"Then why didn't you let her in when she came home?" The words came out louder than Muhammad had intended. Layth nudged him.

"It was nothing." Ziad waved his hand as though brushing away an insect. "I was caught unaware. But I immediately made arrangements for her future well being."

Muhammad was fairly certain Ziad had never changed his mind in his life. He found it hard to believe, but he harbored a small ray of hope that the evening could turn out better than he had anticipated.

"Really?" Layth's voice reflected more interest than surprise. "I understood she was released three days ago. How did you manage to make these arrangements on such short notice?" Muhammad stole a sideways glance at his

184

older brother. Layth made the remark sound like more of a compliment than a question of truth or falsehood.

"Well, it's no great thing to do when one has the right connections." Muhammad wanted to shake the pompous tone out of him. Ziad fell silent as Ferial came in with a tray of tea glasses. Muhammad listened for sounds of Omar and Mustafa. Except for the occasional clink of a small spoon on the side of a glass, he heard nothing. Could they be asleep so early?

Ferial reached him with the tray. "How are the twins?" he asked quietly. "I hope they aren't giving you any trouble."

"The twins are fine." Muhammad thought she looked older than the last time he'd seen her. "They are a handful, though."

"They were more than a handful when they first came, but they just needed a strong disciplinarian to give them a little guidance," interrupted Ziad. "I suppose poor Deena …" Muhammad didn't hear the rest of the sentence. His face grew hot with anger; he leaned forward, angry words filling his thoughts. Ali pulled his arm down and back in his chair. His grasp was so tight it stopped the circulation. Muhammad remembered his promise to keep his anger in check. He gripped the chair until his knuckles turned white, and he was sure he left fingernail marks in the wood.

How could he have let his sons live in a home with a man known for his violent temper? As soon as the issue of Kareema was settled, he'd tell his sister that he was taking his boys home. If that meant he had to stay home to take care of them, so be it. He wasn't getting any work anyway so he might as well be with his children. It would probably be good for him, and it certainly would be better for them than leaving them with Ziad.

Ziad resumed his speech when his wife had left the room. "I have a lot of support from my contacts in the Brotherhood of the Faith. Through those contacts, I located a businessman in another city who's looking for a second wife. If we hurry, we can have her married before word of her disgrace spreads beyond the confines of the camp." He paused with a satisfied expression on his face. "So you can see, I have done my duty by the girl, in spite of the disgrace she has brought to this family." He was proud of himself for finding her a place as a second wife? Kareema had already suffered so much humiliation. He bit his lip to keep from blurting his outrage aloud.

"But she hasn't brought disgrace to the family," said Layth. "That's the reason for our visit. We have proof that Kareema is innocent, and the rumors are false."

Ziad's face flushed as words whipped out of his mouth. "I should've known you wouldn't appreciate what I'm doing for her. It's your fault that Kareema got herself into this mess in the first place. It's your fault that she insisted on going to high school where she picked up all those ridiculous political views. If she'd stayed home after her preparatory education, she'd never have been in this trouble. If you hadn't encouraged her, she'd have been married last year."

"At fifteen?" Muhammad didn't know how Layth managed to make the remark so conversational. He was on the verge of shouting his opinion.

Ziad ignored the interruption. "Kareema brought the ultimate disgrace to this house. I don't know what she told you, and I don't care. She has a history of deception and twisting the truth. I have it on good authority that she acted improperly with an Israeli soldier. Even you must see that she has to be married immediately. She's lucky I have such extensive contacts. I was able to find a good match for her, even though she's damaged goods. "

Muhammad shook off Ali's restraining arm. "Damaged goods?" His voice was too loud again. "How can you talk about your own daughter as though she were a sack of potatoes? She's not 'damaged goods'; she's an intelligent, caring, and quite wonderful young woman." Muhammad paused for breath, and allowed Ali to grab his arm once more. He had to remember that his anger could harm Kareema.

Layth took the doctor's letter out of his pocket and extended it to Ziad. "I don't know about your 'good authority', but we have a medical statement that says quite plainly that Kareema has never done anything to justify your accusations."

Muhammad was shocked when Ziad glanced quickly at the paper and crumpled it with an expression of disgust. "This paper is meaningless—worse than meaningless. If Kareema is as innocent as you claim, she'd never have allowed a man to examine her. It's obvious to me that either you bribed the doctor to write this letter, or you passed of one of your own daughters as Kareema. Either way, I find it offensive." Ziad's eyes went from one brother to the next, stopping at Layth. "You boys could benefit by spending more time on religion and less on politics." He heaved himself out of his chair. "Have Kareema here by noon tomorrow so we can get the papers drawn up for her marriage."

"I'd like to see my sister for a few minutes," said Muhammad, starting toward the kitchen. He couldn't stomach the idea of talking to Ziad about taking his boys home. The man's brain was made of cast iron, and the mold was one that should have been smashed a century ago.

"Ferial will see you at the door. She's busy packing the rest of your belongings."

"What?" Muhammad whirled to face Ziad. Was Ziad talking about his children as belongings, or had he misheard? Ziad didn't bother to answer, but merely walked toward the front door. Muhammad jammed his fists into his pockets and dug his fingernails into his palms. He stared at Ziad's back for a few seconds before he followed. At least it spared him the need to ask for his boys back.

"We will tell Kareema what you said. If she agrees to wed, we will bring her here tomorrow," Layth said stiffly.

"I've gone to considerable trouble on her behalf. If she doesn't appreciate my efforts, that's her problem. She got herself into this mess, and she can figure her own way out of it. She disgraced my house, and my last act as her father was to find a suitable match for her." Ziad turned and left the room.

"That sounds like a definite split between the families," said Ali in a low voice.

"Papa!"

"Papa!"

"Uncle Ali! Uncle Layth!"

The two boys ran to their father and grabbed his legs. He stooped down and put his arms around them, pulling them into a tight hug. "I've missed you so much," he said.

188

"Are we really going home, Papa?"

"Yes, we'll all go home now."

When Muhammad stood up, Ferial was standing next to him with tears in her eyes. She had brought out several grocery bags of what looked like clothing and a cardboard suitcase.

"I'll get a car," said Ali. He gave his sister a quick hug and left.

"Thank you for taking care of them," said Muhammad.

"She may need this," Ferial whispered as Muhammad gave her the ritual kisses on each cheek. She put something in his pocket. "I believe in her innocence." Before Muhammad could answer, she turned to talk to Layth.

Muhammad gave the boys some of the bundles to carry, and helped them outside to watch for Ali. When he came back for the suitcase, Layth was speaking softly to Ferial.

"I know you say that he's never been violent or hit you, but beating is not the only form of abuse. I just want you to know that you will always have a place in my home. You only have to call me when you decide you've had enough, and I'll come for you."

"Thank you, Layth. I know you mean well, but Bilal is still in high school. My place is here for now." Muhammad picked up the suitcase and went outside. He felt sorry for his sister, torn between loyalty to her children and love of her brothers. He hoped she'd find a way to keep in touch.

The twins kept up a constant chatter on the ride home, keeping Muhammad busy trying to follow their two-pronged conversation and answer their questions. Ali and Layth were very quiet. When the car stopped at the mouth of the alley, the twins hit the ground running, and were

189

banging on the door by the time their father caught up to them. He reached over their heads for the buzzer, but the door opened before he pushed it.

"Omar! Mustafa! I missed you so much!" Amal grabbed the two boys and held them close. "Thank you, Papa, for bringing them home." She pulled the boys inside without even glancing at anyone else.

Kareema stood behind her as though rooted in place. There could only be one reason for the twins to be with them. "It didn't go well, did it?" She looked at her uncles and tears began to flow down her cheeks. They didn't need to answer. It was written on their faces. Muhammad put his arm around her shoulders and led her inside. Ali and Layth picked up the luggage and followed. Ali moved toward the kitchen and put on the kettle. Kareema sank to the sitting mat and waited for her uncles to speak.

Muhammad spoke first. "Kareema, how would you like to live with us? You know those boys are too much for Amal to manage, even under the best of circumstances. We'd be sincerely grateful if you helped us. Would you be willing to stay?"

Kareema spoke slowly. "I don't know exactly what happened tonight, but I can tell by your faces that going home is not an option. My father has barely tolerated me since the new arrangement of school and work. Mother does what she can, but home's been pretty awful." She tried to smile. "Of course I want to stay. It would be an honor to serve the family."

"You misunderstand," Muhammad shook his head, "I don't want you to be here just to do the housework. I want you to be a true sister to Amal, and help her as you would a sister. Help her and teach her things her mother …," his voice caught, but he finished the sentence, "her mother would have taught her—if she'd been given the time."

"Thank you. I'll try to be the best big sister that any family had. Thank you, Uncle, for making this easier."

Ali came out of the kitchen with a tray of tea glasses and the kettle.

"Will you tell me what happened tonight?" She didn't want to hear it, but she had to know.

Layth described what happened. Kareema didn't interrupt, although she couldn't suppress a small gasp when he described the second wife proposal. Layth paused and took a drink of tea. "He says that if we bring you home tomorrow before noon, he'll make the arrangements for the marriage. It's your decision."

Kareema looked down at her tea glass. Amal broke the silence by bringing the boys to the bathroom. She looked through the bags until she found their pajamas. Kareema knew what her answer was, but putting it into words wasn't that easy. The boys nearly spilled her tea as they made their rounds with good night hugs and kisses before disappearing again into the back room.

The men waited for her to speak. "Uncle Muhammad, thank you for inviting me to stay before I heard this. I'm glad I accepted the invitation before I knew the alternative." She took a shuddering breath, but did not look up. "I know exactly what second wife means in this case. It means I'll be an unpaid servant who has to leave the bedroom door unlocked—and for the rest of my life I'll constantly be reminded to be grateful for my position."

Layth shrugged. "Perhaps, but maybe you should think about this a little more. Forgive me for stating the obvious, but this is a decision of tremendous importance for you. I know that right now you're pleased to be here. For the moment you find it more comfortable than your own home, but think it through. There are fanatics on all sides of this conflict, and they do not spare women or children."

"Yes." Kareema shuddered as she thought of the brilliant university student whose body was found in an alley — his head was found in another alley. Usually the deaths were less gruesome, but no less final. She forced herself to listen to Layth as he continued. "We all hope this silly rumor dies down. There's always another rumor to grab the attention of susceptible minds, and people may forget you. However, if they *don't* forget you and the ridiculous ideas, you will continue to be in danger of being recognized by the fanatics. Who knows how long it might be until you can lead a normal life? I'm not saying that will happen. The most likely outcome is that you'll be forgotten in a week or so, but no one can guarantee it. Do you understand?"

"Yes." It would be too much to hope that she'd be forgotten. Those women would never forget her.

"I know your first reaction is to stay here, but think about it." She didn't want to think about it. It was too horrible. "Being a second wife is not an ideal life, but you'll be in a different city where no one will think to notice you, and you will have a life — perhaps not the life you dreamed of having, but a life nonetheless. You have until noon tomorrow to accept the offer."

"I've heard stories of such arrangements, but I always thought they were tales told to frighten young girls into behaving. No, Uncle, I'd slit my wrists first." She wasn't going to shed another tear over this.

Layth hesitated before adding, "Your father said that would be his last act as your father. If you accept the offer, he considers he has done his duty; if you reject the offer, then it is your own doing and he no longer considers you his daughter."

Ali spoke for the first time. "Kareema, you don't know this man. It's possible that he's a kind person who heard of your plight and is willing to shelter you from harm."

"I have to disagree, Uncle. I do know the man. I don't know his face or his name, but I know his soul as well as I know my father's. You know my father's opinion of me. He'd never have presented me in a light that would encourage a kindly man to take me in, even if such a man exists among my father's network of friends. In all probability he's not even very well off and this is an opportunity to get a wife without buying any marriage gold or making any promises."

"I agree, you probably can't expect any marriage gold."

"Without marriage gold, I'll have nothing but a promise of a roof over my head as long as I please my husband. Not to mention that if pleasing the new husband happens to displease the old wife, my days would be a living hell as well — until I'm divorced and kicked onto the street with nothing. I'm sorry, Uncle, if it's your opinion that I ought to grab at this hope of safety and stability, but I'd rather take my chances of a quick death at the hands of the fanatics."

"Just think about it," said Layth.

"Did Mother hear all of this?" asked Kareema after several minutes of silence.

"I don't know if she heard, or if he anticipated our visit and told her earlier. All we know is that she was standing by the door with the bundles of things that belonged to the twins, and a suitcase we assume has your things in it," Muhammad answered.

"I choose to take that to mean that Mother agrees with my choice." Kareema gave a small smile. "If she expected me to show up in the morning, she'd never have packed my clothes, would she?"

"So—welcome to the family. I know this isn't the way you'd hoped the evening would end, but some part of you has to admit that this is probably the best outcome we should have expected. At least your father didn't insist on removing you from our house to marry you to the merchant." Muhammad got up and gave Kareema a brief hug.

"I know I'll be very happy living with you, and I'm happy to have such a heartfelt welcome." Her face belied the happiness in her words.

"You don't have to pretend, Kareema. We all understand that this isn't a happy occasion for you."

Ali and Layth rose and also embraced her as they left. After they'd left, Muhammad motioned for Kareema to sit again. "Your mother was crying when we left. We all told her that we think of her often and if there's anything we can do to make her life easier, she just needed to send word to us. Layth even told her that if she was afraid of your father, she'd be welcome in his home any time." That started Kareema's tears again. "She told us that your father had never hurt her and that she was needed there." He reached into his pocket and pulled out the small package. "She gave me this for you. She said to tell you she loves you very much and that she knows you're innocent. She believes in you."

194

Kareema could barely see through her tears as she opened the handkerchief wrapped package. There in her palm lay one of her mother's precious gold bracelets. She gasped in surprise. "She sent this for me?"

"She said you might have need of this someday." Kareema sobbed quietly. "I told her that you still have a family, and I am honored to act as your father. That was all the time we had." He got up and grabbed his jacket. "I'll sleep at Ali's tonight. You sleep in this room and we'll sort things out later. You need time alone to think."

Kareema spent a night of deep thought and fitful dozing. Sometimes she cried, sometimes she was angry, but she never wavered in her belief that she had made the right decision. Her last thought before finally drifting into sleep was that spending the rest of her life within these walls was better than spending it in jail or in the situation her father had offered.

Kareema and the boys had almost finished breakfast when Muhammad came home. Omar talked about the school Aunt Ferial took them to, and Mustafa kept finishing his sentences for him. Soon they were all laughing. After breakfast, he cleaned up and changed clothes.

"Aunt Hanan brought some grape leaves. We're going to stuff them for supper tonight."

"You and the children go ahead and eat when you're hungry. I'm not sure when I'll get home."

Kareema moved a mattress into the back room that night, intending to sleep on the floor with the boys. Amal argued that she should have the bed. In the end, they moved the bed into the front room, and they all slept on mattresses. Kareema woke up with every movement,

195

expecting her uncle to come home. As the hours passed, she became more and more anxious. Did she have anything to do with him staying away? She resolved to talk to him about it as soon as she had a chance.

Muhammad did not come home the next night either. The boys asked several times where their father was. Kareema gave the vague answer that he was busy and would be home as soon as he could, but that night when the twins were asleep, she asked Amal if she was worried.

"Maybe a little. He used to go away a lot, but that was right after Mama died." Kareema heard a catch in Amal's voice, and she blinked back tears of sympathy. "I thought he was getting better."

"Do you think he might be staying away because I'm here?"

"No, I think it's still about Mama." The whispered words trailed off into silence. After a couple of minutes, Kareema decided that was all Amal was going to say, but another sentence floated through the darkness. "He doesn't seem to like being around people much now."

Kareema understood that all right. When the people around you didn't share your fears and problems, it was hard to be sociable. She had avoided her friends back when she was trying to catch up with her work and living in terror of being married off to someone she'd never met. She'd thought that was the worse time of her life. Ha! Now she knew that things could always get worse. What she wouldn't give to have some time with her friends now. She shut her eyes and took a deep breath. She *would not* cry. She was lucky her family, or this side of it anyway, believed in her. She was lucky she wasn't still in that awful cell. She was lucky she was alive. She could have been shot during the demonstration. If she was so lucky, why was she so miserable? Stupid question … because she was afraid to stick her head out the door.

She stared at the ceiling, listening to the even breathing of the three children. She mustn't feel sorry for herself. Maybe Muhammad wanted to be alone. She used to go for walks when she was angry or upset, but not for days at a time. Amal must be wrong. She had to know, and the only way to find out was to ask her uncle.

Muhammad came home the next afternoon, and Kareema was burning to ask him where he'd been, or more important, why had he gone? She'd been thinking about how to phrase her question all day. When it was time for the boys to go to sleep, she suggested to Amal that they might like a story. She made tea and brought the tray with two glasses. "Uncle."

"Yes?" Once she had Muhammad's attention, all her carefully prepared words flew out of her head. There was nothing left but the blunt question.

"Are you staying away from the house because I'm here?" His face registered such complete surprise that she almost dropped her tea with relief.

"Of course not. I could never take care of the boys, or run a house, and it wasn't fair to Hanan to ask her to take care of two houses. I'm thankful you're here. How did you get that silly idea?"

Kareema looked into her tea and inhaled the minty steam. How could she explain without sounding as though she wanted to know where he went and what he did? It was not her place to ask him for explanations. "It's just that you've hardly slept at home since I came, and I thought maybe it was me."

197

"No, it has nothing to do with you. Well, in a way it does." Muhammad stretched his legs out in front of him and cradled the small tea glass between his hands. "I'm working on something with a couple of friends. They both have day jobs so we do the work at night. You being here makes it easier for me because I know you'll get Amal off to school and take care of things when I'm gone."

"You can't be working *all* night if they have to go to work in the morning." She hoped that didn't sound like she was scolding him for staying out.

"It's a long walk home from the workshop, and I'm tired when we finish. Besides, if I come here and sleep in the daytime, the boys would have to stay quiet." He gave Kareema a grin. "Staying quiet is too much to ask of them, so I sleep in the workshop."

"Thank you." She wondered what the project was, but her uncle didn't tell her, and she couldn't ask. It was enough to know that he was safe at night, and that she was not to blame for his absence. She'd tell Amal that he was working nights. That would make Amal feel better, too.

After a few days things began to fall into a pattern, and Kareema adjusted to it. Her fear that her accusers would seek her out in her uncle's house lessened, although she was still afraid to leave the house. She wished she could let just one friend know where she was, but the risk was too high.

Muhammad came home for a few days and disappeared for a few days. When he was gone, Kareema gave the boys lessons to replace kindergarten. It kept her busy, and they enjoyed it. Each time Muhammad came home, they had a mini-celebration. On nice days, he played soccer in the alley with the twins, or took them on walks through the camp. Sometimes they even came home with baked treats for dessert.

Chapter XI
❧ NEARLY NORMAL ❧

Suicide blast shatters Mideast peace talks
Toronto Star; May 8, 2002

Arafat faces exile after failing to end suicide attacks
Bristol Evening Post; May 9, 2002

Israeli Troops Sweep Through Jenin In Retaliation Raids
Birmingham Post; May 29, 2002

Israeli forces on alert to prevent attack in Jerusalem
BBC Summary of World Broadcasts; May 28, 2002

Muhammad winced as he scraped the last of the lather and two-day stubble off his face. He really needed to buy new blades. It felt strange not to hear voices at this time of day. The house was almost never this quiet and empty. Kareema must have taken the children next door. He rinsed off his face and picked up the towel. Someone that sounded like Amal asked a question. They were back. He smiled and came out of the bathroom—but no one was there. Yet he was sure he'd heard Amal's voice.

"Amal? Where are you?"

"I'm here, Papa." The voice came from the back room. Was she sick? Maybe Kareema took the boys so she could sleep.

"Are you all right?" He opened the door. She looked all right. She sat cross-legged on her mattress with paper and a pencil, but no one else was in the room. "Who were you talking to?"

"No one. I was just talking to myself."

"Since when do you ask yourself questions? What's going on?"

"Nothing."

"I thought 'nothing' was what the twins were doing whenever something got broken." Amal squirmed and blushed. He leaned against the doorway, waiting for her to tell him what was happening. She acted as though she'd done something wrong. Maybe Kareema left her home as punishment. Amal was usually unbelievably well behaved; maybe a little rebellion would put some spirit in her.

"I don't want to talk about things that might upset you."

"If what you're doing might upset me, then it's probably something you shouldn't be doing."

"Papa, please don't be angry. I'm not doing anything wrong." He sat down next to her. "I was talking to Mama." Her words were so soft that he barely heard them. "I tell her everything that happens, and sometimes I ask her what I should do." Her eyes brimmed with tears when she looked up at him. "Please don't feel sad. And please don't tell me I shouldn't do it. I feel better when I talk to her." A single tear spilled over and began to roll slowly down her cheek.

Muhammad didn't know what to say. Part of him wanted to tell her that she couldn't talk to someone who was dead, but he didn't. She said it made her feel better, so what's the harm? "Does she answer?" he asked hesitantly.

"Sometimes. No. Well, I mean not really. What I mean is, she never talks to me with words, but sometimes I feel like I know she's proud of me, or sometimes I picture her smiling at me. Sometimes I tell her I just can't do something, and she tells me that she knows I can do it, and I only have to try a little harder. I think she listens." Amal looked at her father. "Do you think I'm foolish ... or ... or ... crazy?"

Amal was so fragile and vulnerable. She looked as though a single word could crush her. Muhammad put his arm around her and pulled her close, remembering the little girl who used to sit in his lap and fall asleep with her head on his chest. It pained him to think that her dead parent gave her more comfort and guidance than her living one, but that might be for the best in the long run.

Kareema and the boys returned from their visit; they ate; they watched television and talked. All of this happened around him, as though it was happening to someone else, even when he took part in the conversation. He couldn't stop thinking of Amal talking with Deena. When the boys got ready for bed, he suggested that Amal take care of them so Kareema could stay and watch the news.

"Kareema," he said softly, "did you know that Amal talks to her mother?"

"Yes. I've heard her whispering when she thought I was asleep."

"Did you know she thinks her mother answers? She doesn't answer in words, but sometimes Amal says she knows how her mother feels about some things."

"Who's to say it isn't true?"

Muhammad stared at the flickering screen for long minutes. He probed deep inside himself. Great empty places and seas of guilt rose and their waves beat on his

202

being. Did he know what Deena thought about things? All he could find was his own longing to be with her again.

Maybe Amal had found a peace that eluded him. He envied her the belief that she could feel Deena around her. "She was afraid to tell me she talked with her mother. She thought that reminding me would make me sad. Imagine that—my little baby girl was trying to protect me."

"She's not your little baby girl," said Kareema. "She is now officially a young woman."

"You mean she started … You mean she … She's too young." His mind stumbled over the concept, and his tongue followed suit.

"She's a little young, but not unusually so. She's been through a lot lately."

"Oh, my God. And I've been blind to all this?"

"Don't worry about not knowing. Fathers are always the last to know." There was more than a hint of laughter in the reply. "She'd never tell you. And besides, it only happened today."

"Today?"

"That's one reason I took the boys next door for a couple of hours. I wanted to give Amal time to think and be with herself. This is a major milestone in the life of a young girl, yet it's one she never feels comfortable talking about, and she has to deal with it by herself."

"I see." Muhammad nodded slowly. He wasn't convinced that he did see. He didn't even know what to think about his baby becoming a woman. Of course, he knew it would happen. He and Deena had often lain awake at night dreaming of their children's future, but it had always been in some undefined someday. And now he was facing that future alone. He felt himself sinking into the black loneliness. He couldn't let that happen again. Not now. He yanked his thoughts back to what Kareema was saying.

"She asked me if this meant she had to cover her hair now. I told her it was entirely her decision. She's small and still in blue. Of course, some girls wear head scarves from the time they begin school, but most girls wait until later. They usually decide to cover when they begin to get self-conscious about their physical development."

"She's still a little girl." Even as he said the words, he knew she wasn't, but it was so hard to accept. She was still so small and frail.

After a long pause, Kareema spoke again. "Uncle, please try to let your vision of your daughter, the way you think about her, be something that is as alive as she is. Let her grow up in your mind and heart as she grows up in reality. Don't fix her in your mind as a photograph of a little girl that never changes."

"She'll always be my little girl." He tried to imagine her as a woman with children of her own. He failed.

"Mama once told me that Grandfather always thought of her as his little girl. That's why he chose my father for her. He thought she needed someone who would always walk in front of her and show her the right way to go, someone strong, who could protect her from all the horrors that exist in our lives. If he'd recognized her as an adult who could think and make decisions, my life might be very different."

"I'm sorry." Muhammad wondered if his life would have been different if his father had been around as he grew up. He didn't think he wanted to know any more about his father.

204

"I'm not looking for sympathy. I just don't want you to make the same mistake with Amal. She's a very special young woman. See her as what she is. Let her grow up in your thoughts as well." Muhammad nodded. Kareema picked up the tea tray and gave him a peck on the cheek on her way to the kitchen.

The next day Muhammad came home in the evening wearing a grin and carrying a large package. Amal came running to take it from him, but he kept it out of her reach saying it was a surprise. Amal's face lit up with pleasure.

"A surprise?" Omar came running out of the back room with Mustafa on his heels. "For us?"

"Everyone sit down and be still." Muhammad held the package over his head until the boys and Amal were seated. "You too, Kareema." Kareema came out of the kitchen, drying her hands. "This is a very special holiday." Amal looked at Kareema, who merely shrugged. "This is the holiday of Half Eid." Muhammad caught the looks the girls exchanged and laughed. "Come on, come on. Sit down." Muhammad could barely sit still himself, seeing the happy faces in front of him. It had been too long between moments of joy in this house.

Amal frowned. "I thought I knew all the holidays. Eid is a Muslim holiday, but I never heard of anything called Half Eid—and it's not time for Eid now."

"When was the Eid, Amal?"

"Maybe in December?"

"Very good. Now when will the next one be?"

"Maybe next December? I know it moves eleven days on our regular calendar every year. So I think it should still be in December this year."

"Excellent. You're right. Last year it was December seventeenth, and this year it should be December sixth. Now how many months is that, if we count December of last year?" He looked at the boys. "How many months in a year?"

"Seven," said Omar.

"That's days in the week, silly. Twelve months." Mustafa laughed and poked his brother.

Muhammad cleared his throat and frowned at them. The boys instantly grew quiet. A stab of guilt reminded him that they'd lived under the same roof as Ziad far too long. He reached out and ruffled their hair, then held out his hands with his fingers spread. "Count on my fingers as I say the months. December, January, February, March, April, May. How many is that?"

"Six."

"Right. And six months is half a year. Do you understand?" They nodded. Muhammad wasn't sure they knew that six was half of twelve or if they just wanted to give him the answer he expected. It didn't matter. "So this is halfway from the old Eid and halfway to the new Eid. Do you know what that means? What do you get on the Eid?"

"Pennies!" shouted Omar.

"For candy!" shouted Mustafa.

"Sometimes you get something new to wear, too," said Muhammad. "I noticed yesterday that your good sister, Amal, has nearly washed your shirts away trying to keep you clean."

He opened the package and reached his hand in very slowly, drawing out the suspense. First, he pulled out two knit shirts. The thrill of pleasure at the sight of their smiling faces was almost painful in its intensity. They wanted to snatch the shirts, and he could almost see the effort it took for them to wait. He put the shirts into their outstretched hands and grinned at their thank yous. After they became quiet again, he pulled out two pairs of sturdy long pants with elastic waistbands.

"They look a little long," said Omar hesitantly.

"You're growing fast, and you won't be wearing long pants very much now that the weather is so warm. You can roll them up for now. I'll bet Kareema can take your old pants and cut the legs off and make them into shorts for the summer."

The boys looked at Kareema for confirmation. When she smiled and said she could and would, their smiles returned.

"That's like getting two new pants!" said Omar, bouncing with happiness. "We get new shorts from our old pants ..."

"And we still get the new long pants!" Mustafa finished.

"And for the ladies of the house," he reached into the package again. "I reach into the magic bag and what do I find?" With a flourish he pulled out two identical head scarves and continued talking as he presented them.

"For my new daughter, who has blessed this house with her presence."

"And for my little girl, who has grown in so many ways. This one is special." Muhammad smiled and watched Amal struggle to hide her disappointment. He placed the scarf in her hand, and his smile broadened at her surprise that it did not bend over, but stayed in a stiff square.

"The scarf may be put away until the day you decide you want to wear it, but the special part is inside." She pulled the layers of scarf aside and found a book of stories with bright pictures. "I know you love stories, and I thought you'd like this. The man in the book store said it was just right for your age." Muhammad thought of the gift as a bridge between the little girl and the woman, but he kept that thought to himself.

Amal ran her hands over the colorful cover and hugged the book with both arms. "This is beautiful. Thank you, Papa."

Then Muhammad solemnly handed Omar a few coins and gave him the traditional good wishes for the Eid, modified slightly for the occasion.

"May every year (and half year) find you in good health."

Omar bowed his head in acknowledgement and gave the proper reply. "And may you be in good health." He repeated the ceremony with Mustafa. The boys almost bounced with their desire to go to the store with their new wealth.

Muhammad laughed, remembering his own pleasure when he'd received coins for the Eid as a small boy. "It's too late to go to the store tonight, but you can go tomorrow. Tonight you can think about all the different treats in the store and decide what you want to buy."

"I'm going to buy chocolate," said Omar.

"Hard candy lasts longer," said Mustafa.

"Why don't you go in the other room and try on your new clothes?" They scampered off with their treasures.

He turned to Amal and handed her some bills, giving the same ritual good wishes. Amal looked inordinately pleased. Children always got coins. Adult children and adult female relatives got folding money. He went on to give Kareema her Eid gift. Finally, he handed Kareema a larger bundle for household expenses.

"Don't put them together," he said. "I don't want you spending your gift for the house." He held out his hands, including both girls. "This is a peace offering. I want to say I'm very grateful for your patience with my inexcusable behavior."

When Amal bent close to her father to kiss him good night, he whispered in her ear, "Are you going to tell Mama about the Half Eid?"

Her cheeks turned a delicate pink; her eyes sparkled with happiness and she nodded. "I have to let her know the family is well, and the house is turning back into a home."

The house seemed much larger when the weather turned warm and the boys could play in the courtyard. It also made it easier for Kareema to help Amal with her homework. As much as she loved her uncle's boys, their constant chatter sometimes exasperated her.

"Kareema, can I ask you a question?"

"Of course, Amal."

"Remember how happy Papa was on the Half Eid?" Kareema nodded. "Why doesn't he seem that happy anymore? I thought he was over feeling bad about Mama. I mean, I know he'll always feel bad, but I thought he was over the part where he couldn't be happy. Now I think he's sad again. He doesn't laugh."

"Healing is a process, not an event. When you have a bad cold, you don't go to bed one night feeling awful and wake up the next morning feeling wonderful. You might wake up one morning feeling better, but by evening you're tired and sick."

"You're right. I still cry at night sometimes, and sometimes in school I look around at all the girls that still have mothers, and it makes me cry." Amal's eyes filled with tears.

Kareema pulled her close and stroked her hair. "It's all right to cry, sweetheart. Life isn't fair." No, life wasn't fair to either of them—and that didn't even count the overarching unfairness of being born in a refugee camp under military occupation. The occupation she had once vowed to fight for the rest of her life. Well, this was the end of life as she'd known it. She closed her eyes to hold back tears. Ever since she moved in with Amal, she watched as little news as possible. She knew exactly how her uncle felt. Her entire life had been stripped from her—work, school, friends. She held the younger girl close, drawing as much comfort from the closeness as she gave.

After long minutes, Amal sat up and wiped her eyes. "I'm so glad you're here with us."

"I am, too." Kareema got up and checked on the boys. They were still amusing themselves with little bits of wood their father had collected from various job sites. Some were whittled into small cars, and the boys never tired of rearranging the others into roads, buildings and unnamed obstacles. Maybe being twins made them closer than regular brothers. They almost never argued, unlike her own childhood with Bilal. She glanced over at Amal. She was sitting in front of her homework, staring into space. "Do you know where your father's working?"

"No. I never know where he works. He never wanted us to ask questions about his work. He always used to say he was happy to leave the place and didn't want to be reminded of it again until he had to go back." Amal picked up her pencil. "It must be a good job, though, because he wouldn't have brought us present unless he'd already given Aunt Hanan money for food. You're right, Kareema. Just knowing he'll be home at night is a big step. The laughter will come back later."

But it didn't.

Kareema became more and more anxious as Muhammad became more withdrawn and morose. It seemed almost as though he was stepping backward through the grieving process. Sometimes he scowled at the television and withdrew into his own thoughts. She wanted to ask questions, but it wasn't her place to question him. She should talk to his brother, but it was hard to know what she could say without stepping over the bounds of household privacy.

Privacy was a precious commodity in the close quarters of the camp. This house, like all the others, was full to overflowing. A privacy code grew out of close quarters and thin doors. Kareema often joined the twins in their play, or went into the kitchen to give Muhammad a semblance of privacy with his daughter. Kareema wondered about an overheard snippet of one conversation between father and daugher, but the "privacy code" forbade her from asking about it.

"You will always be taken care of. I have fixed everything." What had he fixed, and how?

Several nights later, Amal ran to open the door when the buzzer rang. Kareema heard her stammer out a greeting. "Papa! Wha …What's happening? Why are you—?"

"Aren't you going to let me in?"

Muhammad stepped through the door and Kareema understood Amal's amazement. He wore a black suit, a white shirt and a striped tie. Amal stood with her hand on the doorknob, her mouth open in astonishment. "Papa, you couldn't! Are you getting married?" she asked in an incredulous whisper. Kareema understood her confusion. Amal had never seen her father in a suit, except in the wedding pictures.

It took Kareema mere seconds to connect the suit to pictures of other men wearing black suits. All the pieces came together in one terrifying picture. In an instant, she understood who Muhammad's new "friends" were, where he got the suit, and why he was wearing it. She had to stop him. "No, Uncle!" she screamed, and everything went black.

Muhammad's attention was on Amal until he heard Kareema scream. Then everything seemed to move in slow motion. Kareema crumpled and fell just beyond his lunging grasp. His peripheral vision registered the boys' appearance in the doorway, and Amal's open-mouthed reaction. Then they all heard the awful thud as Kareema's head hit the cement step up from the courtyard into the house.

"Kareema!" The name came from all directions. He knelt by her side. Blood poured over the concrete. He felt for a pulse. She was alive. Thank God! His breath come in short bursts, and his hands were suddenly ice cold.

"Kareema, wake up! Can you hear me? Kareema!" Nothing.

"Amal, get an ambulance."

Amal whirled and flew out the door. He listened to the flap, flap of her plastic sandals for a few seconds then turned his attention back to the twins. "Omar, get me a blanket. Mustafa, as many towels as you can find." The white-faced boys ran to get what he needed. "Kareema, can you move? Can you hear me?" The limpness of her body told him she could do neither.

"Here, Papa."

"Thank you. Now get your shoes on and run next door. Tell Aunt Hanan that Kareema fainted and hit her head when she fell. She may need stitches. We're taking her to the doctor." By the time he wrapped a towel around Kareema's head and wrapped her in the blanket, the boys had their shoes on. "Hold the door for me and close it behind me. Lock the outer door and put the key in my pocket. You can get in using the ladders." He surprised himself by giving such clear orders. His heart was pounding, and he felt paralyzed by fear. What if Kareema died? How would Amal cope? It would be all his fault. He couldn't do anything right.

He moved along the alley with his burden, muttering to himself. "Please don't let her die. Please don't let her die." Who was he talking to? God didn't listened to him last time, why would he listen this time? He reached the end of the alley. Why had he brought Kareema out here? He should've waited for the ambulance and the stretcher. He moaned in frustration. He didn't get this right, either. Should he go back? How would he get the door unlocked?

A car honked. "Papa!" Amal jumped out and opened the back door. With the driver's help, they got Kareema situated with her head on Muhammad's lap. The car started with a spin of the tires that spat gravel and dirt behind them.

"Your little girl nearly got herself killed. She ran right out in front of me and started waving her arms. I don't do the hospital run, but she promised no birthing. I had a birthing in my car once and had to change the back seat. Swore I'd never do it again." Muhammad was proud of Amal's quick thinking, but he wished the driver would stop talking and pay more attention to speed. "She's been sitting on the edge of her seat telling me to go faster, faster, faster." Yes, faster, faster, faster. They had to get help.

The driver kept talking, but the words blended together. Every time the man looked in the rearview mirror Muhammad nodded. Drive faster. Watch the road.

When they approached the temporary checkpoint leading to town, Muhammad closed his eyes. Unlike the checkpoint between Kalandia and Jerusalem, the one between Kalandia and Ramallah was seldom manned unless there a curfew was in force. As long as Muhammad didn't see it, he could pretend it didn't exist. Though small and unmanned, it was the checkpoint that had killed Deena. Muhammad brushed tears from his eyes. Was he crying for Deena or Kareema? It didn't make any difference to the pain in his chest. He struggled to keep from getting lost in his emotions. He had to keep his head today. Kareema needed him, and he had promises to keep.

They pulled into the emergency entrance to the hospital. Amal jumped and ran through the doors shouting for help. An alarm bell began to ring, and men came running with a stretcher. They pushed Muhammad out of the way, got Kareema on the stretcher, and started to run. One of the men tried to take her pulse while they ran.

214

Muhammad took some bills out of his pocket and thrust them into Amal's hand. "Pay the driver." He trotted after the stretcher.

A man in a white coat grabbed his arm. "You can't go in there. They'll come out and let you know what's happening, but you have to wait over here."

Amal came in and sat next to him and leaned against his arm. He patted her knee. He had nothing to say. He couldn't think of anything comforting to say. They waited in silence. He wanted to look for someone to ask what was happening, but he couldn't move. At last, a nurse came toward them, her rubber soles making squeaking sounds on the waxed tiles. Muhammad tried not to think about the blood on her blue cotton pants as he hurried to meet her. "How's my daughter?" He wasn't exactly lying. "Did she lose too much blood? Can I give blood for her?"

"Closing the wound was the easy part. Fortunately, the skull isn't fractured, but we have to worry about internal bleeding. That's the real worry because intracranial pressure will put pressure on the brain. We're waiting for the neurologist to arrive."

"Will she be all right?"

"We need to get a CT scan. If we don't see evidence of bleeding, she should be fine, but we won't know for sure for twenty-four hours. In the meantime, we need to keep her calm. We don't want to sedate her because she needs to be responsive when the neurologist arrives. She's extremely agitated, and we're having trouble getting her to stay still. She keeps calling someone named Amal. Is that her aunt or her mother? Could you find Amal and bring her here? It's vital to get her calm."

"I'm Amal."

The nurse looked at her doubtfully. "Are you sure there isn't another Amal?"

"I'm the only Amal in the family."

"Very well, follow me." She held the door open for Amal. "Only for a few seconds. She mustn't talk too much." Muhammad moved forward, but the nurse put out her hand and stopped him. He paced three steps in one direction and three in the other. The nurse didn't sound reassuring. Why had they called a specialist?

This was all his fault. He should have said something earlier. He'd rehearsed it often enough, but he'd never figured out what to say. He whirled at the sound of the door opening. "Well? What did she say?"

"I'm not sure." Tears rolled down Amal's cheeks. "Her voice was barely a whisper … but I think it's about you. Her words don't make sense to me. I think she knows something about you that I don't know. I need to know what's happening." She searched his face as though answers might appear on his forehead. Muhammad put his arm on her shoulder and led her back to the chairs in the waiting room. He hadn't counted on this. He'd expected a quick good-bye with the details coming later in a letter. "What are you doing, Papa? Why are you wearing a suit, and how do you have so much money to give me for the car?"

She was too young to understand the overwhelming emptiness and despair that filled his heart—the same heart that had once overflowed with love. A child should live in a world of love. Yes, he'd start with love.

"Papa—"

"You know I loved your mother very much. I still love her very much." Amal nodded. "Your mother was my

216

world. Without her I have nothing. I'm empty now. I have nothing inside me. Without your mother, I'm only a husk of a man with no soul. Without a soul a man isn't a man anymore."

Amal grabbed his hand. "Oh, no Papa, you have a wonderful soul. That's why you hurt so much when Mama died. If you had no soul, you would have gotten over it easier. Everyone knows that."

Muhammad shook his head. At least she saw his pain, even though he could never explain the depth and intensity of it. And that was as it should be. A child should not have to know and understand despair. "Thank you, but I don't feel like a whole man anymore. I'm empty inside, and it hurts. It hurts every minute of every day. It hurts to turn over at night and not feel your mother next to me. It hurts to get up in the morning and not see her in the kitchen. It hurts to go through the day knowing she's not waiting at home for me. I can't work; I can't sleep; I'm not good for anything."

"Where'd all this money come from? Why can't you work?"

Muhammad groaned. He thought he'd had it all figured out—all except how to explain it face to face. That wasn't part of his plan. Now it had come back to haunt him, like all the other failures in his life. He couldn't even think of a plausible lie, even if he could lie to her. "I tried to go back to work, but I couldn't do it. I got in a car to go look for work, but when it got close to a checkpoint I felt my blood rising. The anger was so strong that I knew if a soldier spoke to me, I'd try to kill him with my bare hands."

"But you're getting better."

"Not really. It was like I was living in a thick black fog of anger and pain—and not seeing or feeling anything else. But you woke me up. I began to think again. The pain and anger never got any better. What you saw as improvement only meant I could see the world again. I saw it through and around the pain. I looked and saw Kareema under what amounts to house arrest; I saw my little boys deprived of a mother's care; I saw you, my love, deprived of a mother and trying to be a mother to her brothers. I saw everyone I love suffering because of the life we lead. What have I done about it?" He paused for breath.

"Papa, you've done a lot. You've stood fast. Everybody knows that takes courage. There are songs about standing fast, boys paint it on walls, and when things are bad and you ask someone how they are, they answer that they're standing fast. You've stayed and kept your family. You taught us to respect the land and ..." Tears filled her eyes.

"No, compared to you three girls who stood in front of tanks and shouted your anger, I'm a coward."

Amal's tears disappeared, and her eyes flashed with anger. "First of all, I didn't shout at the tanks. They were there when we got to school. All I did was shout at Imahn to come home. Second, you don't have to carry a gun to be brave. It takes courage just to live here. That's what standing fast is all about. You work so hard just to feed us and buy the things we need to live."

Why was she making this so difficult? It would have been easier in the letter. "Don't you understand, Amal? That's part of the problem. I can't provide for you. I can't go to work every day. I just can't do it; I can't work anymore. I can't provide for you that way. I am a carpenter. That's what I know how to do, but the only

218

place where there's enough work to keep me employed is on the other side of the checkpoints. I can't get there without flying into a rage and throwing my life away in the dust—so I can't work. That path is closed to me forever. Every time I see a soldier I want to make him pay for the life he took from me—yet he has the gun. I feel such a deep anger and a rage and a need to make someone pay for our loss that I can't control my actions. It's like living through the Nakba, the Catastrophe of expulsion from our homeland all over again."

"But you don't have to leave your home again."

"In a way, my home left me. It was your mother that made that little house into a home." Tears sprang to Amal's eyes, and Muhammad realized he'd said the wrong thing.

"I'm doing the best I can."

He pulled her as close as the hospital chairs let him. "You're doing a wonderful job, better than I could have imagined. It's just that I'm not doing my part." This was going in circles. He was either going to have to start over, or keep tripping over his own tongue.

"But you're getting better, Papa. I know it. You laugh with the boys when they're silly, and you hear me when I talk to you. If you don't feel it, it's because you're having a bump in your healing. You *are* better."

"Yes, I've been able to act more normal lately, but it's because I've thought of a way out of my problem. I found a way to make everything right—and I've been training for it."

"You found a different job? One you could do?" Hope sprang into her eyes, and the only trace of tears were the damp paths they left on her cheeks.

"Let's get back to your question about the suit. When have you seen men in suits?"

"At weddings."

"Where else? Where have you seen pictures of men from the camps wearing suits? Think."

"Well, I've seen posters sometimes in store windows, but those are the ..." Amal's face drained of color. " ... martyrs," she said in a whisper. "Kareema knew, and that was why she fainted." He watched Amal's face as the full impact of her words made sense to her. Her expression went from understanding to astonishment, and on through disbelief to pain. He wished he could undo the pain. "This is the suit you'll wear for the photograph on the posters, the suit you'll wear while recording your video to tell the world why you're doing this." Her voice got quieter and quieter as the true meaning of her words sank in, ending in a whisper. "This is the suit that will cover the bomb."

He took both of her hands in his own as though to warm them. "I could be with your mother forever. I'd be whole again. It wouldn't hurt to wake up; it wouldn't hurt to go through the day; it wouldn't hurt to lie down at night on an empty mattress."

"Oh, Papa, we're already without a mother. How can you think of leaving us? What will become of us? How will we manage?" She had not realized how her wail had escalated until a nurse shushed her. "Papa, how can we live through the loss of another parent?" she finished softly.

"You don't think I've thought of that? I've been thinking about this for a long time. You'll be provided for. You'll get money every month, and you'll never go hungry. Of course, you won't be wealthy, but you weren't expecting that anyway, were you?"

220

"Papa! You expect us to live our whole lives on charity?"

"What do you think you've been living on since your mother got sick?" he asked bitterly. "I haven't earned a penny in months."

"That's not charity, Papa. That's love. Your brothers love us, and they're taking care of us until you get healed inside. Papa, you just told me you're a carpenter, you're not a soldier in the PLO. This isn't your job."

"It isn't the PLO."

"Then who is it?"

"Just friends of Palestine. They aren't part of the PLO."

"So these friends of yours bought you the suit and gave you the money?"

"Yes, so I could provide for you."

"And our Half Eid presents came from their money? From your ...your blood money?" Amal's voice escalated again, heedless of the hiss from the nurse behind the counter.

"No. I sold a small piece of your mother's gold. I bought the presents because I loved you all so much for being good to me and patient with me. I gave the rest of the money to your uncle because he's been spending so much on food for us because I can't work anymore."

"Papa, don't say you can't work anymore. Maybe you still hurt too bad to cross checkpoints but, thank God, you're healthy and strong. If you can't make a living as a carpenter, you could do something else. You could cook in a restaurant or in a hospital. You could do a lot of things in a hospital. They need men to roll the patients around, other people run tests and things, or shine the floors. You could work in a coffee shop or the market or fix things. There are thousands of ways to make a living. You just have to heal a little more."

How could she understand? How could anyone understand? This pain was deep; it was permanent. Unlike a physical wound, this would never heal and form scars. "It's not just about the job. Not being able to work is a result, not the problem. I can't stand the pain of living without your mother. It hurts all the time, and I can't stand it. I've been bleeding inside ever since that night. The life has bled out of me. I walk around, but inside I'm dead."

"If you were dead inside, you wouldn't care about Kareema, you wouldn't have bought the gifts for everyone."

It was useless trying to explain his emptiness to Amal. Words can't describe what the hearer can't imagine. He had to try another way. He didn't want to talk about Deena's death. He wasn't sure he could talk about it. The ambulance driver had told the doctor, and the doctor had told the family. He never had to put it into words, until now. "Amal, you know what happened to your mother. She had a sickness that killed her, but it was a sickness that the doctors know how to cure. If she'd been here, in the hospital, they could have cured her. But she *wasn't* here. And the men who killed her are walking around out there. That's not right. There has to be justice somewhere. I can do something about it. I can be a fighter. I can fight back. I can help get justice—not just for your mother, but for all of us."

"Being a fighter isn't the only way to help your country. Raising your family also helps keep the country strong. You give your life for us every bit as much as a fighter. The difference is that you give it to us one day at a time."

"But I can't do that anymore. I can't because when your mother died, she took a vital piece of me with her. This way I can be with her again. I can be whole again."

"Mama wouldn't want you to leave us alone. What do you think would happen if you saw her again and told her that you left us all alone? I don't think it would make her happy at all. How would you feel then? What if you did see her again, and she was mad at you? You can't go back and change this—it's forever." Amal began to cry.

Muhammad felt a slight tremor of doubt. Then his world steadied again. Amal was a child; she couldn't fathom the depths of marital love. Of course Deena would understand his decision. Besides, there were all the other men who were already committed. "The plan's already in place. Everything's been arranged, and I must be there tonight. Months have gone into the planning of this operation. Men have already risked their lives to get me the papers I need and the information I need to do this right. Many more good men are risking their own lives to be at the right places at the right times to get me where I have to go. Everything is set. It involves a whole chain of men all along the line, and the timing has to be perfect. I can't back out now—I've given my word."

"Please, Papa, please just tell them you can't leave your family." She was now sobbing too hard to say anything more.

"No need to cry, Amal." Muhammad jumped at the nurse's voice behind him. He looked up and saw the nurse that had taken Amal to see Kareema. How long had she been standing there? "Your sister's going to be fine. She sat down next to Amal and put her arm around her. She looked over Amal's head and addressed Muhammad. "I have good news. The CT scan looks good. We'll keep her overnight and if nothing changes, she can go home."

Relief flooded through Muhammad. "Thank you very, very much." At least he hadn't caused any permanent harm. He asked the nurse what time it was. "I have to go. I'm already late for an important appointment—but I had to stay for Kareema. Sorry, but I really have to go now. I'm so glad she's going to be all right." The words tumbled out of his mouth.

"Papa …"

"You stay with Kareema until your uncle comes." He gave Amal a tight hug. "I love you very much," he whispered. "Take care of your brothers." Amal's body was stiff and unyielding. He turned and walked to the door; her anguished wail followed. He quickened his step and broke into a run.

Chapter XII
❧BEST LAID PLANS❧

Bomber gets past security; Fifth suicide attack in a week shows Israel's vulnerability to the tactic
The Globe and Mail (Canada); May 28, 2002

Bloodshed becomes an expected part of everyday life
Toronto Star; May 19, 2002

Boy Killed As Army Opens Fire In Camp; Israeli Troops Move Back Into Refugee Camps
Belfast News Letter; May 18, 2002

Israel hits back with West Bank grab
Israeli tanks and troops yesterday poured into three West Bank towns, Nablus, Jenin and Qalqilya, where they declared curfews and began arresting suspected Palestinian militants. Israeli police have arrested about 1200 Palestinians in the past 24 hours after finding them on Israeli territory. Most were sent back to the West Bank, while the rest were detained for trial, Israeli radio reported.
The Age (Melbourne, Australia); June 30, 2002

Muhammad left the hospital with Amal's words ricocheting around in his mind like bullets and, like real bullets, causing unbearable pain. He found a cab and took it to the outskirts of Kalandia. Once he cleared the last of the little shelters built beyond the UN defined borders of the camp, he started walking across country. He always did his best thinking while he was walking. Why did Amal's arguments hurt so much? He'd said all the same things to himself over and over again. He'd countered every argument either Mazin or Abood could think of as they tried to talk him out of it. Not only did they raise every point Amal brought to bear, but another one of their own. They'd said his rage made him a liability. They couldn't afford a berserker endangering the mission. Running away from life was one thing—being part of a complex, well-planned operation was quite another.

It had taken a long time to convince them that he could handle the mission, in spite of his problem. If he didn't have to go through a checkpoint, and he wasn't in a closed space with soldiers, he could manage. His steps quickened as he remembered the hours he'd spent learning basic Hebrew and practicing with Mazin. He strode along, talking aloud as he held a mock conversation with himself. It sounded good to him. By the time he arrived at the bunker, he wasn't sure if he felt more nervous or more excited. He would soon be with his beloved Deena again. He was about to do the most meaningful thing he'd ever done.

As Abood set up the video camera, phrases from the speech he had prepared went through his mind. He'd read it many times, and the words flowed easily. He paced in the small space, rehearsing it quietly. "No one spends his life easily. It is the most extreme measure an individual can take to call attention to his plight and that of others like him. I do this as an act of desperation. I want the Israeli citizens and the rest of the world to understand the despair and hopelessness of our lives under occupation. I have nothing to look forward to; the life I lead now is not worth living … The Israeli army is not killing our soldiers—we have no soldiers; it is killing our entire population, and the death toll includes more women and children than men."

The operation they had planned was perfect. It would not be a random bombing. He wanted to be better than that. He had no desire to kill random Israelis. Soldiers took the life of the person who meant more to him than his own

226

life, and he wanted to exact justice from soldiers. However, that type of operation required a lot more planning and coordination than boarding a bus and blowing it up, or self-destructing in a store. It involved weeks of planning and an unknown number of people. The plan was as well put together as a fine piece of furniture, with every piece carefully chosen and fitted into the plan. Men had already risked their lives getting the intelligence and making sure the communications were set all the way, and more men would risk their lives to be at the right place at the right time to make this work. His was the pivotal role around which the entire plan revolved. Yes, he would be spending his life well.

The rest of the night was too busy for him to think about anything other than the tasks he had to perform. They took his picture, recorded his video, and gave him some time to write personal letters. He wrote the letter to Layth first. He poured out his feelings, something he never did in person. It was easier than he'd imagined it would be. When he signed it and sealed the letter, he felt a weight lift from his shoulders. He ended that tie with the letter. The next was for Ali. Again the words flowed easily, and the ending was almost satisfying, as though he was getting a little farther away from the real world.

Amal's letter was the hardest, but he managed that one, too. He told Amal that she was young and resilient and that eventually she would recognize that he had given her a better life while at the same time doing something he needed to do. She would have a much better life with her Uncle Ali than he could ever give her. "I know you think I betrayed and abandoned you, and it hurts me to cause you this pain. I beg you to think kindly of me now, and read

227

this letter again a year from now, and again five years from now. I'm sure you will grow to understand as you grow into your adulthood. I love you more than you can imagine. Please think of me as happy to be reunited with your mother." When he read it over, it sounded thin and inadequate. He only hoped that in time, she would understand the emotion behind the words. Her life would be better now. How could she grow up happy with his misery always there in front of her? It was much better this way.

He thought about writing a letter to be given to the boys when they were older, but decided against it. They were so young. Soon he would be only a distant memory. Why revive it when they were older? He gave the letters to one of the men to deliver after the operation was completed.

Then came the delicate process of attaching the explosives to his body in a way that would not be visible as he walked around, while still being comfortable enough to allow natural movement. Abood turned out to be the explosives expert. He stood still while Abood sewed the harness and wired the charge, listening to Mazin. Mazin kept going over and over the plan with him.

"How will you know you're going the right direction?"

"The taxi driver will point. Once I crest the first hill, I'll find small piles of stones every thirty or forty paces." The words came out like poetry, thrilling him like no poem he'd ever read or memorized. This was his path to Deena.

"How will you know to stop?"

"I'll stop when there are three small trees on my left. That will be within sight of the car that is coming for me."

"Describe the trees."

Muhammad closed his eyes and pictured the trees. He'd never seen them, but he'd seen a photo. There would be no mistakes. He recited the description, welcoming the trees into his mind as friends he was anxious to see again.

"What are you doing here?" The harsh tone of the question in Hebrew jolted him out of his mental journey, back to the reality of the harness of explosives being sewn together around his body.

"I am so sorry, sir. I must have gotten turned around. Do you know how I can reach ..." He heard the Arab accent in his Hebrew, but that was all right. He just had to be good enough not to arouse suspicions.

"Good." Mazin grunted his approval. The destination Muhammad asked about would depend on where he was challenged.

"That was smooth. You didn't jump or flinch—and you sounded relaxed and innocent." Abood echoed Mazin's approval.

"I am relaxed and innocent."

Muhammad knew every move to make and every landmark along the way. He knew the exact time he was expected at each point in his journey to his target. He responded to questions without hesitation, whichever language he used.

At last he was ready. The letters were written; the video recorded; the harness secured snugly and comfortably around his body. There was nothing left to do but wait for the car. The three men sat around the upturned crate. Abood made tea and they sat and waited. Conversation came in fits and spurts. Mazin had no more questions to ask, Abood had no more jokes to tell, and Muhammad was quietly attentive to their remarks. He felt unexpectedly detached himself from the ties of this world. He played a mental video of the anticipated journey in the background while he listened to the men trying to make conversation.

The car came, and he got in with a short greeting to the driver. They drove for a long time, or maybe it just seemed that way. Muhammad felt time stretching out in front of him like a tangible thing that he could twist and pull. He had memorized the map. They were headed toward a part of the border between Israel and the West Bank that was as deserted as any place in this area could be. The land was poor and rocky. Water was so far beneath the surface that wells were hard to dig and unreliable. Muhammad faced the window, seeing, but not registering, the thinning houses and dustier roads. Lost in his own thoughts, he had no need to notice this part of the scenery. His thoughts were ranging ahead — and far behind.

The roads kept getting smaller and smaller. Finally they left any type of road and drove over open ground. The car bounced over large rocks and outcroppings of bedrock where the surrounding soil eroded away a little more with each winter's rain. When the car could go no farther without risk of serious damage, the driver got out and opened the door for him. The driver put a hand on his shoulder and pointed to a hill. Muhammad noticed the yellow-stained fingers of a heavy smoker. He smelled tobacco on the man's clothing. He listened carefully to the driver's detailed descriptions of everything along the way to the next contact. Muhammad barely heard the words. Mazin had told him the same words until he could recite them by heart. He even described a pile of rocks that Muhammad would find when he reached his destination.

230

Muhammad watched the driver's mouth and nodded. Then it was time to go. The driver shook his hand, and wished him Godspeed. Muhammad started walking.

"Hey!" Muhammad turned around. Had he forgotten something? The driver was holding out a package of cigarettes. "Take these. You might need them."

"Thanks, my friend. Think of me while you smoke them on your way home." Muhammad smiled and waved, his heart suddenly filled with love for the driver without a name. The man had offered him what comfort he had available.

The rounded hills rose and fell on every side of him, with scrubby little plants clinging desperately between the rocks and patches of bedrock. Deeper soil nurtured clumps of wiry bushes and even an occasional tree or two, stunted by soil that could not retain the winter rains. Although each hill was different and each patch of vegetation was different, taken in a single glance, the landscape showed remarkable uniformity. It would be easy to get turned around. One had to pay attention to the few landmarks available.

"From there you'll see the next car waiting for you," the driver had said. "We're running right on schedule, or even a few minutes early." As Muhammad walked his confidence rose. Every description he'd been given matched what he saw. He found the piles of rocks — exactly as the instructions said he would. He found the trees that exactly matched the photograph, but there was no car waiting. Hadn't the driver said they were early? The car would come along soon enough. He walked toward the scraggly trees that poked up above the scrub and leaned against the largest one to wait.

The minutes ticked by and became an hour. He walked around the trees, then he measured out a square with the trees at one corner. Pacing the square was easier than standing still and counting seconds.

It was nothing to worry about. The car could have had a flat tire. That could take time. There might have been an accident that held up traffic. Maybe the driver's watch was broken.

Another hour ticked away. Pacing for two hours drained the nervous energy. He sat under the tree. He could brush off his suit before he got in the car. When his legs stopped moving, his thoughts began whirling. Amal's last wailing plea echoed in his mind; her tearful face appeared on the insides of his eyelids. He tried to chase away the memory by reciting his instructions aloud. He practiced the Hebrew conversations he had memorized.

As the third hour advanced, Muhammad's anger outgrew his patience. Didn't the driver understand how much effort had gone into this operation? Did he have no regard for the risks other people took to get all the arrangements made? Not to mention the hours spent in training.

The sky grew dark, and still he waited, afraid to lie down for fear that the car would come and the driver wouldn't see him and would leave again. He leaned against the tree. His head drooped and he jerked awake. He mustn't sleep. He got up and paced in the dark.

When dawn broke with still no car in sight. He admitted to himself that something had gone terribly, irretrievably wrong. Even if a car arrived now, the plan wouldn't work. The passes that should have been prepared for him would all be dated for the previous day. It was over. He knew it hours ago, but every time he started to think about it, he'd stoked the flames of his anger. He could no longer deny that the opportunity had passed, along with his hopes for getting justice for Deena. Anger petered out, leaving him drained and sad.

He sent up a silent prayer for the driver of the car that never arrived. He laughed at himself — praying to God, who never listened. What now? He was hungry, thirsty, tired, and lost.

He thought briefly of trying to find another target, but looking around at the barren landscape he knew it would never work. A man in a suit and tie was as conspicuous in this setting as a peacock in a henhouse, even if he knew where to go to find a target. His instructions said the car would take him to the next stop. The instructions did not include a street map — that was the driver's role. He began walking back the way he had come. With luck and a little help, he'd probably find his way home.

It wasn't too difficult tracking the landmarks backward, and he soon reached the place the car had left him. He continued walking in the direction he thought the car had been driving until he reached a road. He followed the road to a village. The stone buildings and low stone walls separating the fields told him it was a Palestinian village. He'd been over twenty-four hours without food or water and with scattered minutes of sleep. He was near the end of his endurance.

He wanted to knock on a door and ask for something to eat and drink. Maybe he could sleep for a few hours, and perhaps even get a ride back in the direction he needed to go. He rolled his head back and forth on his neck and made little circles with his shoulders to relieve his muscles of the strain of the unaccustomed weight of the harness. He couldn't knock on a door and ask for help—he was still a walking bomb. He couldn't remove the explosives—they were never meant to be removed. For the first time, he felt fear.

He did not fear for himself. The thought of his own death now only made him sad. His death now would be wasted. It would have even less of an impact than if he'd gone berserk at a checkpoint. How was he going to get home without the help of his fellow countrymen? He couldn't walk back unaided. Without food or drink, he'd never make it home alive. If he didn't get some help along the way, he'd surely die. If he took shelter in a village and the bomb went off, he'd take some innocent family with him. On the other hand, if he didn't take shelter, he could die from hunger, thirst, or exposure. Someone was bound to find him and no matter how long it took, the explosives would still be there—ready to do their job.

To avoid the village, Muhammad left the road, but stayed within sight of the buildings and tried to continue in the same general direction. He got hungrier and thirstier. He stumbled and fell to his knees. Had he fallen asleep while walking? He couldn't go on. He looked around for some shelter to keep him hidden from view and curled up on the ground under a tree. He'd start walking again after dark. Even the discomfort of the harness and the rocks beneath him couldn't keep him awake.

He woke up from the cold. The moon was bright enough for him to find the road. He hadn't walked far when he wandered into a vineyard. The grapes were barely forming, but he picked some leaves and thought of the delicious grape leaves Deena used to cook. He pictured a plate of steaming grape leaves, each rolled around a spicy mixture of meant and rice. He could almost smell the aroma. It wouldn't taste as good, but at least it was food. He ate a couple and found that chewing them made him a little less thirsty, especially after he'd swallowed the initial bitter taste. Food was food, regardless of the taste. He stuffed his pockets and kept walking, eating the leaves slowly. He walked past plowed fields on either side of the road, but it was still early in the growing season. None of the plants were at a stage where he could find food. He kept chewing on grape leaves.

His feet turned into lead weights and his walk slowed. Grateful for the cloudless sky, he concentrated on putting one foot in front of the other. His stomach hurt. Maybe hunger pains? He shoved more grape leaves into his mouth, ignored the pain and moved forward, one step at a time. What else could he do? The pain got stronger. Bending forward seemed to help, so he walked on bent over, holding his arms over his abdomen. At the next field of grape vines, he stopped and refilled his pockets. Not many steps later, he started to throw up. The cramps got so strong he couldn't walk anymore. He stumbled to a sheltered spot where a stone fence divided two fields and his legs collapsed under him, then he vomited until his throat was raw. His stomach spasms continued, and he had no control over his body's reaction. He wretched again and again. His mouth filled with vile nastiness of who knew what—there certainly wasn't any food left. He alternated between groaning in unbearable pain and listening to his teeth chatter as the chill of the cold ground invaded his body.

His body spasmed painfully. Was this what his beloved Deena had gone through? He saw Deena floating before him. She smiled at him and he reached his hand to touch her face, but the image faded. In the distance, a dog howled. His stomach clenched in yet another spasm. He would have screamed with the pain, but the spasm had stolen his breath. No, it wasn't a dog. It was Kareema screaming. She reached her hand toward him. He remembered the nurse saying there could still be bleeding in the brain. The worst had happened. Kareema was dead, and it was all his fault.

"Oh God, I'm so sorry." A breathy whisper was all he could manage. Deena and Kareema were coming for him. He was dying, unless he was already dead. NO! He couldn't die and leave the bomb to kill some innocent. He fumbled for the string as the stars went out and blackness descended on him.

He woke up with the blessed feeling of water in his mouth and running down the sides of his face. A blazing light backlit the face of an angel drizzling water into his mouth. As full awareness returned he felt sharp rocks under his head.

"Are you back with us, son?" asked the angel. No, it wasn't an angel. He wasn't in heaven. Sharp rocks bit into his head, and the voice was that of an old woman. He struggled to sit, and a surprisingly strong arm slipped around his shoulders and helped him. Once she was no longer silhouetted against the blazing sun, he saw that the old woman's face had the familiar beauty of wisdom and old age, not the legendary beauty of the angels.

"You must get away from me, Auntie," he managed to croak through his rusted vocal cords. "You're not safe here."

"I know." She gave him a smile that made him think of angels again. "I am old and there are worse things than a quick death." She offered him the cup with water. "Can you manage this? Drink slowly." Gratefully he took the cup and tried again to make her move away from him.

"Thank you."

"My grandson found you and thought you were dead. He ran for help, and his father, my son, guessed that you carried explosives." She paused and took the empty cup from him. I made everyone else leave the field and brought some water to see if I could revive you. I felt your heart beating in the veins of your neck. You were cold, but it was the cold of night, not the cold of death."

Muhammad gave a wan smile. "It fooled me, too. I didn't expect to wake up in this world today."

"But I'm sure you didn't plan to leave this world from our small field." It was the kind of statement he could answer with either a nod or an explanation.

He chose to explain. "Something went wrong with the plan. My contact never arrived, and I had no idea where to go. I didn't even know if I had crossed into Israel or was still in the West Bank. I was in a barren border land with no idea of my location, so I came back."

She nodded and remained silent for a couple of minutes. "Wait here. I'll get some food." He watched her walk to the small house two fields away and disappear inside. He didn't know how many hours he'd slept, but he felt so tired. The thought of food was nice. He couldn't even think beyond food and rest. She returned within minutes, carrying a bowl of bread soaked in fresh goat milk and the inevitable teapot and small tea glasses. She set the tray down by his side and told him to eat slowly. She watched him eat and once reached over to hold his hand, slowing the next bite. "Slowly."

He nodded.

"Can you satisfy my curiosity?" she asked. "Why, since you were determined to blow yourself up, did you try to kill yourself with poison? It makes no sense to me."

"What do you mean?"

"Why did you poison yourself?"

"I still don't understand. I waited for my contact for a whole day without food or water, and I walked a long way. I ate some grape leaves to give myself the strength to walk. Raw grape leaves aren't very tasty, but surely they aren't poisonous. That was all I ate because the crops weren't ready yet."

The old woman shook her head and clucked her tongue. "The leaves are not poison," she said, "but the white powder on them is."

"White powder? It was dark and I didn't see any powder on the leaves. The truth is that even if I'd seen it, I would've assumed it was dust. I grew up in the camps. What do I know about real plants and how they look?"

She went on to tell him that in the old days they would sometimes lose a whole year's crop from different pests. Farmers today use pesticides and fungicides and whatever else they could to prevent this. To his surprise, she started laughing. "The bugs seem to figure it out. Must be pretty embarrassing to know that you can't figure out what a bug can. You were very lucky that your stomach rejected what you ate. Your stomach is smarter than the rest of you. If

238

you'd kept those leaves down, you would have had a different ending."

It took Muhammad a bit more time to see the humor of the situation, but he eventually smiled back at her. "I hope my children never hear that their father's dumber than a bug."

The mention of children wiped the smile off her face. "Take off your coat and shirt." He did as she asked. Might this clever woman be able to remove the harness? His heart did a little dance in his chest as he dared hope. He sat perfectly still for long minutes as she studied the harness from all angles.

"I'm sorry." The woman shook her head, and he wanted to cry with the disappointment. "I can see where the explosives are sewn into the harness around your body, but there are so many wires, and they're all over the stitching ..." She shook her head again. "I can't."

"It's all right." It wasn't all right, but what was one more disappointment in his life? She was afraid to try to remove it. She helped him move to the next field where there were some olive trees to provide shade. He was too weak to walk alone. She brought him a blanket. "Take a nap. I'll be back later."

"Thank you." Muhammad suddenly realized how tired he was. It wasn't just the miles and miles of walking, but the strain of the past few days. He sank to the ground and folded his jacket for a pillow. The old woman tucked the blanket around him, and he fell asleep almost immediately.

The sun was low in the sky when the old woman returned. "Are you feeling stronger?" At his nod, she went away and came back with a bowl of lentil soup and a loaf of home baked pita bread. Following her directions, he ate slowly. Her son came out after the sun went down and brought some rice and stew. He sat at a respectful distance and they drank a glass of tea together.

The next day the old woman spent hours with him. They talked randomly and sat companionably during long silences. He had no trouble telling her of his family. Amazingly, he was even able to tell her about Deena. There was pain; there were tears, but the rage had gone. He had no energy for rage. As though talking to himself, he remarked on this absence.

"No," she said with a smile. "It has nothing to do with lack of energy. I have been listening. Your soul is too full of love to give rage a foothold." Muhammad smiled at her. She was so much like his mother when she began talking about God. It must be nice to find comfort in thoughts of God. He smiled in appreciation of the pleasure her faith gave her.

The old woman pronounced Muhammad well enough to travel later that evening. She brought him a donkey and gave him directions to the next village. She told him to leave the donkey tied to the first fig tree he saw. The boy would go and get it later. Muhammad waited until the day grew cooler then set off on the donkey.

It took him two nights to get back to Kalandia. He moved carefully and napped in the daylight and travelled by night. He begged food from solitary farmers by calling to them from a distance. They, in turn, called blessings on him and left sandwiches and fruit for him to collect later, when they left the field. Many assumed he was a freedom fighter hiding from pursuit. He had lost his tie long ago, and his suit was rumpled and covered with dust. They didn't converse; they didn't want to know. What you don't know, you cannot tell.

His head felt clearer than it had been in a long time. A few times he'd been offered a ride in the back of a truck, but more often walked for hours at a time, lost in his own thoughts, often talking aloud to himself. He began thinking of Amal and the boys. Amal's last conversation kept echoing through his mind.

At first, he went over and over the conversation exactly as it had taken place; then he began to think of all the things he should have said. He walked for hours with the hospital waiting room clearer in his mind than the road he followed. When his feet would no longer carry him, he found the best shelter he could behind a stone fence and fell asleep. The conversation went on, but soon faded into dreams. He woke the next morning with the vague memory of Amal telling him that she had spoken with Deena and she knew what she would say. Why couldn't he remember the rest? What would Deena say?

It took the entire two days, but he finally managed to work it out for himself. He was walking down a dirt road without a building in sight when a small bubble of genuine laughter formed somewhere inside him, followed by another and then another until he had to stop walking and grab his sides with laughter.

"Amal, you were right, but I had to work it out for myself before I could accept it. I have been out-loved, out-thought, and out-done by my own daughter! What could make a man more proud?"

As the land around Muhammad became more familiar to him, he began to look ahead. He had to get the bomb harness removed. The only man who could do that was the man who had put it on him in the first place. As much as he wanted to go home and see his family, he couldn't get anywhere near Kalandia with the harness. When he finally located the entrance to the small carefully hidden cave-like shelter, he found it locked. No one was there. That made sense, in a disappointing way. Mazin and Abood didn't sleep there. Why would anyone sleep in a bed of gunpowder that could go off at any moment? He'd been doing it for several days, and it was not the best way to sleep.

He had to wait. He did his best to hide himself between the rocks. Not too difficult, he thought ruefully. He'd been traveling so long that enough dirt and dust to become camouflage covered his clothes. He dozed fitfully, trying to ignore the increasing thirst and hunger. His lips were cracked and his feet were so swollen they barely fit in his shoes.

The sun rose and set again. At least he thought it only happened once. He didn't think he could get up if he tried, but he didn't try because he had nowhere else to go. He moved, sometimes seamlessly, from waking to sleeping while having conversations with himself, Amal, his mother (or was it the old woman who gave him food?), Mazin, and Abood. His lips moved with his silent conversations, and blood trickled from the parched cracks. Reflexively, his tongue flicked out to soothe his lips. He tasted the metallic salinity of blood and the coppery smell filled his senses. The confines of the ambulance closed in around him. "Deena, beloved, don't leave me." It was his blood. Deena's teeth had split his lip while he was trying to breathe life into her. He swiped his sleeve over his mouth, and the grit of dirt and sand grated against his face and stung his bleeding lips. The sting brought back the present. He wasn't in the ambulance. Deena was gone, and so was his soul.

How had he thought that he could just go back home and take up the threads of life? He could never face another checkpoint. He couldn't work; he couldn't support his family; he couldn't even die properly.

He realized he was slipping into something akin to delirium. He would die if he stayed here much longer, but that was all right. It saddened him that he could not take even the first step toward justice for his wife and his people, but at least his body would be found by someone who might know what to do with the explosives. He was too close to centers of population to go anywhere else. He had to wait.

"What the hell? Is he alive?" Muhammad's eyelids fluttered. "This is getting to be a habit." Was this another one of his conversations with the wraiths of his dreams? Strong hands gripped his arms from either side and lifted him, then half carried, half dragged him into the shelter.

Cool water splashed his face, and sweet tea dribbled into his mouth on its way to his stomach and brought him back to reality. What was he going to say? He'd rehearsed so many conversations, and now he sat, empty of thoughts. Two men sat facing him. Mazin and a man he didn't know. Mazin dribbled more over-sweet tea into his mouth. Muhammad sputtered and coughed. He struggled to sit. Mazin lifted his head enough for him to drink.

"Think you're going to live?"

"Maybe." Muhammad's voice sounded like a cat coughing up a fur ball. Felt like that, too. The two men didn't say a word. Mazin held the glass to his lips and he drank hungrily. "No one came for me." His words slurred through his painfully cracked and swollen lips. "I waited about twenty-four hours but no one came."

Mazin nodded. "We know. They arrested your contact. We lost two good men on that. We thought we'd lost three. We were sure they'd found you, too. Guess he wasn't as weak a link as we'd thought if you waited a full day and they still hadn't come to arrest you, too."

Muhammad wondered what was going to happen to him, in the way one might wonder about a character in a television show. He was empty of feelings, empty of words. Would they give him a new target? If they asked him to do something else, he'd do it. He had confessed his weaknesses and said good-bye to everyone that mattered in the last two days. He knew the conversations hadn't really taken place, but he had emptied himself of emotion.

"Don't drink too fast, you'll throw it back up. Just rest." Muhammad closed his eyes. He heard the others move toward the rickety table.

"What's his story?" asked the unfamiliar voice.

"Same as yours, more or less." Mazin's voice kept changing direction, as if he were moving around. Muhammad heard grunts and thuds. Maybe Mazin was moving sandbags. Muhammad dozed, or maybe just floated without the will to move.

"How did *he* find you?"

"Same as you. Desperation finds a way."

"You sending him back out?"

"No. Poor bastard's been through hell already—more than once."

"His harness'll fit me. You know I'm ready. I've been training for weeks. All I need is a target. Think of how much easier it'll be for Abood. He won't have to build it from scratch."

"I'll make some calls. Go get Crazy Abood."

He heard movement and assumed it was the nameless man leaving, but by the time he gathered enough energy to turn his head and look, Mazin was the only one in the room. Mazin ran to the door. "And bring food," he yelled after the other man.

Muhammad's eyes closed, and he slumped into a sleep that closely resembled a coma. He woke to the sound of angry voices.

"Do you understand what you're asking me to do?"

"Yes, I do. If you can *do* it, you can *un*do it."

"Oh, yeah? You never heard the proverb about the crazy man throwing a rock in the well and ten sane men not being able to get it out? It was never meant to be removed. It doesn't work that way. I could blow us all to smithereens trying to cut the right wires. Do you think I'm crazy?"

"As a matter of fact ..." The talking paused for a few seconds, then soft chuckling grew into laughter.

"You have a good point. They don't call me Crazy Abood for nothing. Is sleeping beauty awake?"

"Me?" Muhammad turned. Were they talking about him?

"Yeah."

"Don't risk your lives for this. I'm not worth it. Send me back with a new target."

"You're kidding. You don't even have the strength to stand up."

"Then take me somewhere safe so I can set it off without killing anyone else. It doesn't matter anymore."

Abood shook his head. "You're as crazy as I am. You walked all the way here. There must have been places where you could have done that on the way, but you didn't. Why?"

Muhammad shrugged. He looked at the two men, both of them willing to risk their lives to save him. He owed them the truth. "I thought about what my daughter said, and I was coming back to her." It was all so clear in his mind. How could he tell them how broken he was? How could he explain that a drop of blood on his tongue brought it all crashing down on him again?

"And?"

"And I realized I'd never work again. I can't go through a checkpoint. I couldn't do it the last time I tried, and I can't do it now. If I can't work, I'm more of a burden than a help to my family. It's better if I leave now, while the boys are still too young to remember me for long."

Abood looked at Mazin. "I don't know about you, but it sounds to me like a man with a checkpoint problem, not a man who wants to die."

Pointedly ignoring Muhammad, Mazin nodded. "I knew a man once who went nuts whenever he saw a spider."

"Yeah, and I knew one who couldn't get in a car with the windows closed."

"This isn't a joke. If you try to take this thing off and fail, you die with me."

"Here." Mazin handed him a bowl with pieces of stale bread soaked in sweet tea. Poor man's breakfast. "Eat this and stay out of our way." The men carried or dragged the crates out of bunker. They moved the sandbags and stacked them in front of the door to the other room, leaving

246

a small space for the door to open. By the time Muhammad scraped the last of the food from the bowl, Mazin pulled a large desert-camouflage tarp out of the cupboard and went outside, closing the door behind him.

"Come on, then. Let's get to it." Abood motioned toward the door behind the sandbags.

"No, I told you I didn't want to risk your life with mine."

Abood stood over Muhammad, looking more bear-like than ever. "You know I could wrestle you in there with one hand tied behind me, but I'd rather not. You've been wearing that harness for how long?"

"I lost count of days." It didn't matter. The way Muhammad felt now, Abood could probably beat him with both hands tied behind him, but nothing mattered anymore.

"You've moved and stretched, you've fallen down and gotten back up, you've slept on rocks and twigs. That thing's taken more punishment than it was made to take. Who knows which wires are out of place or damaged. It probably wouldn't be a good idea for us to wrestle right now, but I'm game if you are."

Muhammad shuffled into the other room. He sat where Abood told him to and stripped off his clothes, revealing the harness that had become so much a part of him that he no longer felt its weight or noticed where it chaffed against his skin.

Abood rooted through a box until he found what he wanted. He held up a small pair of scissors with very thin blades. "My mother used to use these for her embroidery." The soft affection in the voice of this big brute of a man almost startled Muhammed. "Sit up straight and don't move." He moved behind Muhammad, and the sound of the scissors snipping thread punctuated the absolute silence of the bunker.

"Why are you doing this?" Muhammad asked, more to cover the snip snip of the scissors than to hear the answer.

"Stop talking. You talk you move, your breathing changes. Don't move."

The command sounded ominous. A man who was sentimental about his mother's scissors shouldn't have to die. Snip. Snip. Silence. Snip.

"I'm doing it to save you. Without you and men like you, they win. I risk my neck every day, and I do it for all of you—men who want to go to work in the morning, give a good day's work for their pay, and raise their kids the best they can. That's the real Palestine." Snip. Snip.

Abood moved to the front. Muhammad watched the beads of sweat form on his forehead and trickled down to the stubble on his cheeks. "I'm not worth saving."

"Stop talking." Snip. Snip. "You can't even control whether or not you can get to work anymore. They even strip away your dignity and self-respect at the checkpoints. Get off the bus, go over there, sit down, stand up, what's in your pockets, show me your ID, get on the bus, show me your ID, bark like a dog, crawl on your belly." Snip. Snip.

"Uh-huh." Muhammad felt each word vibrate with his own thoughts. Yes, that's it. Truth has a solid feel, like good wood in your hands.

"And then it's only a short step more, just one more order. Go where I tell you. Do what I tell you. Stop breathing." Snip. Snip. "And remember I have the gun that makes you do what I say." Snip. Snip. Drops of sweat gathered on Abood's chin and dripped onto Muhammad.

Abood stepped back and wiped his sleeve across his face. "Time for a break." Grateful, Muhammad filled his lungs. "Did you always work in construction?"

"No, I used to make custom furniture. Really beautiful pieces with inlays and carving …" Muhammad smiled at the memories.

"So you're good with your hands."

"Yeah." Muhammad flexed his fingers and looked at his hands.

"Break's over. Now for the hard part." Abood put the scissors back in the box and brought out another small tool. "Clippers." He moved to the back again. "Don't move. Don't even think about moving."

"Uh huh." Was that talking? He froze, barely breathing.

"What would you say if I told you …" Muhammad felt slight pressure on his back. He suppressed a shudder as a trickle of his own sweat ran down his spine. Snick. He felt the whoosh of Abood's breath on the back of his neck. "… that a young girl walked into the YFP office asking where she could sign up." Abood's fingers forced their way between his back and the harness. "She said she could go places without anyone paying attention to her." Snick. One more wire cut. "She said her parents were dead and she might as well."

"What?" Muhammad jerked as he connected the words and their meaning became clear.

"You stupid bastard!" Abood's slap nearly knocked Muhammad off his seat. "I told you not to move!"

Muhammad leapt to his feet. "Did you put a harness on her?" His hands clenched, and his breath came in short gasps. "Was that my Amal?"

"Don't be absurd. The YFP doesn't do that."

"I swear to God if you put a harness on my little girl, I'll kill you right now."

"Don't make me laugh. You don't have the strength to kill me."

"I don't need strength to pull a string." Muhammad gestured to his side, in the general direction of the string that should trigger the explosives.

Abood walked around and put the clippers back in the box. His shirt was soaked with sweat. "You stupid fool. You lost one person you loved, and you fell to pieces. Your little girl thinks she lost her entire family. What would be more natural than for her to follow her father's example?"

"No. It can't be." Muhammad's knees felt weak. He sank back in his seat and covered his face with his hands. "I never even thought …"

"That's your problem right there."

"Then get this damned thing off of me and let me go home. I have to talk to Amal."

Abood picked up the scissors again and moved behind Muhammad. "Talk to her? What will you say?"

"You told me not to talk while you're working." What would he say? He closed his eyes and tried to picture himself in front of Amal. He tried to think of words, but the only words he could think of came from his image of Amal. The only scene that came to him was the waiting room of the hospital.

Her words echoed in his mind. "Papa, you have a wonderful soul. That's why you hurt so much when Mama died. If you had no soul you would have gotten over it easier." Amal had a wonderful soul. Why had he thought she would get over the death of her parents? Because she was young? He should have known better. He was younger than that when his brother was shot, and he still hurt inside when he thought about it, and he still had occasional nightmares. How could he have assumed she'd get over it? He didn't think. Abood was right. He was a stupid fool. Abood, right again.

A voice shouted through the door as the harness slipped off his shoulders, pinning his elbows to his sides. "Everybody all right in there?"

"We're just fine." Abood shouted. Gently, he helped Muhammad slip his arms out of the harness.

"We're just fine." Muhammad's whisper lagged by seconds. He was free of the bomb. It hadn't exploded. He turned and looked at Abood. His lips stung as he stretched the dry chapped skin into a smile.

The voice beyond the door spoke again. "The kid's back with a feast. He says he wants to share his last meal with friends."

Abood threw his arm around Muhammad's shoulders. "After we eat, I'll take you to my place so you can bathe before you go home. It'll be enough of a shock when you walk through the door without you killing her with your smell."

Muhammad hadn't noticed the rank fetid atmosphere of the closed room until he smelled the fresh air coming through the open door. He took a deep breath and smelled onions and cinnamon. His mouth watered in anticipation. Surprisingly, he really wanted to eat. "Thanks."

"You're a lucky so-and-so to have a loving family still hoping you come home."

"But you said she thought—"

"I said, 'What would you say if I told you.' Besides, you can't believe anything I say. Everyone knows I'm crazy."

Muhammad just stared at Abood. He couldn't believe the man tricked him. Who would do a thing like that? "You dirty—"

"By the way, I know someone who needs a good man to mind his shop while he takes care of other business. You interested?"

"Really? Who?"

"Me."

Abood was right again. He *was* a lucky so-and-so. "Let's eat. I have to get home."

www.ingramcontent.com/pod-product-compliance
Lightning Source LLC
Chambersburg PA
CBHW060414180626
46817CB00007B/2582